The Adventures of Jack and Joe
TIME GENTLEMEN

Craig P. Kelly

Chapter One – The Present

At one time they did have an office. Not a very nice office, granted, but an office is an office. "A good place to do business," remarked Joe at the time. He was wrong. Jack and Joe did very little business there. Sure, Joe kept himself busy and Jack did a lot of drinking, but aside from the case of Mrs Gilhooney's missing cat, business was slow. And slow business is no business (like no business I know). Which means no money, which means no rent, which means no office. You get the picture.

And so we find them. Two brothers, two colleagues, sitting in the front two seats of a fifteen year old family hatchback filled to bursting with the remains of a proud, if dirty, live-in office. The one in the driver's seat was Joe. His hands were clamped tightly onto the fake leather steering wheel with his rigid arms stretched out and his gangly body pressed firmly against the seat. His dark-haired head rested, eyes closed, against the headrest with his thin-bridged nose pointing upwards towards the broken, leaky sunroof. Joe's well worn and weary suit and tie seemed to fit his average build well with a smartness that clashed considerably with his elder brother, Jack. Jack was sitting uncomfortably in the passenger seat of the car and snoring loudly from the crumpled up wasteland he called a body. His baseball-capped head faced down, occasionally rolling from side to side as if in some hazed dream. Obvious drool wet his unshaven chin and his arms flailed by his side like a rag doll being electrocuted.

Tap, tap, tap.

Joe's eyes opened. His face centred, slowly waking from his slumber.

Tap, tap, tap.

"Wha...?" murmured Jack from the passenger seat, shaking his head gently. A hand rose to his face as if to stop it falling from his neck. Joe, slightly more alert than his brother, wound down his window.

"Can I help you, constable?"

A broad shouldered policeman dressed in traditional force blue leaned down to Joe's eye level and snarled. "Cut out the coy shit, Joe."

"Hi, Cadley," said Joe, waving a hand in vague recognition. He stretched and fought a yawn as he spoke. "What's up?"

"Cadley!" cheered Jack from the passenger seat. Clearly he had woken up. "Got any beer?" Jack was fairly short and fairly round with fair hair and a fair beer gut. His stubby fingers tugged at his outer Hawaiian shirt which he wore over his inner Hawaiian shirt in place of a jacket. When asked why he wore two brightly coloured shirts at once Jack would generally respond with violence.

"Hello Jack," smiled the policeman, Cadley. He tussled at his coarse curly hair. "Look, I know you guys are in a bit of a bad way but you can't park on the hard shoulder of a motorway."

"You did," smirked Joe, thumbing the police car behind them.

"Yeah, but I can, because I'm a copper and I can abuse my power. You guys have no power to abuse." Cadley shook his head sadly. "Look just get a move on will you?"

"And do what exactly?"

The constable sighed. He'd known the brothers for years and

he knew they weren't bad guys. But even so they'd come close to serious trouble a few too many times for his liking. "Come on guys. Just follow me and we'll get some breakfast." Jack and Joe hesitated and reluctantly PC Cadley sweetened the deal. "I'm buying."

It took Joe a few minutes to get the car started. It was old and the lure of breakfast didn't do much for it. It did for Jack and Joe though and, ignition achieved, they quickly tailed Cadley's police car. They knew instinctively where Cadley was heading. 'Greasy Bob's Café', the finest spot in the whole of Scunchester. The place was off the next junction about ten minutes away but it took Joe only five minutes to realise something was wrong. Joe's eyes flicked to the rear view mirror.

"Someone is following us," he remarked deadpan.

Years of dedicated training led to Jack's next move.

"No shit?" said Jack. He spun his significant weight around, spilling a bag of crisps, and heaved himself between the seats, cranking his head in search of the pursuer. "The black car?" he asked. He waved at it, a broad, cheeky smile across his rubbery face.

"Yes." There was a time when Joe would have used the old cliché, 'don't turn around but…' or given some other such warning. But it never made any difference. Jack was as subtle as two dead bricks and he learnt that if he didn't want Jack to look at something the best thing to do was just not to tell him. As Jack pulled faces, Joe flashed his lights twice at Cadley in front. Cadley wasn't sure what that meant, but he figured it was probably bad news.

"He's getting close," Jack told Joe. "Can't we go faster?"

"Not without breaking traffic laws. Can you see who it is?"

"Nah," said Jack, swinging back into position. He scooped a handful of crisps. "Flash car, a Beemer. Black windows. It's probably just some idiot. Is there any salsa dip left?" He twisted forwards to open the glove compartment and peered in curiously. He sifted through the out of date documents, crumpled forged tax discs and blackened banana skins but the search left him disappointed.

"There's some in the fridge," said Joe. The fridge was wedged between Joe's seat and a suitcase. It took Jack a bit of skilful manoeuvring to gain access, but fridge-breaking was his speciality. He slung his right arm around the corner of the seat at an angle that suggested that either Jack was double jointed or his arm was in fact broken. His fingernails prised at the rust encrusted plastic seal that ran around the rim of the fridge door and he wiggled his fingers, slowly edging his hand into the larder within. He wafted his hand blindly inside groping for the familiar lid.

"Got it," Jack said, before dropping it with the impact. The car had just been rammed. "Shit!" He looked behind. "Did he just ram us?"

"Yes."

"No shit?"

"No."

"Shit."

"Hold on." Joe slammed hard on the accelerator pedal and veered into the middle lane. Cadley held his lane and dropped back while switching on his blues and twos. The mysterious driver in the black car swerved out to follow the hatchback and got a honking from the car it cut up in doing so. It sped forwards and gave the creaking Maestro another ram. The older car couldn't take such a pounding and the boot swung open with a crunch, losing a chest of drawers.

"My underpants!" cried Jack. The black car swerved to avoid the falling debris before it urged forwards and rammed again.

As the hatchback jolted, the black car pulled out into the outside lane and rolled effortlessly alongside Jack and Joe's ailing vehicle. Cadley pulled up behind it, lights flashing and siren blaring. Jack scrambled back over his seat and perched himself dangerously with his left leg caught painfully twisted around his seat belt. He clung on to various household items with as many limbs as he could manage but couldn't stem the steady leak of wardrobe and office equipment from the exposed boot. Joe rammed right hoping to go on the offensive. Jack rolled across the car hoping not to fall out. The rear passenger door swung loose causing a suitcase to spill its load and half the contents of the fridge to dump out.

"Easy!" Jack bellowed. "That was the last of the milk."

"Hardly a dent," cursed Joe. The black car had suffered minimal damage, unlike the side of the ageing Austin Maestro which had ripped like it was tin foil. "Hold on."

"I am!" screamed Jack. And he was. He held on to the fridge like his life depended on it.

With a fresh burst of speed the black car slammed hard into the hatchback. There was nothing Joe could do. It simply wasn't built to withstand this amount of abuse. Two wheels gave out under the pressure and the hatchback flung out of control. It spun through the air like it was a dice in a crap game, crashing over the outer two lanes and colliding with other drivers who had foolishly got their cars caught up in the melee. Cadley's police car swerved to avoid the pile up but clipped the front of his car on a nearby Ford Focus and spun backwards to a juddering halt. Cadley could only watch on as the hatchback bounced three times on the floor and skidded on its roof into the barriers at the side of the hard shoulder. The mysterious black car simply sailed on into the sunset (figuratively speaking. It was half past ten in the morning).

As the dust settled Cadley rushed out of his police car and over to the hatchback. The one remaining door of the car opened and Joe half fell out. Jack followed after his brother, clutching the remains of the fridge. After a moment of collapsed silence, the pair gingerly stood up and walked over to Cadley.

"That was close," remarked Joe, brushing himself off.

"This salsa is good," noted Jack as he crunched through a pack of tortilla chips.

The car exploded.

Chapter Two – Just Before That, A Long, Long Time From Now

The Instructor looked over the strange clock with an unhealthy interest. His third eye swirled into action, erecting fully and closing to a tight focus on the deep grain of dark wooden casing. The clock was as tall as a tall human, but something seemed odd about it. For one thing it had just one hand. And for another it had slightly too many numbers on the face. The face itself looked like it had been carved from crystal and was secured above an elegant wooden rectangular frame. A rimmed door ran the down the front of the frame, perhaps a little over five foot high. There was a slot for some kind of key in one side but no key. The door was locked shut and for some reason no matter how hard anyone pulled, picked or bashed at it, the door would not open.

It was a grandfather clock, not that the Instructor knew that. There had been no grandfather clocks for a long, long time. This one had an inscription on its face. It said 'O.M. (Scun.).'

"Impressive," he strained through his voice box. The Instructor peered closely looking for signs of power, but he could see none. The hands were not moving and the clock did not tick but he could sense that the machine harboured a hidden power of awesome proportions. The Instructor removed his third finger and screwed in a drill bit in its place. The bit began to rotate with a harsh whirr. The Instructor grimaced and pushed his finger at the wood. The wood resisted and despite firm pushing and the Instructor's arm having the hammer-action setting enabled, the bit broke. The end flew acrobatically through the air, thudding to a halt in the forehead of the male standing behind the Instructor. The male didn't seem to notice.

"Maybe with a masonry bit?" suggested the male. He was a large, well, man, for want of a better word. He'd be what a man looked like if you filled him full of air for a few hours with a foot pump. He was around seven foot high with vein throbbing muscles that perhaps would be better suited to the cover of various specialist magazines. He was wearing a black ribbed vest which only just stretched over his chest. His short hair made it easy to see that even his skull was bulging with muscles. He wore dark sunglasses tight into his face to the extent that it didn't look like they could be removed without surgery. Unusually, perhaps, his nose was made of metal and had a large stud ring in it. He had 'goon' written all over him. Not literally of course.

"Shut up, Bolt," twisted the Instructor snarkily. The Instructor was also difficult to define exactly as a 'man'. 'Robot' would probably be a little more to the point. The Instructor didn't have a face, just a mesh where his mouth should be and three robotic eyes that peered from his forehead in various directions and turned purple when he was mad. Which was often. The Instructor was a lot shorter than the goon next to him and his body was hidden by a dark blue robe so that it was difficult to tell just exactly how much of him was robot and how much was human. If any.

"The holo-video-gram replay shows the humans had a key of some kind, a pendant in the shape of a cross. Did you see it?" The Instructor was talking about the two humans who had recently raided his impenetrable fortress somehow and leapt through his portal of power. He had no idea how the humans got through his defence system. Even more bizarrely they had brought with them the clock, despite it weighing a bloody ton.

"Yeah," replied Bolt.

"Good. Download the necessary files. Capture their images. You, my little friends, are going on a trip." The Instructor referred to Bolt and his two war buddies, goons both.

"But where did they go?" asked Bolt. He meant the humans, not his war buddies. His war buddies, Jug and Goldfish, were out back pulling bullets out of each other with tweezers.

"The more correct question is when did they go. We shall access the portal file and determine their trajectory. I should be able to make a reasonable prediction. Give or take a day."

The Instructor walked meaningfully towards the portal. The portal was, as any good human slave knows, the Instructor's source of power. However it was also a huge drain on the planet. The Instructor used the enslaved human race to keep the power going. The portal was the Instructor's life's work for it also served as a time machine. He'd perfected travelling through time. Almost. The Instructor could send living matter through the machine with only minimal data lost. Perhaps 5% of brain tissue was erased, but as humans only used a small fraction of their brain most of them wouldn't even notice until they'd had a fair few trips. However for machines such as himself it was a different matter. The portal would wipe his entire robotic memory. He knew it did this because he'd tried it once before and had spent many hundreds of years wandering aimlessly in the past until Bolt and his cohorts rescued him to the future. He presumed he must send them at some point to rescue himself in the past, bring him back to then and revert to his backup data at that point whenever that point might have been. He made a mental note to get that done, once he could figure out the finer details. *Like how the hell would I be able to manipulate the past from a future that shouldn't exist. Meh.* It was better not to think of such things. It all usually worked out anyway.

He sent a surge of oil to his brain to relieve the robotic headache that had just kicked in. The clock-workings in his gear systems started sloshing the juice around, calming his neuron pathways back to their steady hum. His heater fans whirred to life and he went into standby mode.

Chapter Three – Breakfast, Later On But Much Earlier

Picture the grimiest, slimiest burger bar you have ever been to. Pretty grim, eh? Grease everywhere, dirt on the floor, rats in the kitchen, spit in the soup, you know the kind of thing. Got it? Okay, now add a big, fat bald man with a boil the size of a small country glued to one of his chins. Give him an off-white apron dripping, and I mean this, dripping with dripping. Got that? Okay, now add his wife, a four foot eight demon with an oddly shaped head vigorously rolling and shaping burger meat (the term meat is used loosely here). Okay? Great. That's Greasy Bob's café. Oh, and the big fat man? That's Stevie. He bought the place from Greasy Bob a few years back and cleaned it up a bit.

Jack bit into his triple whammy special and swallowed. A yellowy-red goo slurped from the far end of the burger and fell to the table in a gelatinous heap. He mumbled something as he ate, which Joe translated as "This is a damn good burger."

Joe and Cadley talked amongst themselves, toyfully playing with the bacon butties that sat sadly in front of them.

"Any idea who it was? In the black car I mean?" asked Cadley. As he did so he lit up menthol, flouting the smoking ban. He reasoned the cigarette smoke would actually make the place smell better.

"No," said Joe. He took a sip of his Coke through the straw he felt obliged to use – Stevie insisted he had one. "But whoever it was was trying to kill us. Who would want to kill us?"

"You mean apart from the Vamenti brothers?" remarked Cadley.

"Well... yeah," managed Joe. It was true that the Vamenti brothers had a lot of ill will for Jack and Joe, ever since Jack had apparently accidentally shot Ma Vamenti in the leg. "It's not their style though. They'd want us to know it was them."

"For the last time, it isn't true!" moaned Jack after swallowing a mouthful of food. He was sick of hearing about an incident that he was sure didn't happen. Although he was pretty drunk at the time. "I did not shoot Ma Vamenti in the leg. She's nuts! She made up that story just because I refused to sleep with her. I mean, please. She must be a hundred years old."

"So if it isn't them who else have you managed to piss off recently?"

"The landlord?" suggested Joe.

"My bank manager," added Jack between munches. "Or One-hand Sam, he got really mad last time I saw him."

"Why was that?" asked Cadley, breathing in his smoke.

Jack hesitated. "It was because I called him One-hand Sam. He's still a bit sensitive I think."

"Still...," Joe began. He didn't get chance to say anything further because it was at that moment the café doors flung open with a loud and unearthly bang. Shards of glass cracked and fell on to the grease-congealed floor, forming what would have been a reasonably protective barrier if it were placed on the top of a tall brick wall. As it was, the three hulking figures that entered through the shattered doors merely crunched the glass under their large booted feet as they strolled casually into the joint. All three held large pistols in all six of their oil-stained hands.

The largest of the three, who possibly was an inch under seven feet tall, took a further few steps forwards. The smallest brute (about six five) twisted side on and provided cover to the door. The remaining bad guy merely held his ground swinging his guns to face the few diners who dared to move. The large guy spoke first, cocking his weapons as he did so.

"Nobody move or the fat guy gets it," he said in a low monotone. He thrust a pistol forwards and positioned it so it was several inches from the head of Greasy Bob's proprietor. Jack was sitting several feet behind and edged his seat quietly to one side. A short pause followed as the middle bad guy surveyed the scene, glancing slowly from customer to customer. He was a thinner man than the other two, just, with more hair. While his companions had short dark militaristic hair, he had long dirty mangles of hair flopping in every direction. His outfit too was subtly different. He wore a deep blue bulky jacket slung over an Adidas T-shirt and khaki pants. The others wore tight fitting vests, better to show the size of their combined muscle which, Joe had to concede, was considerable. All three wore traditional bad guy dark glasses, although the big one seemed to have a metal nose. The smallest of the three smoked a smouldering half-finished cigar while the largest had several noticeable teeth missing which Jack thought was cute. *If you like that kind of thing*, he hastened to think. *Which I don't*, he added.

The blue jacket eyed Joe. Joe frowned slightly and Jack once more edged quietly away. PC Cadley remained quiet, hands resting suspiciously by his side. The blue jacket looked at his watch a moment, then back to Joe.

"He is one," he told the others. He then looked to the pretending-to-be-invisible Jack. "He is another."

"Me?" questioned Jack with every ounce of surprise. "No.

I'm someone else!"

The largest bad guy swung his pistol forwards, knocking Stevie heavily to the ground with blood streaming from the nose that had just broken. Joe couldn't be certain but he thought he heard Mrs. Stevie mutter a curse about health and safety. The big baddie lumbered around and raised his two pistols so they pointed at their two respective targets: Jack and Joe.

"Who the hell are you?" demanded Jack as he gulped. Sweat rolled steadily down his forehead and into his eyes, blurring his vision, which was okay because all he could see at the moment was the barrel of a very nasty looking gun. He was a squeeze away from death. He sure as hell hoped no one sneezed.

"I am Bolt," said the big guy in his laboured low voice.

"Bloody hell, Bolt," shouted his smaller companion in a strange accent Joe couldn't quite place. "Why the hell did you tell them who you are?" As he talked his cigar rolled periodically from one side of the mouth to the other.

Bolt was obviously a little upset about his mistake. A frown crossed his otherwise emotionless features and just for a second he lowered his guns. "I'm sorry Goldfish."

"Shit Bolt!" muzzled Goldfish chomping his Cuban. "Just tell them who I am, for damn's sake."

Bolt looked puzzled, but his shoulders gave the impression of a shrug. "Okay." He raised his weapons to eyeball height. "That guy is my friend Goldfi..."

"Bolt!" shouted the blue jacket. "Enough." Bolt remained expressionless but silent. The blue jacket pointed to Joe and opened his mouth to speak.

"Sorry, Jug" interrupted Bolt.

Jug rolled his eyes, and then waved a gun at Joe. "You. Give me the pendant."

Joe blinked. "The what, now?" he said.

"The pendant. Give it me now or die."

"What pendant?"

"Don't play games with me. Where is it? Do you have it here?"

Joe was a little flustered. Jack tried to help out: "We don't have it, you've got the wrong people, idiot." He regretted the 'idiot' as soon as he said it. Suddenly he was feeling a little hot under the collar, and tried to loosen his shirt without moving his hands.

Jug frowned. He lowered his twin weapons and thrust them into two over-sized holsters at his hips. He raised his right hand to his chest and felt inside his jacket. After a moment of fumbling he removed a small computer pad like you'd see if you were watching an episode of *Star Trek*. He looked at the display intently and pressed a few invisible keys just below the pad. He took a few steps towards Jack and Joe and waved the pad around a bit. He pressed a few of the invisible keys again and frowned some more. The pad bleeped tonelessly. "You haven't got the pendant." He took a few steps back, and asked quickly, "What day is this?"

"Tuesday," said Joe, relieved by the easier line of questioning.

"Shit, we're early." Jug looked desperately to his colleagues. "Come on!" He turned and jogged out of the café. His two pals backed out slowly with their weapons still keen. No one in the café moved, apart from a lady who fainted as she'd forgotten to breathe. Bolt was the last out, and disappeared to the right with a blur. There was an uneasy pause broken finally by the screech of Jack's chair. He stood up and raced to the door. Cadley was the next to act mumbling quietly into a radio attached to his collar. One or two of the customers began to stir. Some of them even rushed to help Stevie as he lay on the ground clutching his face. Joe was the last to move. He slowly stood up and followed Jack out of the building.

"They've disappeared, brother," Jack told Joe outside the doorway.

"Who do you owe money to, Jack?" Joe asked quietly as he pulled firmly on the hem of his suit jacket.

"Only Denny, I swear!" Denny the Dog was a bookie Jack flirted with. He owed him for a few missed bets, but Denny was a friend of sorts and didn't have the kind of contacts to hire three wackos with large guns to bust him up. Not over fifty pounds anyway.

"Okay, so who was that and why did they want us?"

"I dunno," said Jack. He held up his hand and made a small pinch with his finger and thumb. "But I came this close to kicking their sorry arse."

Chapter Four – Gone To The Dogs, A Bit After Before

"Are you mad at me, Denny?" asked Jack. This was several hours later. After running out of alternatives on the list of 'people who want to kill us' Jack and Joe found themselves at the greyhound track. Denny had a small stand in the rear corner of the bookmaker's terrace. It comprised of two wooden boxes on top of each other and a faded sign in front listing the odds on the latest hare chase.

"Me?" said Denny innocently. "Why would I be mad?"

"£10 on number six." Joe handed over a note as he made his bet. Denny passed him a slip and odds of 8 to 1. Joe was standing to one side, reasonably eager to watch the race, which was about to begin.

"Because I owe you money?" said Jack to Denny.

"Yes, but you are going to pay up like a good boy before I break your knee caps. You know that and I know that, so everybody's happy." Denny gave a thin smile. Jack nodded uncomfortably.

"Yeah, that's what I figured."

A bang and the race was on. The fake hare shuttled past the released hounds and the chase began. Six steroid-pumped greyhounds thundered around the track and after a few seconds the race was over. The hare won, of course, closely followed by a mottled brown and white greyhound wearing a smart blue coat bearing the legend '6'. Hundreds of losers threw their torn tickets to the ground in disgust. Joe calmly handed his winning ticket to Denny whilst reading the Greyhound News he'd bought for the form for the next run. Someone must have had the newspaper before him and had marked some of the dogs with a uneven circle in blue biro. *The cheapskate vendor must have sold the paper twice,* Joe reckoned. It wouldn't be so bad but the vendor had also sold him a blue biro. He pocketed the pen in his jacket.

"Here you go, Joe." Denny said to him, holding out Joe's winnings. "Another lucky win."

"Luck has nothing to do with it." Joe gave Jack five ten pound notes, then handed the rest to Denny. "This on number 4 in the next."

"Okay." Denny marked down the bet, and gave Joe a slip and the odds of 5 to 1.

"Here's the money I owe you Denny," said Jack dutifully. He handed over the £50 Joe had given him. He was tempted to make a bet instead, but figured Joe would be annoyed when he lost it. Which he invariably did. That was probably why Denny liked him so much.

"That's only the twenty interest you owe me, then."

"Twenty interest!" Jack shook his head. It didn't matter though. The next race was already over and the dog to finish first was a dark brown mutt who bore the marking '4'. Joe collected his winnings, and gave Jack enough to pay his bills. "I hope you choke on it," he muttered grumpily as he handed over the crumpled twenty.

The brothers hung around the track for maybe another hour. Jack sulked throughout, unable to place any bets and Joe unwilling to provide him with any further monetary contributions. Joe did have a few further flutters and considered himself fortunate to have a reasonable run on poor odds. He was puzzled though. Every dog that won had been circled in the newspaper by the previous punter.

"The guy who had this paper before me could have made a fortune." Jack ignored Joe's comment. He was having a piss behind a tower of wooden pallets and therefore busy trying not to get his shoes wet.

The brothers sloped off through the rusted corrugated iron that served as the trackside entrance, wandered past the neighbouring yellow plastic factory and headed off towards downtown Scunchester. With no further encounters for the remainder of the day with any gun-toting goons, they idled the time away in boredom. With the remainder of Joe's winnings the two secured a room for the night in a cheap bed and breakfast in the seedy side of town, quite near their old office. Without a television for comfort it was silently decided an early night was in order. Jack hogged the bed, and Joe folded uncomfortably on a rickety chair and fell straight to sleep.

Chapter Five – About The Same Time Only In The Far, Far Future

The Instructor re-did the calculation for the third time. The time portal was extremely unstable and it was difficult to give it a precise point on the space-time curve on to which he could beam his ugly goons. The first two times had been too early. He needed to get the pendant from the humans but he had to get to the part of the life-stream when they actually possessed the ankh shaped key. A day or two more should do it, according to the calculation. He'd just forgotten to carry the four last time. Once he had the pendant he'd have control of the strange device that the mysterious humans had inadvertently delivered to him. His three goons were standing idly by waiting for new coordinates to be entered. Jug and Goldfish oiled their weapons, but Bolt was happy to stand around and occasionally pick his nose (it kept dropping to the floor).

"I have programmed the portal to take you further into the future of the life stream of the humans," droned the Instructor through his crisp, digital voice box. "It is interesting, is it not, that the life stream is so far in the past." His logic circuit reasoned that the clock was also a time machine of some sort, only far more stable than the one he possessed, and that was how the humans had stumbled upon his realm without detection.

"Do we have to keep using the portal?" asked Goldfish. "It

makes me go all fuzzy." Jug hit him hard with the butt of his gun.

"We shall try once more. This time do not return until you have the pendant." The Instructor's eyes glowed an eerie purple and swirled around his face like angry kaleidoscopes.

The goons stuttered reluctantly forwards and picked up their equipment, including a big yellow button on a grey plastic frame that sat neatly onto a clip on each goon's belt. The button reset the time stream and would return them to the future upon completion of their mission. Although something about the Instructor's voice told them they wouldn't have much of a future if they didn't manage to recover the pendant from the humans.

The translucent vortex within the portal shimmered with an increased velocity as the Instructor inputted his calculation. The power drain of the portal was huge and it would take a lot of his stored human capacitors to generate the amount of juice that he'd need to keep the thing going long enough to pass his three envoys through. It annoyed the Instructor that he needed the human slaves to generate the power that kept him and his machinery going. He'd have killed the whole bloody lot of them years ago otherwise. *It's such a pain to remember to feed them.* Sometimes he'd forget altogether and they'd all die. Luckily he kept a lot of spares in frozen storage.

The portal turned from green to orange, a familiar colour that meant the goons could now step through. Jug went first and vanished as he entered the vortex. It was as if his entire atomic structure had suddenly disintegrated. A closer look and it was possible to see a stream of Jug's particles flow through the portal like sand in an egg timer. Goldfish and Bolt followed moments later. The portal shuddered and turned green, the shimmering vortex steadying with a placid hum. The transfer was done.

Somewhere deep within the Instructor's citadel a thousand human souls died in agony as electricity was sucked from the limp and lifeless bodies. A robot cleaner tutted and started the furnaces.

Chapter Six – Back in the Present

Jack woke refreshed at perhaps twenty past noon. He considered twelve hours of sleep to be essential to modern living. Without fully recharging the old batteries, he reasoned, he couldn't be his usual alert self. Sure, he could sleep for less. He'd been known to live off nine hours of undisturbed kip. But twelve was the optimum. For peak performance.

"You've missed breakfast." Joe told him. He was sitting in the corner of the room on a wooden chair reading a daily paper of some sort. He spoke without looking up from the paper.

"Yeah, well. Who needs it." Jack moaned as he stretched himself awake. "I can quite easily start the day with lunch."

Joe folded the paper and put it down on the out-of-order trouser press that served as the room's only table. He looked at his watch briefly. "You've almost missed that too." He sighed and straightened his tie. "Come on, get dressed. We've got work to do."

"Work? What work?"

"I don't know, but we are out of money. We best go and see Drager."

Jack slumped out of the side of the bed, dressed only in his boxer shorts. They were Christmas ones with little Santas flying on little sleds filled with little presents. "Bloody hell, no." Jack looked worried. "We can't go and see Drager, he'd laugh in our face." Drager was a prosperous rival private detective and while

Jack and Joe didn't exactly get on with the goof-ball, Drager often hired others to do some of his grunt work. They'd worked together on a few occasions. "The Polish pillock," added Jack.

"He's not Polish, he's Bulgarian." Joe replied. "He's not even that. His parents were Bulgarian, he has an American passport I think."

"He's still a pillock."

Joe stood up and reached for the Hawaiian shirt Jack had thrown to the ground the night before. He picked it up, shook out the spiders that had taken residence overnight and flung the multicoloured monstrosity to his brother.

"Get dressed, pillock," he said.

It didn't take long. Jack put on his pants and socks. He threw on his shirts and his ageing leather shoes and the job was done. He would have had a wash, but the water wasn't particularly clean. Mind you it would have probably killed off a lot of germs.

Drager's office was on the south side of Scunchester, above a snooker club, and it didn't take them long to get there. The secretary ushered the brothers in quickly (primarily so she didn't have to listen to Jack's horrendous attempts at flirtation). Drager's office was rather grand, for an office, with corniced walls lined with polished wooden bookcases holding volumes of ancient and largely unread law journals. The thick rug underfoot seemed vaguely Persian, as did the vase sat atop an ornate stonework pedestal. All in all the room was as pretentious as its owner.

Drager was sitting at his desk writing something down on a notepad. He did a lot of that. Writing things down. He was very meticulous in that respect. Or a bit of an anal fuck-wit, as

Jack liked to describe him. Drager knew Jack and Joe were standing a few feet in front of him, waiting. He ignored them anyway. His golden rule was to always keep people waiting and he would speak only when he was ready. He would bide his time until just the right moment, so that his words had more poignancy, so his...

"So, what's up Drager, you anal fuck-wit?" It was Jack, not one to be kept standing around. He'd marched forwards and plonked his backside on Drager's tidy hellhole he called a desk. Jack's trousers, reasonably loose with the absence of any belt, rolled down slightly at the back affording a not pleasant view for any one who cared to look (i.e. no one). He picked up some kind of executive toy and toyed with it.

Drager was momentarily stunned. Joe swore later that he actually noticed Drager's jaw drop. Not a common sight as Drager was famous for his Vulcan-like emotionless appearance. It didn't take him long to recover.

"Jack. You are sitting on my wife."

Jack squirmed his backside round a bit. Sure enough a small portrait of a lady lay half-broken underneath his left buttock cheek. Drager carefully pulled it out from underneath and placed it to one side.

"That your wife? She's quite tasty, Ven. I think I saw her last week in a lap dancing club, I slipped her a fiver..."

"My name is John." Drager's real name was Ven Dragovich. But he hated it. So he changed it. A few people still called him Ven. His Mum. His Dad. And Jack. But he hated it. "And you call me Drager, understood?"

"Whatever you say, Ven," Jack said, still perched on the desk.

Joe remained standing a few feet further away, glancing casually at the ceiling. *Let them fight it out*, he thought.

"So," Jack continued. "What've you got brewing? Any work for your old buddies Jack and Joe?" He sniffed as he spoke and wiped his nose on the sleeve of his shirt. Hawaiian shirts are brilliant for that sort of thing. Wipe your nose and no noticeable change in colour at all.

Drager watched Jack with solemn interest and sighed. He placed his pad and pen tidily to one side of the desk and folded his arms. "I don't know." His quasi-American accent very rarely showed signs of foreign influence, remaining a perfect balance of neutrality. The odd Eastern European slant was known to pop out occasionally but only at moments of great stress. This was not a moment of great stress.

"Come on," said Jack. "We know you must need some work doing. Have we ever let you down before?"

Drager was tempted to answer the question honestly but didn't. "From what I hear you guys are in a little bit of bother. No office, no equipment, no car."

Jack shrugged a little. "We don't need any of that stuff anyway."

"I did have a job lined up for you but it's a stake-out. You can't have a stake-out without a car. Pity. It was a nice job too." Drager smiled thinly. He seemed quite pleased with himself.

"Ah, come on, Ven!" Jack pleaded. He was about to plead some more but Joe interrupted. A good job too. Jack was a miserable pleader.

"We've still got a car." Joe said. Drager look at him intently trying to fathom out whether he was lying or not. He picked up a HB pencil and played with it between his thumb and forefinger. Joe remained expressionless.

"You do?" queried Drager, unsure. "I thought your car got trashed."

"Damaged," Joe countered waving his right hand. "Not trashed. It's at the garage awaiting collection." He paused a moment. Jack gave him a funny look but Joe ignored it. "Tell me about this stake-out Drager."

Drager frowned. He didn't like it when his information was wrong. But it didn't matter. He did have a job that needed doing and decided that he may as well take advantage of the situation.

"On the outskirts of Scunchester is a small warehouse. My client has a vested interest in the warehouse. But he suspects that all is not well. I need you to watch the place overnight. If anyone breaks in or out I need to know about it. Tail them if you can, as long as I get some answers." He shoved a card across the table with the address of the warehouse emblazoned on it in cheap gold pen. Jack picked it up and pretended to read it. Drager looked to Joe. "Any questions, Joesph?"

"When do we get paid?" asked Jack from his perch.

"After the job is done." Drager told him calmly. "Now get off my desk, and get the hell out of my office." The pair left Drager's office hurriedly and descended the stairway to ground level. They walked along the busy street, straining to hear each other over the throng of honking traffic.

"What car?" asked Jack. He smacked Joe's arm as they marched. "It was a wreck, Joe, we can't do a stake-out."

"I gave Charlie a call. His boys are working on the car."

"Charlie can't fix for shit!"

"He's still our mechanic."

"He'll never fix it for tonight."

"So we don't use a car," said Joe calmly.

"Don't talk daft. You've got to have a car for a stake-out."

"Why?" asked Joe.

"Why? Because it gets cold in the middle of the night. Because if you have a car you get to sit down and not freeze your backside off watching nothing happen for twelve hours. Because if on the off chance you *do* see something happen you can't chase the bad guy's car on foot!"

Joe frowned. "Do you want to get paid or not?"

"You're nuts," waved Jack. "I am not doing a stinking cold stake-out perched on the wall of some nearby garden. No way, bro."

Chapter Seven – That Evening

Perched on the wall of a nearby garden Jack supped a steaming liquid from a half-melted polystyrene cup. Joe sat on the kerb a few feet in front, eyes staring diagonally across the road to the warehouse beyond. It was a clear night but with a cold, crisp breeze that made Jack wish he'd worn more than his two Hawaiian shirts on top of each other. A barely full moon shone down brightly, affording a reasonable view for those who, like Jack and Joe, needed it. They'd been at it for just over an hour and a half and so far seen pretty much what they'd expected. That is, absolutely nothing.

"The problem with stake-out work," complained Jack as he hoisted himself up onto the loose brickwork of the crumbling garden wall, "is that ninety-nine point nine percent of the time all you do is sit on your arse so out-of-your-mind bored that even if something actually did happen you wouldn't bloody well notice."

"That's because after a few hours at it," Joe grunted, "you are always asleep. If you paid more attention you would learn a whole lot more."

"A whole lot more of what? There is nothing happening at that warehouse tonight."

Joe sighed. "Take a look around, brother. What do you see?"

"I see a crap-shit old mill, a dozen council houses, a derelict scrap yard and two cold, dozy idiots sitting outside in not the nicest area of town and who will both probably die when the pubs shut and the drunken local residents return home and find us two loitering."

"Anything else?"

"There is nothing else to see!" Jack crumpled his now empty cup and heaved it backwards over his head into the garden behind him. He shook his head sadly and then had a furtive glance up and down the street. Joe must be getting at something. "I dunno? Twenty or so cars most of which are in as poor condition as ours and..." And he spotted it. "And a brand new Mercedes with foreign plates."

"Yup. The latest model with four alloy hub caps and a dozen other mod-con features which won't be there in the morning if the owner doesn't return soon." The car was a little way up the road, further along than the warehouse but on the opposite side of the street. It was a metallic indigo colour and logic permitting it was not the kind of car that would usually reside on a poor council estate.

"So what are you saying? That some hot-shot is in the warehouse right now?"

"I'm not sure," replied Joe. He looked towards the dark warehouse. "No lights on that I can tell. The Merc was here when we got here, so either a posh relative is visiting a down-trodden cousin or it's something to do with Drager's client."

"Okay, say our baddie is in the warehouse. He comes out, and we tail him yeah? Presumably by running along side the car, but not so close that he notices us, right?" He tried to be as sarcastic as possible but Joe didn't seem to notice.

"Don't be stupid," said Joe as he climbed to his feet. "Come on."

Joe walked slowly up the road with Jack following. They

stopped maybe a dozen feet away from the out of place vehicle.

"What do you think?" asked Joe.

Jack eyed the car. He looked at the seal tight windows, noted the central locking system was operational, saw the flashing LED and the tacky "I've got a big alarm" stickers. He saw the car registration imprinted in the car's tinted windows, the automatic lock on the boot of the car, the low suspension of the back wheels and a rather nifty CD and radio player with a security code lock-out. The car also had an aerial that had been snapped off and replaced with a bit of coathanger.

"I could probably open it, but it's fifty-fifty whether I could get it to go. And there is an outside chance the alarm would go off as the manufacturers intended." Jack considered further for a moment. "Why would you want to steal it anyway? Piss the owner off?"

"I don't want to steal it. I want you to open the boot and climb inside. That way we don't need to tail it because you will be already in it."

"Oh, good plan, Sherlock." Jack shook his head in mockery. "It's not going to work though. The car is already over heavy. Look at the suspension. It's low and the rear wheels are down. Something is already stashed in the back." Joe frowned, but nodded. Jack was an expert on motor vehicles so he always bowed to his brother's superior knowledge. Jack was no mechanic of course. He just knew how to break into cars and steal them. But even that had an art to it and Jack was a prince among men when it came to a bit of taking without owner's consent.

"Want to see what they've got?" Jack grinned. Joe gave a slow and silent nod, as if giving his permission unwillingly, and let his brother get to work. Jack glanced down the street casually, giving a silent whistle. He edged his backside to the rear of the vehicle and slowly started to push his bum onto the metal. He shunted the car gently, as if testing just how far he could go without the alarm kicking in. He pushed a bit harder, then twirled around with his fingers quickly at work at the rim of the boot. He had a slender silver wire that he wiggled between his thumb and index finger. Jack gave himself a smug grin as he felt the clumsy locking mechanism with his wire. He knew exactly what he had to do.

Several minutes later the boot was open and an alarm was ringing loudly. It wasn't a good alarm, surprisingly, but rather the type that honks the car's horn repeatedly for about twenty minutes. A nuisance, but it allowed Jack and Joe a bit of time. After all, who looks outside when they hear a car alarm go off? Especially in a rough neighbourhood like this. Car alarms go off every fifteen minutes. In this neighbourhood people only look outside if a car alarm *isn't* going off. No, the car alarm wasn't the problem. The problem was what to do next. The contents of the boot had stunned both Jack and Joe. It was partly because it was actually a he. It was partly because he was dead. It was partly because of the blood oozing from a large gunshot wound. And it was partly because his eyes were still open and staring upwards with a large, purple and well bitten tongue hanging out of his mouth. Whichever, it was not a pretty sight.

"Jesus!" said Joe. Jack reacted better and slammed the boot shut.

"Come on, let's run!" Jack screamed and started to run for the old derelict scrap yard where he could get better cover. The alarm horn was still honking away. Joe shook himself awake and began to run. A thought stopped him though, and instead of running he scanned the road for a brick. He didn't have much time. Out of the corner of his eye he noticed a light flicker on in one of the side windows of the warehouse. Joe raced to the nearest garden wall and dislodged a half-slashed red brick. He ran back to the Mercedes and smashed the passenger window. More lights flickered on, up and down the street. Joe reached into the car and grabbed the front of the CD player. He wrenched what he could away from the car and then ran for all he was worth, his legs pounding the floor like they belonged to an unfit Linford Christie. A nervous half-glance behind him revealed two figures standing outside the open door of the warehouse. They had probably seen Joe run in the dark but it was too late for them. He'd made enough ground away and darted quickly around the next corner. And he didn't stop.

Jack meanwhile hid amongst the rubble of the poorly lit scrap yard and watched what happened next. He just wished he was a bit closer so he could hear what was going on. He squinted in the hope that squinting actually helped. Which it didn't of course. The two figures, neither of which Jack could identify at this distance and in this light, lurched slowly towards the car. A heated argument raged although Jack could not make out any of the words clearly enough to determine what the argument was about. He guessed it was probably the first guy asking why the second guy left the car with a dead body in the boot parked outside in a dodgy area of town with a large neon sign above it saying 'steal me'. The first figure looked at the car, while the follower examined the boot. The first figure looked peeved and shouted loudly at the second fellow. The second fellow just seemed to shrug it off, and indicated with a hand gesture that the first guy should a) shut the fuck up and b) get in the car and drive. The first guy complied.

Jack heard a creak and glanced to the warehouse for the

source. A third guy had appeared and was opening a pair of bay doors. He silently waved the car in and then, after a moment, closed the bay doors once more. The remaining figure outside returned to the entrance from which he had come and, finally, a level calm returned to the street.

Jack remained in his squat position watching nothing else happen for the rest of the night and at about 3am he fell asleep.

Chapter Eight – The Far, Far Future, Once Removed

Alyssa, High Priestess of the Castle Carranock, Enchantress to the King, level nine Spellchanter, was standing with her arm held up high and her right boot firmly pressing down on the head of a cave troll. She thrust her raised sword swiftly downwards, green gore splurting upwards onto to her Radley leather armour. She twisted the sword in the neck of the pitiful creature and pushed it deeper into the wound. With a troll you can never be quite sure. The buggers regenerate so you have to make it hard for them to get all the pieces of themselves back together again. With a little effort she ripped the head from the body of the corpse, hacking at the thick gooey strands of spinal cord that came up with it. Once the head was free she tossed it to her companion, Rascal the Thief. Unfortunately he was too busy searching through the corpses of the five henchmen they'd hired to help them on the quest, and the troll's head thwacked him on the back before dropping to the floor.

"Ouch, that hurt!" yelped Rascal jumping upright, rubbing at his back with blood stained hands. "I think the bloody thing bit me. If I get rabies you are in big trouble."

"Drop the head into the Chasm of Burning Fire, and quickly," replied Alyssa ignoring the thief's threat. The troll's head was already beginning to move, the remains of the attached spine squirming around on the floor like a snake, desperately trying to find its way home. "I don't want to have to fight this thing all over again."

"That's a right shit name for a chasm," said Rascal calmly as he picked up the troll's head by the ears. He paused a moment to pry a bluetooth headset out of one of the lugs. "I mean. It's a chasm with a fire at the bottom. Its bound to be burning. Who came up with these stupid unoriginal names?"

"The Instructor, probably. It's his game."

Rascal just shrugged before flinging the head into the deep chasm with a grunt. The head smashed into the far wall, the spinal cord trying to get some purchase to save itself from the sudden descent. Unfortunately for the troll there was no purchase to be had and the head tumbled down into the flames far below. "They should probably turn off the fires anyway. It's a huge waste of oil and prices are sky high at the moment."

"The owner probably got lucky and managed to get a fixed tariff."

"And think of the environmental impact, eh?" Rascal crouched down and got back to the business of pilfering from the dead. The ultimate form of recycling, he reckoned.

"Ironically I don't think Troll's are very green." Rascal didn't bother to laugh. Alyssa wiped the blood from her sword on her armour and picked up her shield. "The witch said the golden egg should be in the caves beyond here."

"You really think the egg will free us from the Instructor?"

"So the prophecy says."

"Yeah, well," stuttered Rascal standing up and stretching his back. "The prophecy also says only the Code Spell can deliver us from destruction."

"I'm working on that."

"You know the Code Spell?" Rascal folded his arms, unconvinced.

"No. I'm hoping the egg has something to do with it."

"Forgive me if I'm a little sceptical but I don't trust the witch."

Alyssa said nothing and, strapping her shield to her back, headed for the carved passageway at the cave's far edge. She picked up a burning wicker torch from a bracket screwed into the wall and made her way into the gloom.

"I'm really not being paid enough for this," grumbled Rascal to himself as he tied a bag of swag to his waist. With a heavy heart he lightly jogged after the slowly vanishing outline of Alyssa ahead. "I must speak to the union about industrial action when I get back."

Chapter Nine – Back to Jack (Briefly)

Jack woke up groggily at around half eleven. He had woken earlier, when dawn broke, but he shrugged it off, crawled under an old derelict Volkswagen and slept in the shade. But a scrap yard, no matter how derelict, can only provide so many hours of comfortable sleep so Jack eventually decided to get up. He crawled from his hole and dusted himself off. He staggered forwards to the street and glanced towards the warehouse. It looked pretty much as he remembered it. Warehousey.

Once he was satisfied he wasn't being watched by anyone he hopped over a narrow wall and out on to the street. First order of business. Find Joe. He worked his way down a few streets and eventually found a working telephone booth. He squeezed in and dialled the operator.

"Reverse charges on John Drager, Scunchester," he said to the operator. A voice garbled in his ear. "Tell him it's his Mum. You heard. I'm Mrs. Drager. Yeah, you too lady, now put me through." A moment later he was through to Drager's office.

"Err, Mum?" said a nasal voice.

"Hey, Ven, it's Jack."

"Ummm." Drager was a little wrong footed. "Okay, Jack, what's so urgent that you had to pretend to be my mother?"

"Nothing. Listen, have you seen Joe?"

"You called me up, pretending to be my ailing Mother to ask me where your brother is?"

"Yeah. You seen him?"

"No, I've not seen him. I…" he paused. "I've got a call on the other line. Hold a second."

Rather lifeless music tinkled through the earpiece for about half a minute.

"Jack? Joe is on the other line. He says you should meet him at Charlie's in twenty minutes."

"Drag…" the line went dead.

Chapter Ten – An Hour Or So Later

An hour or so later Jack arrived at Charlie's garage. Joe was sitting in an old open-top convertible out front, a large 'For Sale' sign across the windscreen. Jack swaggered over and leaned on the passenger door, sweating wildly. A trickle dribbled off the end of his nose and dripped onto the fake leather interior. He breathed heavily trying to speak, but it took a few attempts before he could even get his first word out.

"Do you know how long it takes to get from Greenings Estate to here?" he snorted eventually, lifting his baseball cap with one hand and wiping his forehead with his Hawaiian sleeve.

"About twenty minutes if you take the number seventeen bus," replied Joe matter-of-factly.

"Yeah, about twenty minutes if you've got bus fare. About an hour and a half if you've got to walk all the way, fuck-face." Jack was not best pleased. In fact, if he wasn't so knackered he probably would have punched him one. He panted some more. Joe shrugged.

"Anything else happen after I left?"

"Nah. They just parked the corpse-mobile in the warehouse and that was it," Jack panted. "What the hell was with you anyway?" He nodded towards the ripped out stereo from the Mercedes that was in his brother's lap. "I hardly think that yesterday was the ideal time for us to start a stolen car stereo racket."

"True," Joe conceded. "But at least they think we were only after the radio. They don't know we've seen what was in the boot."

"So?"

"So. There is a good chance the body will still be there when we break into the warehouse tonight."

"Break into the warehouse!?" Jack shouted rather too loudly. A few passers-by threw nervous glances in his direction before scurrying off to carry on with their own misdemeanours. Jack carried on in an angry whisper. "Are you out of your bloody mind?"

"I've spoken to Drager and he wants answers. He's already paid up for last night's action. He's paying double for an ID on the body."

"Double?" Jack shook his head. "You should have asked for triple. We're going to get killed."

"I did ask for triple, but he threatened to hire Brownlow."

"Brownlow couldn't do the job, Joe, he's an idiot. You should have asked for triple."

"No, I mean he was going to hire Brownlow to work with us, not instead of us."

Jack considered this for a while. "Oh," he concluded. "Double will be fine."

Joe opened the car door and stepped out. He wandered into the garage workshop and Jack wearily followed him, dragging his well worn heels across the pot-holed concrete. Inside they saw the familiar face of Charlie standing over the familiar shape of their car. They'd known Charlie a few years and had in fact bought the Maestro from him in the first place. Charlie was a half-decent mechanic who charged very little, a quality greatly admired by the brothers. The car had had to be repaired on numerous occasions and Charlie had been known, like today, to work absolute miracles.

"It was hard work, mon," baritoned Charlie gently. "You'd ripped it pretty bad. We had to strip the engine and straighten the chassis." He spoke slowly and with great care rolling each word around his mouth before releasing it through his thick red lips.

"Plus we fixed the creaking door." An oil-drenched mechanic wheeled out from underneath the Maestro. It was Charlie's garage monkey, Bronzer, a wiry creature covered from head to foot in grease. He grinned as he talked allowing the white of his teeth to shine brightly in contrast to the rest of his face.

"Did you save the fridge?" asked Jack.

"We did our best, Jack mon," Charlie told him. "But it was too late." He nodded towards the back wall where Jack's prize possession lay in two separate pieces. The door of the fridge swung gently open and a liquid ooze seeped out over the floor. As Jack looked sadly on, a shelf collapsed inside the unit and a hiss whistled softly. Jack removed his cap and lowered his head, offering a small prayer to the ancient Greek god of refrigeration.

"Give us the keys, Charlie." Charlie complied and gave a battered set of keys to Joe.

"Can we get paid, Joseph?" asked the mechanic with doomed optimism.

"Erm, add it to my bill," stalled Joe. "We'll pay when the jobs up, okay?"

"Okay. I will add it to the rest, mon," nodded Charlie. He was pretty much used to this by now.

Chapter Eleven - That Night, Back At The Warehouse

Jack and Joe arrived on the street on foot just after midnight. Keeping out of the moonlight they edged their way forwards along the pavement before eventually taking advantage of the cover offered by the derelict scrap yard. The street was deserted and ill lit, with only a few of the nearby council houses showing any sign of life. The warehouse too was in darkness, any street lighting in the area long since vandalised by Scunchester's local school children.

The brothers kept their position in the scrap yard for a good forty minutes, looking for even the smallest indication of activity near or in the warehouse. Ideally they wanted to see whoever was in there close up shop for the night and leave, but they doubted they'd get so lucky. They didn't even know if someone was in there or not, but Drager had said that his boys hadn't seen anyone leave all day. That only left the period when Jack was asleep unaccounted for.

A third dark figure emerged from the darkness and took position next to a rather surprised Jack and Joe.

"'Ello again," said the figure in a friendly but whispered voice. He was a stunted male dressed darkly, holding a screwdriver carelessly in his gloved left hand. He had short but uneven hair greased tightly to his scalp with a wax that smelt vaguely of cooking oil. His chin was unshaven and his thick muscular neck was covered in misspelt tattoos.

"Don't try number fir-teen," advised the figure "The man, 'e's got 'imself a big dog."

Joe nodded very slowly to the stranger. "Thanks," he managed.

"No problem," whistled the figure who then hoisted himself up. He stooped right and lurched into the darkness.

"That's just what we need," said Jack to his brother with a nudge to his ribs. "A friendly burglar."

Joe shrugged. "Come on," he ordered.

The pair scrambled through the vehicle graveyard tripping over the odd rusted engine part and generally being noisy in the way people are when they are doing their damnedest not to make a sound. Nearer to the warehouse they stopped, just close enough to check for any security devices that might hinder the covert operation. It was a squint to see in the darkness. An alarm of some sort was obviously in place, its warning light blinking passively in a manner that fooled no one. No other security precautions were visible, save for the display of cemented glass shards that decorated the skirt of the rooftops presumably to prevent unwanted climbers from reaching its lofty summit. Jack and Joe preferred to use the door. They located a first floor fire exit partially hidden by trees and climbed the rusted metal ladder that was clamped to the wall underneath. Joe nodded to the door and Jack nodded to Joe. Jack peered at the door closely, placing his eye to a tight crack running vertically downwards bang in the middle of the exit. Joe kept watch, looking out for any possible danger lurking in the darkness. It took Jack a few minutes to pick the lock, longer than usual, which was odd, but finally the door silently swung open. Jack had taken the precaution of oiling visible hinges in order to minimise detection, only spilling a little bit onto the fire escape.

The two tiptoed tentatively through the doorway. Joe quietly closed the fire door leaving the brothers in the kind of semi darkness that makes you wish you'd thought on to bring a flash-light. Edging forwards it was obvious even in the darkness that the fire escape had led them into an office corridor of some sort, although the stale smell and shattered windows suggested this particular part of the warehouse complex had not been used for some time. Joe felt the braver of the two and took point, leading the slow advance down the silent corridor by feeling his way along the brittle plasterboard wall. Jack hovered by the door for as long as he could get away with, but eventually and with a marked reluctance he followed his brother.

Ahead of Jack, Joe stopped. He could hear a voice. Several voices, in fact. Very faint voices, but certainly coming from within the building. With even greater care he edged forwards a little further. He could make out a bend in the corridor just about visible in the darkness and it wasn't long until his frantically feeling fingers found an edge as the wall took an abrupt turn to the right. Joe paused a minute to allow Jack to gain a few yards behind him. The turn led them to some kind of metallic gantry that trailed like a giant balcony across one half of what was presumably the main warehouse storage area. Perching themselves in a corner near to the corridor they had just appeared from, Jack and Joe achieved a perfect vantage point from which they could view the majority of the warehouse underneath.

The near and far side of the large chamber lay in darkness, but large chunks of debris were clearly visible. The car with the corpse had been parked just in front of the huge garage-like grill doors that dominated the front of the warehouse. A pathway, large enough for the car to drive along, lay clear from the front door through to the back part of the warehouse where the voices could still be heard. Jack and Joe had to squeeze forwards and lean between the rails of the gantry to view the back of the warehouse. Fair light shone from several small lamps, which helped. The brothers watched and listened.

The lit area was spread out like a makeshift lounge. A long, battered old sofa lay across from a flickering but silent television set. An easy chair of a suitably contrasting colour to the sofa sat uneasily to the left with plumes of sponge peeking out of the tears in the mouldy fabric. Between the two was a small oblong table that was used variously as a footstool and a pizza box storage area. Behind the mock-up lounge was a mock-up kitchen, partially hidden in a plasterboard alcove. A wooden decorating table poked out from the alcove supporting a microwave, a kettle and a pop-up toaster. Four figures intermingled between the various parts of the makeshift hang-out.

"'Ere," said a short, red-headed runt spread-eagled on the sofa, his belly popping out of his hooded top. "You guys won't be gone long will you?"

"We'll be gone as long as we 'ave to," said the lanky one with the good hair. "Mr. Smith wants us to do some jobs for 'im don't 'e." The two others, twins, were standing just next to the lanky one and sneering.

"An' you gotta watch the warearse fer us," said one of the twins.

"Importan' job, warearse watchin'," said the other twin.

"I don't wanna stay 'ere wit' dead body!" protested the ginger youth.

"It's a lot o' responsibility," said the lanky one. "If you wanna join the gang proper you gotta do wot we tells ya. Got it?" The ginger youth nodded meekly from his half-folded position. The three others picked up various bits of equipment and moments later they were gone. The ginger youth watched them leave through the garage doors and then picked up the remote control for the television and began watching Perry Mason.

Chapter Twelve – Two Hours And Two Minutes Later

After thirty-six minutes of watching the lack of events beneath them, Jack had fallen asleep. An hour and twenty-six minutes later, the short ginger youth, long since bored of watching eighties reruns, followed suit and started slipping zees. Loudly.

Joe nudged his brother. "Wake up," he whispered.

"Wha'huh?" drooled Jack as his tried to regain focus. "Whassat?"

A few minutes later Joe had successfully woken his brother.

"Let's go," he said. They edged along the rim on the metal platform, the quiet clink of their feet just about muffled out by the sound of the television. Joe noticed the ginger youth stir slightly but so far he seemed undisturbed by Jack and Joe's delicate movement. Half way along the metallic balcony between a support strut and the near side wall a circular hole opened up onto a ladder that delved downwards to the ground floor below. The pair descended the ladder and made their way through the derelict storage area towards the sleeping ginger youth.

Joe stopped.

"We could use this," he said. He bent down and scooped up a roll of half used packing tape. Jack gave a quick nod and a wink. They both took a deep breath and rushed towards the sofa, Joe tearing the tape with his teeth. It didn't take them long to secure the ginger youth. He woke up half way through the process to protest, but Joe was quick with the packing tape. Under and over the sofa it went, securing the youth like a badly wrapped Christmas present, with bits of him sticking out everywhere.

"'Ere, get off," he said, squirming to move an arm.

Jack rested his foot on the table and grinned. "What's your name, kid?"

"Billy," said Billy. "Lemme go!" Billy gave a pitiful scream, half of fear, half of panic.

Jack ignored him and looked to his brother. "Now what?"

"Now we get the body."

They left Billy squirming. Jack managed to stop him screaming by ramming a slice of leftover pizza in his mouth, but it was only a temporary solution at best. Jack looked at the car and scratched his chin. He pulled a small knife from his trouser pocket and fiddled with the lock of the boot anxious not to set the car alarm off this time. It took a few moments longer than the last time but Jack managed to jimmy the boot open with only a few minor scratches and, thankfully, no alarm honk. The dead body was still inside, and didn't look any healthier. Joe grabbed the legs and half yanked the body out of the car. He nodded to Jack to indicate he was to grab the head.

"No way, Joe. He's staring at me, it's freaking me out. I'm not touching the bloody head."

"Pick up the head, Jack," ordered Joe. Reluctantly Jack bent over and grabbed the upper half of the body. His right hand disappeared behind the back of the body to pull it forwards. He felt something wet and sticky and quickly jerked away, showing his blood soaked hand to his brother.

"Get a load of this red shit," moaned Jack. "He's still bleeding."

"Stop moaning and get on with it."

It took a while longer than Joe had hoped but they finally got the body from out of the boot and dragged it feet first towards the living area, leaving a slug-like trail of blood behind them. They just got back as Billy gulped down the last of the wedge of pizza.

"Martin is gonna be mad when 'e gets back," warned Billy. "You better put th' dead guy back."

Jack propped up the body against the TV while Joe searched the body's jacket for a wallet and ID. Nothing in the jacket pockets, so he stuck his hands into the dead guy's trousers and gave a jangle. Nothing. Nothing worth mentioning anyway.

He looked at Billy, "Billy, do you know who this guy is?"

"Yeah, 'e was called 'Arry Sommat, Mar'in said. Can I have some mor' pizza?"

Joe grabbed a slice of cold pizza and threw it towards Billy who caught the slice skilfully between his teeth.

"You got a phone?" he asked.

Billy gave a grunt and nod towards the makeshift kitchen. Jack and Joe dragged the body with them. With a heave they propped the body against the work surface near the back wall. The body's head slumped backwards at right angles to his torso.

Joe picked up the phone and dialled.

"Who are you calling?" asked Jack, smearing the blood from his hand across his outer Hawaiian shirt.

"Drager," Joe replied. The phone gave a quiet click. "Hey, Drager, it's Joseph. We got the stiff, but no ID."

Joe listened a moment.

"Yeah. We got a kid here, thinks he was a Harry. Yeah, I don't reckon he knows too much."

Again, a quiet pause.

"No, we haven't found anything like that."

A long pause. Every few minutes Joe would nod a quiet uh-huh. The phone gave a click and very slowly Joe lowered the receiver. For a few minutes Joe didn't say anything.

"Well?" said his brother. "What do we do now, smart-arse?"

"Drager says the guy is probably Harry Mantei, his client. He says he should have some kind of necklace on him."

"Necklace? Those fuckin' loonies would have taken it," Jack shouted.

"Yeah," said Billy munching the last of the slice of pizza. Somehow he'd manage to squeeze his left hand up through the tape, giving him a few inches of pizza-eating movement. "Mar'in were lookin' for somethin' like that for the Mister."

"The Mister?" asked Jack.

Billy squirmed a little, possibly remembering what Martin would do to him if he told anybody what they were doing and who they were working for. He was quite fond of his testicles. "Yeah. I don't know 'is real name," he lied (unbeknownst to him his lie was actually accurate).

Joe straightened his tie and frowned towards Jack. "Drager thinks Mantei may have eaten it."

"Eaten it? Great. So what's he want us to do. Haul this guy's backside to Drager's office and hope he has a post-death involuntary movement of the bowel? No thanks."

"No. Drager says we are to leave the body here."

"That's more like it. Let's get out of this place before the ginger lad's friends get back. It's getting late and it's probably past their bedtime."

"Yeah, any chance you could untie me?" asked Billy, struggling a little on the sofa. "Me Mum will be wonderin' were I've got to."

"Shut the fuck up," shouted Jack, "before I nail your testicles to the wall."

"Figures," mumbled Billy under his breath.

"Drager also says we can't leave without the necklace," said Joe.

"Great. What does Drager want me to do? Stick my hand up his arse?" Jack waved his hand about for his brother to see. Joe said nothing, but instead watched Jack's hand. After a moment he looked Jack in the eye and without speaking gave him an answer he didn't want to hear. Jack slowly started to shake his head.

"No, no," stammered Jack.

"You'd better take off your digital watch."

"Hey, just a minute. Why can't you do it?"

"You're already covered in blood, what difference is it going to make. We could always toss a coin for it."

"That is so unfair," argued Jack. "You know I always lose a coin toss." An old gypsy lady had cursed Jack when he was six and as a result he had unmanageable hair and an uncanny ability to lose a coin toss.

"You don't have to go through the rectum," pointed out Joe. "We could cut him open. We just need to get to his stomach." He wandered over to a sink and removed a bread knife and a small paring knife.

"Oh that's brilliant," Jack told his brother as he walked back. "A bread knife, the tool of the professional surgeon. Drager better pay us good for this." He removed his baseball cap and rubbed his forehead, suddenly feeling a tense headache pushing itself through. Jack took the bread knife from his brother and held the blade up, letting the lamp light glint off the metal. He shook his head and pushed the body of Harry Mantei flat on the floor.

Moments later the operation was underway. Joe pulled up the corpse's shirt and Jack pressed the knife against the flabby skin of the exposed belly. He pressed down as hard as he could and drew the knife towards him. The dead flesh tore underneath. Joe winced as the first lines of blood seeped out of the dead man's abdomen. A dank smell drifted from the open wound and hit Joe's nostrils with a surprising amount of violence. Steadily Jack shoved the knife back and forth. The blood clung to his hands like a dark red paint and if it wasn't for the knife in his hand and the corpse at his feet a casual observer would probably think he'd been doing a wall at home and not had chance to wash.

It took several random incisions and the removal of a lengthy amount of intestines but they found it. A metal pendant about an inch high. It was a cross of some kind. The shortest end had a little loop on it, a short length of chain through it enabling the pendant to be worn around the neck. The base of the short end was wide curving inwards to meet the centre of the cross. Two equal length ends stuck out left and right, thick at the tip and thinner towards the middle. The longest end was double the length of the short end and was the thickest of all the points of the cross. The centrepiece itself was a square inlaid with a circle rising upwards, while the backside of the cross was bare.

"Is that it?" Jack wiped some sick he'd drooled during the fourteen minute operation with an oil cloth he'd found on the floor.

"I guess."

"What a fucking waste of time."

"I guess."

Neither of the two said anything for a while. Billy had long since fainted and Jack and Joe were only disturbed from their embarrassed silence by the banging of the main entrance doors as they were unbolted. At which point they ran.

With cumbersome speed Jack and Joe scrambled up the metal rails to the gantry above. Martin and the twins stooped through the opening warehouse shutters and gave confused shouts, unsure as to the extent of the warehouse intrusion. They stumbled quickly into the dimly lit warehouse, their keen criminal senses telling them that something had seriously gotten fucked up.

"Shit," exclaimed Martin as he rushed across the warehouse only to discover Billy taped to the sofa and the butchered body of Harry Mantei dripping over the makeshift breakfast bar-cum-operating theatre. "Shit."

"They's up the gantry," shouted the ugliest of the twins. The gawky pair made chase after Jack and Joe who by now were clumping down the dark corridor at the end of the gantry. Martin, however, didn't run. He picked up the phone and dialled a number. He waited patiently for a few minutes before, finally, somebody answered.

"Mr. Smith?" he said.

"Nah, mate," came a tinny voice at the other end of the phone. "Ya got the wrong number. This is a call box, mate."

Chapter Thirteen – Seconds After Before

Jack and Joe tumbled down the fire escape at the side of the warehouse, Joe first. Jack had slipped on the hinge grease he had dribbled earlier and slammed into his sibling sending them simultaneously sprawling down the rust covered steps.

"Ow," moaned Joe as he picked himself up from the floor at the foot of the rusty stairs. He stretched the curve of his back, clicking several bones back into their rightful place.

"Fuck ow," reprimanded his brother, his hands still covered in Harry's blood. He scrambled forwards. "Let's get the fuck out of here."

The brothers made it to the ill lit road and raced for the scrap yard, jockeying for position with flailing arms and tempered comments. As the pair pushed and pulled each other over the low brick wall at the boundary of the scrap yard the sky roared with thunder and flashed with an eerie green light that seared and arced across the sky like a badly drawn cartoon. Another clap followed and the lightning faded. Joe's fingers grasped the dusty red bricks of the wall and he pulled his body upwards so that his narrow eyes could just see over the brickwork. He blinked quietly and reached down with his right hand. Jack gave a grunt as Joe jerked him to eye-level. It took a moment, but suddenly Jack was looking in the right direction. Or if you think like Jack, looking in the wrong direction.

The three stooges that Jack and Joe had bumped into earlier, the ogres who had bust up Greasy Bob's café, were standing in the middle of the otherwise deserted road. Wisps of ash swirled around their feet as one by one they raised their six unhealthily over-sized pistols and pointed them in Jack and Joe's general direction.

"Give us the pendant," growled the middle stooge, the one wearing the blue jacket. "Erm, this is Thursday, right?"

A horrible silence followed, disturbed only by the cocking of six large pistols.

"I've got a pl…" whispered Joe, but it was too late. Jack had formed a plan of his own and it involved running in the opposite direction very, very fast. Joe, who knew a good idea when he saw one, followed rapidly behind. The pistols opened fire. A hail of lead trailed the darting brothers who dived for cover behind half a Nissan Micra. The stooges advanced and the spray from the weapons quickly disintegrated the brother's limited hiding place. They lunged to the ground as the Micra ripped away under the heavy barrage. The firing abruptly stopped as the stooges took a moment to reload. Jack and Joe took a moment to get up and run like their arses were on fire.

They ran across the scrap yard, between the dead cars and broken debris, with just enough distance and cover to dissuade the three stooges from a further barrage of gunfire. They clambered over another short wall, and darted across the street to where their hatchback was waiting. Jack and Joe hopped quickly into their car. Jack swirled around with an eager grin to watch the stooges disappear into the distance as the Maestro raced into the moonlight. His grin faded as he realised the goons were actually getting closer and the roar of the car engine just hadn't happened yet. He swivelled in panic, gaping at his brother.

Joe frowned, hand still over the ignition key as he watched his brother carefully. "Put your seat belt on," he said stern-faced.

"We're being chased by three gun heavy arseholes and you're asking me to put my seat belt on?" Jack was shouting, clearly upset by the turn of events. He could see the bad guys in the rear view mirror. One of them raised a pistol.

"Put your seat belt on," repeated Joe. Jack blinked but didn't answer back. Instead he slipped on his safety belt with a great deal of haste, fumbling at the catch. Joe twisted the key in the ignition and after the second attempt he pressed heavily on the accelerator pedal. The Maestro lurched forwards with a bang of the exhaust followed by a bang of poorly aimed gunfire.

Chapter Fourteen – The Far, Far Future, Off To The Side A Bit

Rascal rested his arm lightly on Alyssa's forearm and tugged at the strap of her bracer. She snarled in his direction, but quickly realised he was actually trying to attract her attention and not just trying to get a quick feel. She followed his panicky pointed finger and looked at the altar ahead of them, fifty foot tall if it was an inch. A great dais raised at the pinnacle of a winding stone stairwell that circled the great column at the heart of the gloomy cave. It wasn't, of course, the steepness of the climb that worried Rascal, although he wasn't looking forward to the eventual and inevitable journey. It was the five bastard stone golems that were standing in the way.

"C'mon," whispered Alyssa, as she ducked under a fallen granite plinth that had once been a fine kitchen worktop and was now, sadly, dedicated to denizens of evil. She crouched behind a lone stalagmite, the first golem not more than twenty feet away from her. The golem was twice as tall as the enchantress, and twice as wide. His brick coloured fists held a gigantic stone staff in his inch thick fingers. The golem was gently knocking his staff on the floor to a steady rhythm. Alyssa peered around her cover and could just make out two white wires drooping down from the stoney creature's ears. She realised that the golem was actually listening to music, and was even tapping a foot along to the beat. She could swear that she could hear him quietly humming an Elvis tune even at this distance. *Bloody stone golems and their rock 'n' roll,* thought Alyssa.

"What's the plan?" asked Rascal who had sneaked up behind Alyssa. "My old Mammy told me that stone golems are impervious to mortal weapons."

"She did, did she?"

"Yeah. Of course I don't know what impervious actually means. I really should have looked it up. But it doesn't matter. I don't think even you can handle five of the buggers, although I'm prepared to watch you try. From a safe distance." The rogue grinned helpfully.

"No need," came a quick reply. Alyssa fumbled at her Gucci backpack and pulled out a paper wrapped parcel. Her fingers quietly pulled at the string and loosened the brown skin. "I have enchanted a cape that will grant us invisibility." She pulled out what appeared to be absolutely nothing from the parcel and held it up to show her companion.

"Are you sure?" asked Rascal slowly. "I mean, I can't see any cape or anything."

"That's the point."

"Hmm."

Alyssa pulled an invisible end of cloth over her red hair and dangled the cape behind her. She fiddled with her fingers around her neck, tying an invisible cord.

"Get in close behind me and bend over," demanded Alyssa to an unconvinced Rascal. "And no funny business or the stone golems will be the last of your worries, understand?"

"You're the boss," conceded the thief as he lowered himself into position, close to Alyssa's firm backside. He nervously placed his hands on Alyssa's generous hips and waited to be told off. No rebuke came, and instead Alyssa merely tossed the invisible other end of the cape over Rascal's bent back ensuring he was well covered by the sightless material.

"We walk slowly between the golems, right?" she whispered with her head twisted backwards. "Lets just hope they all have mp3 players playing loud music into their tiny skulls so they don't hear our movements."

"Hey, relax. If there is one thing I can do it is move silently."

"As I recall you said that before we ran into the troll."

"I didn't see the bloody troll, alright?"

"Hmm." The conversation faltered as the pair stealthily picked their way between the walking monoliths, turning this way and that to get between the bulky frame of each of the creatures. The pair inched towards the spiralling column. Alyssa felt Rascal's nose nuzzle gently against her bottom and she made a mental note to break his nose once the golden egg was hers. She could hear the scraping of Rascal's sandals on the flagstones underfoot and wondered where exactly the thief had learnt his trade. He should probably ask for his money back.

"Where you goin'?" came a deep booming voice in broken basic. Alyssa glanced left and saw a stone golem standing to one side looking firmly in her direction. The golem's spear was on the floor at his feet, and instead he held a mobile phone in his hands. It looked like he was in the middle of sending a text message, which is difficult on a touch screen when your fingers are like huge sausages. Alyssa and Rascal kept very still and hoped that the golem wasn't actually talking to them. Perhaps he was speaking into the phone. They should be so lucky.

"Woman and bent man. Why you creep here?" The golem was obviously addressing the two of them. He lowered his mobile phone to his side (inadvertently crushing it, a common problem for golems but luckily he had taken the insurance option) and picked up his spear.

"You can see us?" asked Alyssa hesitantly. Rascal slowly rose upright and stretched his back. He started whistling quietly and kicked away some dust with a foot, trying somehow to give the impression that he wasn't actually with Alyssa and was just passing through, all innocent like.

"Duh, yeah," came the slow reply. "I 'ave eyes y'know." One or two of the other golems started to realise that they were not alone and began to remove their earphones.

"Crap," said Alyssa through thin lips to Rascal. "We must have dropped the cape."

"Okay, you now stand still. I come and kill you." The golem laboured to move one foot forwards, hitting the ground with a satifying thud. Several other golems followed, forming a sturdy broken line of stone monsters.

"On three, we run," said Alyssa calmly to her compatriot. Rascal had no intention of waiting for three however, and immediately darted away from the enemy just as fast as his weedy legs would let him. Alyssa twisted around and followed quickly behind him, her crushed velvet boots pounding powerfully on the floor as her thighs pumped her forwards with a surprising burst of speed that allowed her almost immediately to overtake her cowardly companion. The first golem pushed an arm forwards, releasing his spear which could only clatter harmlessly in the space where Alyssa and Rascal had been. Stone golems are a little slow about these things and prefer it when their prey keep very, very still.

A fifth golem was standing between the fleeing heroes and the central column. Whilst still running Alyssa quickly raised a hand out in front of her and chanted a quick spell. Her eyes focussed on the golem, bringing him into a sharp focus as the world seemed to slow around her. She remembered what she was taught at wizard finishing school. The world was just a game and the laws of physics are just a fiction dreamt up by the Instructor in an effort to keep things from floating off into the sky. Alyssa's faced was screwed in concentration as she twisted her hand in front of her as if she'd just grabbed an unseen rug on the floor. She screamed at the top of her voice and yanked her hand back into her midriff, pulling the non-existent rug from under the somewhat perplexed stone golem who had only moments before been minding his own business happily listening to the latest BeeGee's album. Despite the fact that the golem weighed about as much as two fat elephants who had just stampeded through an all-you-can-eat buffet, the golem's feet gave way under him and he fell painfully onto his backside, causing both it and the floor to crack. Alyssa leapt into the air and somersaulted over the prone and rather distraught creature before coming to a halt facing back the way she came. Rascal veered around the golem, and panted up to Alyssa clutching his chest and muttering something about an asthma attack. He'd foolishly left his inhaler with his dragon.

The four remaining stone golems had taken one or two slow steps in chase but were already some way behind. The sight of the fifth golem on the floor and half broken at the waist made the others take stock for a moment and consider their priorities. Most of them were here on minimum wage after all, and no job was worth getting cut in half over. Alyssa simply stared at them, hand held in the air as if to challenge them to come and try their luck. After a moment the first golem put down his spear and fed his earphones back into the appropriate orifice, before turning away and walking off whistling to whatever tune was blaring in his ear drums. One by one the other golems all wandered off and seemed happy to leave Alyssa and Rascal to it.

Alyssa smiled at Rascal. "Now we will climb the stairway column of Abradar and find the Golden Egg."

"Ladies first."

Alyssa punched Rascal hard on the nose.

Chapter Fifteen – The Present, Ten Minutes Later

The needles on the dials on the dashboard of the ageing car flickered into red as Joe thrust up into fourth gear. It had been almost ten minutes since the brothers had watched the three over-sized gun-toting barbarians disappear in the rear view mirror but they'd been keen to make some distance between them and the warehouse. Jack was sweating nervously under his baseball cap but resisted wiping himself with his blood soaked sleeves.

"We've gotta get somewhere safe and we've gotta get somewhere quick," he said. "This is a stupid amount of fuss over a piece of jewellery." Jack unclipped his safety belt and then undid and removed his ruined and bloody shirt, flinging it out of the side window. He twisted his wobbly flesh around and rummaged around in the littered luggage that remained on the back seat. From somewhere he found a brightly coloured shirt, possibly identical to the one he had just chucked, and quickly pulled it over his head pausing only to sniff at the armpits.

A red light appeared on a set of traffic lights ahead and Joe eased on the brake pedal bringing the car to a halt. He reached for the handbrake but before he had time to give it a yank the Maestro was shunted forwards giving the surprised brothers a painful jerk, especially Jack as he hadn't put his safety belt back on.

Joe threw a glance in the rear view mirror. "It's that black-windowed BMW again!"

"Jeez, they came out of nowhere."

Joe pressed hard on the brake pedal and flipped on the hazard warning lights. They could feel the car slowly inch forwards as the powerful engine of the BMW roared behind them. Jack shrugged and lit a cigarette from a pack he'd found in the glove compartment.

"I thought you were giving up?" asked his brother.

"Yeah well, I'm out of patches." He shrugged in reply. "Any idea who is in the car behind us or what their problem is?"

"Nope."

As if to answer them, a door on the passenger side of the BMW opened. Above it a head appeared. It was the shaven skull of Bolt, the largest of the three stooges, and he had a grin on his face. He lifted onto his shoulder a long cylindrical object and flicked upright a set of cross hairs.

Joe didn't hesitate and switched feet quickly from brake to accelerator flinging the car forwards with as much acceleration as its manual gears could muster. Joe pushed hard to the right and screeched the car through the traffic lights and down the junction. Bolt tracked the car and swung the cylinder right. He tugged a trigger on the underside of the pipe. A length of fire whooshed out of the end of the object, hurtling dangerously in the direction of Jack and Joe. Joe was pushing the car's overheating engine hard and the missile narrowly missed the Maestro's tail. Instead it whooshed on, through the thick black smoke that poured from the Maestro's exhaust pipe, and devastated the dining room of a two-storey house, causing one of the occupants to spill his brains across the wall and the other to spill her tea.

Bolt clambered back into the black windowed car, banging his head as he did so. The car screeched forwards leaving skidmarks that any twelve year old boy would be proud of. It veered right and followed Jack and Joe.

"I think these guys are serious, bro," said Jack. "They are after that bloody pendant. Let's just give 'em the thing and get out of this hole."

"No. We have got a job to do. We need to get the pendant to Drager."

"Forget Drager!" The BMW had caught up the lost ground at this point and pounded the Maestro, ramming it hard from behind. Several bits of the hatchback fell off. "We'll just tell the idiot that we mailed it to him and he can take it up with the Post Office."

Joe swerved left, dragging the BMW behind it. He rammed through the side window of a car showroom that had foolishly decided to have its premises on the corner of the junction. An alarm blared out as the window shattered and the Maestro jumped forwards, clipping several new car models. The BMW, caught on the Maestro's bumper, spun left and shunted this year's Ford Fiesta. The Maestro's bumper ripped to the floor and Joe again pressed hard on the accelerator. He sped ahead and broke through the window at the other side of the showroom jumping back out onto the road. The BMW reversed for a moment to straighten up and then followed, its back-end swerving as it accelerated.

The sun crept lazily over the horizon, and the awkward light shone though the Maestro's windscreen. Dawn had arrived and it was only a matter of time before gridlock chaos. Joe fished around under the dashboard, found what he was looking for and put on some sunglasses.

"Jesus," moaned Jack playing with his wing mirror. "They are still behind us."

"I know." Joe twisted the steering wheel viciously right and pulled at the hand brake. The Maestro cried as it swung painfully from the left side of the road to the right. The black BMW sped past braking hard. Joe pushed the accelerator and the Maestro whimpered down a side road. The BMW gave a roar and followed behind. Ahead the side road joined to a dual carriageway that headed into the centre of Scunchester. Already slow moving traffic was beginning to form as the morning rush to work began to make its mark.

"Err, Joe…," Jack began.

Joe pressed hard on the accelerator and swung the car right. The car mashed sideways into a blue transit van, which came as quite a shock to the lady who was driving it. Joe didn't stop and the Maestro scraped on to the pavement, violently swiping another vehicle as it did so. The car darted between lampposts and Joe wildly honked that he was coming through ready or not. The Maestro jumped off the kerb and squeezed over both the first and second lanes. Metal screeched and glass shattered as Joe forced the car through and on to the grassy embankment that separated the incoming traffic from the outgoing. He veered right and drove down the verge.

"I can't see them," said Jack who had swivelled around and searched the traffic for the chasing BMW.

"Hopefully they've given up," said Joe. "Only an idiot would do what I just did."

"Uh-huh," nodded Jack nervously in agreement.

Joe indicated left and pulled off the verge and on to the roadway, leaving half the car's exhaust pipe behind as he did so. The road had come to a roundabout and Joe forced his way ahead of several patiently queuing drivers. The Maestro chugged forwards and suddenly turned away again as the blue lights of a police car appeared from around the corner. Joe turned hard and the Maestro once again lifted itself off the road and onto the pavement, jumping through a fence and into someone's back garden.

"Wouldn't it be easier to get out and run?" said Jack. The police car had turned its siren on and bounced off the roundabout to follow the brother's chaotic journey.

"Probably." The wheels spun hard churning the grass lawn into mud. Jack waved happily and shrugged to the garden's owner who was gawking at them from the window of a large house. Joe pressed on, flattening a trellis, and mowed over a cluster of rhododendrons. The police car followed hard and fast, crushing several rose bushes and destroying a fence crawling with some kind of climbing vine. Joe lurched left and into a greenhouse. The panes shattered and the roof began to collapse behind them.

"Nice tomatoes," said Joe. The car collided through the far side of the greenhouse dragging chains of tomatoes with it. Many had splattered the front windscreen of the car. Joe squirted and wiped, spraying tomato juice onto some nearby conifers. "I hope the coppers don't *catch up*." Jack just rolled his eyes.

The police car knocked over any part of the greenhouse that the Maestro had missed but lost a wheel to a shard of broken glass with a frightening pop. The pressure of the exploding wheel caused the police car to hop left and smash into a conservatory. Its siren came to an embarrassing stop and quite surprised the couple sitting in the conservatory having their breakfast.

Jack and Joe boldly drove through another privet hedge and

didn't spot the swimming pool until the last moment.

"Shit," said Joe as the car jumped into the air above the pool.

"Shit," Jack agreed.

The car splashed to a gurgling halt. The brothers had no choice but to swim from the wreckage and pull themselves to the water's edge. Two police constables ran into view.

"You guys are in a lot of trouble," said the first policeman, holding a sturdy looking baton in his hand.

"Can you call our mechanic?" asked Jack. "I think our car will need a bit of work."

"We're probably still under warranty," added Joe.

Chapter Sixteen – The Present, A Little Later On

"Dammit," said Jack as he paced back and forth in the small holding cell the two brothers were being temporarily detained in. The police had been rather smug when the brothers were brought into the station. Jack and Joe had been bungled through a side door and a desk sergeant had taken their details, adding a few sarcastic comments of his own to the arrest report. Their fingerprints had been forcibly scanned and a dimly lit mug shot photo shoot had taken place. They'd snapped Jack's left profile, which annoyed him because it wasn't his best side. They'd been breathalysed, searched, tested for drugs, searched again, quizzed and beaten up. Finally they'd been dumped in a cell and warned they'd have to wait while the police prepared a room for the cavity search and this was why Jack now paced back and forth anxiously.

"Dammit. Why does this always happen to us?" asked Jack.

"I don't think I recall either of us having a cavity search before."

"No, I mean why do we always end up in trouble for doing other people's dirty work. I wouldn't mind if it was over something important, but a bloody pendant?" Jack thumped at the cold brick wall with the base of his fist. "I'll give Drager a cavity search of his own when I get hold of him."

"The pendant mustn't be that important," admitted Joe. "The police didn't take it." Although in truth he thought that was perhaps down to a slack jawed officer not getting enough caffeine. The dreary eyed bobby performing the search had taken the shoelaces out of their shoes, but not bothered to check Joe's shirt pocket.

Jack frowned and tugged at the pendant. He'd tied it around his neck and it hung uneasily underneath his shirt. The harsh cold metal of the pendant irritated Jack's skin, something else he wasn't best pleased about.

There was a slide of metal.

"Pssst."

Jack and Joe both swung around and looked to the door. Through a small hatch at eye level peered a head covered in a damp yellow cloth.

"Umm, yeah?" said Jack.

"Give us the pendant," began the voice in a deep growl, "and we will get you out of here."

"Who are you?"

The yellow clothed head turned around and whispered frantically to another yellow clothed head behind him. The head then spun back and said hoarsely, "Drager sent us. We haven't got much time. Give me the pendant."

Jack grabbed the pendant and pulled it over his head. He tossed it carelessly at the hatch and a yellow clothed hand grabbed it from the air before it had chance to miss.

"Suckers!" said a strangely familiar voice and then the hatch closed with a scrape and a slam.

"Hey!" shouted Jack. He raced to the door and banged on it a few times. There was no response. "Get us out of here. Damn those yellow bastards."

"Why would Drager send people dressed in yellow hoods to come and ask us for the pendant?" asked Joe who hadn't moved.

"Because he's too lazy to come down himself? Or maybe he had a doctor's appointment?"

"Yeah, but why the yellow disguise? And how did they get into the detention block? The police wouldn't just let them in." Joe stroked his chin and Jack could provide no answer.

"Who cares? If I ever find out which lying sons of bitches Drager sent I'll kill 'em. They promised they'd get us out of here."

"And what do you think they'd do? Just turn a key and sneak us out?"

A loud bang sounded from outside the door. The floor vibrated underfoot. There was a scraping noise followed by the shatter of glass. Then another loud bang as the door to the holding cell shivered under a violent force.

"Hey, that's more like it!" Jack backed away from the door. "C'mon guys, we're in here waiting. Let's get that door down."

"Great, I'm sure the police will let us off with no charge after we escape. Perhaps we'll get a police bravery medal or a community action reward."

"Shut it."

The brothers could hear some loud shouting from the corridor outside the cell. They heard several more loud bangs and a couple of screams followed by an uneasy silence. Jack was about to ask his brother something when the door vibrated again under a heavy force. And again. And again.

Jack backed away from the door some more and found himself with his back tightly pressed against the far wall. Another bang and the six-inch thick door gave way, crashing down to earth with an almighty slap. Jack's eyes opened wide and his jaw dropped to his belly button. At the other side of the door were the three goons whose merry car chase had landed them in the cell in the first place. Two of the goons were carrying their cigar chomping companion and using him as a battering ram. They dropped him to the floor and stomped in over his prone body.

"Give us the key," said the chief goon, raising a pistol to Jack's head. The bad guy moved his thumb and the pistol clunked threateningly. Jack began to sweat uncomfortably and wondered if he'd brought a spare pair of underwear. He itched his left leg nervously as he spoke.

"Um-mm," he stuttered. "We... we don't know what you are talking about."

"The key," he repeated. "You have it. Give it to me." The goon growled and showed Jack his distinctly canine shaped teeth.

"I think he means the pendant," said Joe calmly. He was lying down on the cell bed with his hands tucked behind his head. He had closed his eyes, almost as if he had decided to go to sleep. The second goon took a step towards him and pointed his gun at Joe. Joe took advantage of the fact his eyes were closed and paid no heed to the gun-toting barbarian.

"Give us the pendant," growled the second goon. Joe might not have been able to see the bad guy but he sure as hell could smell his foul breath.

"We don't have it. You got here too late."

"Yeah," chirped up Jack. "Some yellow guys took it."

The bad guys looked at each other a moment. The chief goon put away his pistol and removed a small pad from a jacket pocket. He held it up and pressed something on it with his thumb, then swirled the pad around in the air just in front of the brothers. He looked towards Jack and then Joe. He growled loudly, swung himself around and walked out, carefully treading over their unconscious comrade. The other goon backed slowly out of the room, gun still pointing aggressively. He stooped to grasp his prone colleague and then disappeared, dragging his buddy down the corridor. There was a sudden flash and a bang from wherever they had gone.

Jack ran to the door and peered down the corridor. Several detention officers were unconscious or possibly dead in crumpled piles on the floor but the goons had vanished. He ran to the end of the corridor and could see a circle of wispy crimson smoke slowly vanish from the floor. A crumpled security camera fizzed, dangling from a wire in the corner just above Jack's head. The end of the corridor was guarded by a large metal holding cage which Jack and Joe had been shuffled through before they got shoved in the cell, still intact. There was no other way in or out of the cell wing of the police station. The cage was locked and there was no sign of anybody moving – no police, no goons and no people in yellow. Jack gave a confused frown.

Joe strolled down and joined his brother. "Let's go." He'd picked up a set of keys off an unconscious and possibly dead policeman and unlocked the cage, his hand shaking as he did so. The brothers walked as calmly as they could muster through the open gate and along a wide corridor painted in an institutional green, heading vaguely towards were they thought an exit might be. Everything in the station seemed oddly normal, as if no one was aware of what had just happened in the cells. Police officers and staff paced around here and there and being the dedicated crime fighting force that they were some even looked up and glanced at the suspicious civilians strolling along through the station. Of course they'd didn't go as far as actually stopping the pair and checking who they were or asking why they didn't have identity cards, as they'd all got some photocopying to do.

Jack and Joe reached an exit just next to a card clocking in machine. So as to not look out of place Jack picked up a card at random and popped it in the machine. Joe did the same but just as he slotted his card (or rather Celia's card) in the appropriate hole a big blaring alarm went off.

"Shit! Whose card did you use?" shouted Jack pushing at the door with urgency.

"Someone must have been to the cells." Joe pressed a big green button marked 'push to exit' at the side of the door and the door swung open, causing Jack to stumble out into the courtyard outside. A couple of policemen were standing beside a police car wondering what on earth the loud siren was. One even began to use his radio.

"Slowly now," said Joe as he began to slide along a narrow path at the side of the building. The brothers nodded to the two policemen and gave a half smile.

"Fire alarm, I think," offered Jack nervously.

Between beeps and static the policeman heard something about escaped prisoners and dead detention officers. Jack and Joe bolted for it and ran. They jumped over (or more accurately through) a low thicket at the edge of the police car park and didn't look back. The two policemen stumbled on to the path and gave chase, but gave up after one of them lost his breath. Jack and Joe disappeared quickly into a nearby council estate.

"Out of the frying pan…" muttered Jack.

Chapter Seventeen– Just After Just Before

The council estate was one of the roughest in Scunchester. The police station was built on the edge of it in an inspired hope that it might influence the local residents not to all be baddies and to stop committing crime, but it didn't really work. Some of the locals would even loiter around the police station and when no one was looking would steal something. On many a morning a policeperson would come out to his or her police car and find it up on bricks. Of course the estate had one or two nicer people living in it, but they either had to keep themselves locked up in their houses or just pretend to also be baddies and fake it. Otherwise they'd just be found one morning floating in the canal with the shopping trolleys, beer cans and soiled prophylactics.

"Down this way," said Joe. The pair ran along a narrow side street, and pushed themselves against a worn and heavily graffitied red brick wall, breathing heavily. Jack slid his hands nervously against the rough surface of the rugged wall, his hand sticking on the used gum attached to it by local residents. He looked left to right searching for the best way to get back to one of the more civilized suburbs of Scunchester. "We'll be okay if we can just get to a bus stop."

"Buses don't come down here any more," Jack replied, tugging at his baseball cap. "Not since the locals started stealing them."

Joe slid down on his haunches and looked around nervously,

biting at his thumbnail. "Then we head west. That's the quickest way out of here. We just need to get as far as the trunk road."

"I think it might be too late." Jack slowly raised his arm and pointed his finger back in the direction they had come from. Three burly men were standing in a triangle that pointed towards Jack and Joe. The front one, an ugly, balding middle aged gentleman, had a baseball bat in his right hand which he thumped gently in his left. He was heavily unshaven without actually managing to form a beard, and his ears stuck out of the side of his head like radar equipment. The two others didn't look any prettier. All three of the men were dressed in tracksuits with stripes going down the side and white trainers so bright that they looked distinctly radioactive.

Jack and Joe spun on their heels and ran. Joe took an early lead as Jack was already knackered from the first run they'd done away from the police station. Joe leapt over a number of discarded cardboard boxes piled on the floor, but Jack just clattered through them much to the annoyance of the homeless man who was sleeping in them.

"Hey!" The down-and-out managed before being flattened by the three locals who stomped carelessly over him. Joe turned a corner at the end of the narrow street only to see another two equally tracksuited males smoking roll-ups a few metres in front him, just outside an armour plated newsagents. They turned and stared at Joe as soon as he appeared. Jack thumped into Joe's behind and came to an indelicate halt, shunting Joe perilously close to the smoking gents.

"Crap." Jack grabbed at his brother's hand and jerked him off to the left, darting across the road in the direction of a launderette situated on the opposite side of the road to the newsagents. A couple of tartily dressed girls heavily draped in metallic bling were standing in the middle of the road looking for traffic to stop. The girls both threw their half empty lager cans at the brothers. The cans span acrobatically through the air and one hit Jack firmly on his chest, spilling frothy warm alcohol down his front. More tracksuited males appeared at the laundrette entrance and the brothers veered right along the road to avoid them. Joe slung his head around to catch a glimpse behind them and saw much to his shock that about a dozen males were now giving chase. The first one was so close he could smell the cheapness of his aftershave and see the yellowness of the teeth on his grinning face.

"This way," motioned Jack who was somehow calling on emergency reserves of energy despite being monumentally unfit. Perhaps like a camel he used his layers of fat to get him through difficult times. Whatever it was he found the strength to pull his brother at right angles and down an alley. He realised too late that it was a dead-end, but with so many lumbering males jogging slowly behind them they'd run out of options. *This is it*, he thought, *I'm going to die*. Jack could already see the headlines in tomorrows papers; 'Local Man Wins Bike' (the papers rarely reported on what happened in the estate, but with the prospect of death or at least violent pain imminent he'd stopped thinking straight).

Jack flung himself around to face the baying mob. The tracksuits had stopped running now that their prey was cornered. Joe darted further into the alley trying to open the several locked doors that might lead to salvation, but without any immediate success. Jack dropped to his knees as the baseball bat toting, self-elected ringleader of the estate stepped forward. The man bashed the floor with the end of the bat. Others equally demonstrated whatever makeshift weapons they had brought with them, a long list of clubs, bricks, bottles, chairs and in one case a giant rubber dildo that someone had brought along by mistake (if Jack had listened carefully he'd have heard the owner of the dildo demanding its return from somewhere at the back of the crowd).

"Please don't kill us!" wailed Jack, his fingers crossed together in front of him. "It's a mix up! I left my tracksuit at home. It's in the wash. I didn't know I'd need it today." The baseball bat wielding male edged forwards, shaking his head. Jack picked himself up and edged backwards to the doorway his brother was hammering hopelessly away at. Joe had found a green door labelled '13'. It had a circular metallic knocker in the middle of its wooden struts. Joe was banging away furiously. He'd seen light from a crack underneath the door and reasoned that someone must be home.

"Look, we're on your side," pleaded Jack to the mob as he snuggled close to his banging brother. It was no good.

"Get 'em lads," screamed the baseball bat baddie. He raised his chosen weapon high in the air and the mob behind him roared approval. As one the mob charged, swarming the alley with scant regard for whether there was actually room for any of them to swing their weapons. Some of the men in the mob fell quickly to accidental clubbings from their own and those that fell were quickly stumbled over by further frothy mouthed local youths eager to get a boot in before the ones at the front finished off the job without their valued input.

But it didn't matter. They were too late. Even the guy at the front was too late. The green door marked '13' had suddenly swung open and Jack and Joe had happily fallen inside. Without being touched the door slammed shut behind them and then, strangely, locked itself.

Click.

Chapter Eighteen – After Catching Their Breath

The brothers had been ushered up a flight of steps by an old man and asked to wait. And, confusingly, the old fellah told them that he'd get some money for them. So Jack and Joe waited. The waiting room was dimly lit and stank of old fashioned. The room was far too brown and the tinge of years of not dusting only added to the overall musk of decay. The two were sitting in a pair of rickety wooden chairs, the padding on the seats having long since given out, which made the waiting quite uncomfortable. A single light bulb dangling above them flickered a moment, straining for electricity. The moth circling it was confused by this and went to sit on an oil painting that stood guard on the wall. The painting was cracked with age, which was fine because the painting's occupant had similar cracks of age too. The cracked man was dressed in black Victorian garb and although his eyes were open it looked like the painting had been made post death, someone perhaps thinking they'd best get round to making that family portrait of Grandad now that he'd kicked the bucket. At least he wouldn't have moaned about having to keep still.

The old man re-appeared at the door, much to the relief of Jack's left buttock. "It's ready," he said quickly. The man noticed the small moth beginning to crawl on the surface of the painting on the wall. With a reflex that defied his years his right arm swung from an inside pocket, gripping tightly a metal rod about six inches in length. The rod was attached at one end to a tube that disappeared somewhere into the old man's dark Victorian clothing. The old man pointed the tube at the moth and squeezed. A bright blue flame scorched out from the rod in the direction of the rogue insect. The moth leapt into the air and circled with unfelt pain until its wings gave out under the heat and it fell lifelessly to the floor. The painting cracked even more under the heat. A hole quickly smouldered into existence and began to sizzle into flame. Without blinking the old man twisted the end of the gun-silver rod and squeezed again. This time a stream of white foam shot out quickly dousing the fire. The old man lowered his rod, gave it a quick shake and then returned it to a discreet jacket pocket. Streaks of white foam dribbled down the wall and the odd wisp of paint and canvas floated delicately in the air.

Jack and Joe gave each other a glance before quickly standing. Jack even removed his baseball cap. Joe looked at the old man. He was difficult to age, but must be past seventy, guessed Joe. The old man's brow was riddled with wrinkles and his manicured beard was as white as ghost. Oddly, the rest of his hair maintained a glorious red-black colour. The old man was gaunt and despite a slight stoop was still an inch taller than Jack. The clothes the old man was wearing were out of date by some decades and he even sported a pocket watch on a chain that clung tightly to a faded green waist coat. Above and behind this was a green cravat, the small image of a grey goat sewn delicately to the fabric.

"When do we get the money?" asked Jack bluntly. Jack picked at his nose with the rim of his cap.

"After the tests," the old man retorted. "I wasn't expecting you this soon. You have signed your disclaimers?"

Jack held out the crumpled pieces of paper the old man had given them upon their arrival. Jack had signed his with an 'X'. The old man made no attempt to take the papers but instead beckoned the pair through.

"What tests?" enquired Joe, but the old man just waved his hand quickly to the doorway ignoring the question. Joe went through first, stepping through into a library, books and shelves lining four of the room's five walls. The centre of the room had various tables and desks each generously piled with books, papers, quills and ink. The fifth wall, at the other end of the library, had an alcove in place of perhaps where a fireplace should have been. The alcove was largely featureless and painted a bland tapioca colour. Bang centre in the alcove but oddly not actually against the wall was a grandfather clock. It was tall, wide and wooden and showed exactly the wrong time. The clockface was inscribed 'O.M. (Scun.).'

"Look, there's been a mix up. What's going on here?" Joe asked. Jack quickly caught up with his brother and elbowed him into silence. He didn't want to turn down free money from some clearly-off-his-rocker old fart.

"These things take time," replied the old man as he circled a table and picked up a notebook. He hopped on to a pedestal in the dead centre of the pentagonal room. "Now please enter the clock."

"Eh?" asked Jack eloquently.

"The clock. I want you to enter it. You do speak English?" The old man's voice carried a slight old world accent and Joe wondered if he'd mistranslated his request.

"Enter the clock?" repeated Joe slowly.

"Yes, yes, that is what I said. Here." The old man sprightly flicked a small gold key that the brothers didn't even notice he was holding. The gold shape flew quickly (perhaps too quickly) through the dry air and Jack fumbled as he tried to intercept it. Joe bent over and picked it up from the mossy carpet where it fell. It was surprisingly heavy for a small key and it was an unusual shape that Joe recognised immediately.

"For the clock," explained the old man to Joe, whilst demonstrating by twisting his wrist as if turning a key in a lock. He smiled slightly, although he looked out of practice at it.

The brothers, with not a little confusion, moved warily towards the grandfather clock in the alcove. Between them they threw glances and nods towards the old man, to make sure he didn't mean something else like 'Go and lock the door of the clock.' It seemed that

he didn't. Joe slid the golden hoop of the key into a small hole in the lower outer casing of the mahogany wood and with a well oiled click, the key turned a quarter inch. The door to the clock was over five foot high and perhaps three foot wide. As soon as the key had been turned the door opened under its own power. The brothers looked back to the old man. *What now?*

The old man let out a breath, although he didn't need to. "You must step inside. On the wall are two buttons and a dial. Press the yellow left hand button once, wait ten seconds and then press the red right hand button to return. Do not touch the dial and do not leave the clock until the right button has been pressed. Understand?"

"Eh?" said Jack. Joe nudged his brother quickly in his ribs. After their recent run of (no) business the brothers needed money and were willing to take idiotic risks to get it. And apart from perhaps toppling the clock backwards this one was a no-brainer.

"Yes," said Joe. He twisted his torso and looked at the clock.

It's a tall clock, for sure, but for two people to climb in? The old man is clearly nuts. Just humour the old fellah. He must have dementia. But then there is the small matter of the key to consider...

Guardedly Joe placed a leg in the base of the clock and began to pull himself in. Out of the corner of his eye he could see his brother flicking through a book he'd picked up from a nearby table, which was odd because his brother had the reading age of an ape.

"Oi," beckoned Joe. Jack had a short attention span and was easily distracted. "Come on. Best foot forwards."

Jack frowned, but approached the clock with his ample frame. "I won't fit in there Joe, unless you lose some weight." Jack patted his own belly fondly, rubbing at the Hawaiian shirt that covered his flabby stomach ripples.

"Then breathe in." Joe ducked his head under the top beam of the door frame and pushed the pendulum out of the way with his left hand. He brought his other foot into the clock and pressed himself into the corner. He was crouched only a little; there was more headroom than he'd hoped for and so far no ticking. Glancing awkwardly upwards he couldn't see any actual clockworks, but then there wasn't much light above him.

The clock creaked violently as Jack put the weight of his right foot into the clock. This was going to be tight. He pushed at the pendulum swinging it back towards his younger brother, who caught it like a gentleman (i.e. in his nads). Jack lowered his head and pushed himself at the hole rather like he was climbing back into the womb, something he'd had some practice at. As usual, his girth was causing problems for the narrow entryway and the clock rocked, threatening to imminently timber. With some shoving, some swearing and a lot of squeezing somehow Jack popped in through the gap and brought his remaining size nine into the clock, admittedly only fitting it inside by stepping on his brother's toes.

"It's bigger than you think on the inside," said Jack.

"Yeah," said Joe. "Roomy." He tried to stretch his spine and failed. The old man watched with a keen interest, taking notes on his yellowing pad... height, weight, apparent age and so on.

Joe reached for the door and pulled it round so it was almost closed. He angled his arm around the door, searching half blind for the lock. He managed to wiggle the golden key from its hole, pull his arm back inside and then shut the door. It was dark.

Suddenly a match was lit.

"Good thinking," said Joe.

Jack brought the match to his mouth and began to puff at a cigarette. "Eh?" he said absent-mindedly as he shook the match out and exhaled deeply.

"Don't mind me." Joe coughed as the tart smoke hit his nostrils.

"What? You know I don't like enclosed spaces. I feel like I'm trapped in a coffin all over again."

"Light another match, Jack. We need to find these buttons."

"Who cares?" demanded Jack as he fished back in his pocket and found, to his surprise, an old lighter. "Let's just wait for ten minutes and then split." He flicked the lighter to life, the whiff of fuel adding to the already unhealthy atmosphere. The dancing flame gave the dark wood a red glow and the shadows moved like ghosts as Jack's hand hovered up and down. Against the edge of the wood frame just next to Joe's shoulder was a brass panel that reflected the pitiful light with an eerie dullness. As the old man had told them the panel had two buttons and a dial. The dial had several wheels and was covered in tiny Roman numerals, almost too small to read.

"There is something I should tell you," said Joe.

"What now?"

"Does the key to this thing look familiar?" Joe waved the chain that held the key in front of Jack's face. Jack skilfully re-lit and waved his lighter at it to try and get a good look. It came to Jack in an instant.

"That's that bloody cross I got out of Harry Mantei's bloody guts! How the hell did the old man get it?"

"Keep you voice down, Jack. Something odd is going on and I don't like it."

"So what do we do now?" Jack was tugging anxiously on the door lever.

"We press the yellow button." Joe pressed the left hand side yellow button.

The clock shook violently for a moment, causing Jack's lighter to extinguish. It felt as if the small box was spinning around and around, as if it had been lifted up by a tornado that was taking them on a little trip to Oz. The sudden movements jarred the brothers up and down causing them both to bash their heads repeatedly on the wooden roof above. Jack's stomach was churning and he felt like he was going to puke. He was glad he'd not eaten anything recently. And then, as suddenly as it had started, it stopped. This was followed by an uneasy pause which Joe eventually interrupted.

"Now we press the red button," began Joe, but he spoke to soon. Jack pushed open the clock door and staggered drunkenly out of it. His dizzy head caused him to shudder left and then collapse right. He was on his knees with his hands holding his body just off the dirt encrusted floor. His head was down and he was coughing, making that unique noise that is only heard when someone is trying and failing to be sick.

Reluctantly Joe stepped out of the clock, following his brother. His immediate thought was that the torch-lit room they were now in was not the pentagonal library they had been in only moments before. His second thought, coming to him only milliseconds after the previous one, was to put his hands in the air and surrender to the man pointing a gun firmly in the direction of Joe's forehead.

On the floor Jack heaved his guts. Behind him the door to the grandfather clock gently clicked shut and, as it does when panicked, locked itself.

Chapter Nineteen – Quite A Few Years Ago, A Minute Later

The man holding the gun spoke quietly with a hoarse English accent that sounded almost but not quite genuine. "Who are you?" he demanded. "What are you doing here?" His finger circled teasingly around the trigger of his Parabellum pistol. The man was just a fraction shy of the six foot mark, much to his annoyance. No amount of padding in the soles of his black jackboots seemed to bridge the gap between him and that magic six foot mark, unless he stood on his tip toes and to be honest that usually ruined the brutal countenance he was going for. He scowled his face at Joe, sneering down the length of a long nose that hung just above a well trimmed moustache. His hair was flat with a meticulous side parting and it had the same colour as his 'tache, a subtle shade known colloquially as cow-shit brown.

From the floor Jack fell to his side and breathed heavily, looking up. Jack blinked as he suddenly saw the man with the gun. He couldn't quite focus on the details of the man no matter how hard he tried to focus. Squinting he could make out a tan leather jacket. And not much else. For some reason his mind kept going back to the gun. He shook his head gently and tried again. Yeah, it was definitely a gun.

"I think there has been a mix up," offered Joe mock-pleasantly. "We were just doing a bit of work for the old man." As he spoke he glanced around the room. An odd thought struck him. Although they were clearly in a different room to the one they were in five minutes ago this new room also had five walls. The décor was different, sparse furnishing and not much natural light, but the shape was definitely the same. The clock was even bang in the centre of an alcove, just like before. But as for the books, the tables, the wall charts, the pedestals, the old man... all of it, all gone. The only thing in the room beside the man with the gun was a table with a paraffin lamp on it, sat gently flickering next to a long barrelled rifle. Oh, and there was a ladder propped against one of the walls next to the room's only window, a short flat rectangular shape with the lead framed frame propped open.

"Churchill?" asked the man sharply, his scarred lip hooped in a growl.

"Pardon?"

"The old man? You work for Churchill?"

"God, no," said Jack picking himself up from the floor. "We don't even have car insurance."

The man blinked and swerved his gun over to Jack who, sensing danger, froze. "Hands in the air, mein Freund. It's too late to stop this."

"Stop what?" That was Joe. Jack also did try to ask, but he couldn't get the words out. His lips seemed unable to obey the simple commands his brain was sending to them. That was the fear kicking in, again.

"Today Churchill will be assassinated," gleamed the now-obvious maniac with the gun. He swiped at his hair with his free hand, forcing several strands that had wavered loose over his forehead back to their rightful place on the top of his head. "Oh ja. This official visit to Scunchester will be Churchill's last."

Jack and Joe exchanged looks. Jack made looney-loon eye

gestures whilst keeping his hands firmly in the air.

"Erm," began Joe. "Which Churchill do you mean exactly?"

The man look perplexed, and bashed the side of his gun against his forehead in exasperation. "Winston, of course!"

"Ah, of course. And… you think it's what year exactly?" added Jack in the tone that one uses when asking someone a question as you put the straight jacket over their lolling head.

"Don't play games with me," said the man. "It's 1945."

"It's 1945," agreed Joe slowly. "Of course it is. And Churchill is popping over from the war room to visit Scunchester, that's right isn't it?"

"Don't mock me," stiffened the maniac. "Mein Gott, Germany has surrendered. Surrendered! Can you believe it? I've even heard that Hitler is dead. I will have my revenge today. Hitler will have his revenge." The maniac had started pacing up and down a few metres, ranting largely to himself as Jack silently communicated to Joe with a few nods of his head. He had a plan. A very cunning plan indeed.

"That's right," gave Jack as he nodded his head reassuringly. "I think you… hey, what's that over there by the door! It's Churchill!" Jack shouted loudly and pointed his index finger towards the door that they had come in through. The door that they had come in through when the room was a library owned by an odd old man that is.

Instinctively the male maniac spun on his well oiled heels to meet his nemesis, who of course wasn't there. Jack and Joe burst forwards with frightening alacrity. The brothers swung their four forearms over the distracted maniac and brought him crashing down to the creaking bare wooden floorboards underfoot. The handgun went spilling leftwards and slid gracefully into the propped up ladder against the wall. The foot of the ladder caused the gun to spin and go off. A bullet fired in a random direction, which just so happened to be in to the path of the grandfather clock. Rather than making the expected bullet shaped hole in the wooden frame the bullet ricocheted off in another, far more lethal, direction.

And to make matters worse the ladder toppled.

Chapter Twenty – After The Dust Settled

Jack pushed the ladder off his bruised belly and checked himself. He was all there and had no bullet holes in him. That was a relief. He heaved the Nazi sympathizer off his legs, and heard the low groan of Joe. He looked over to see his brother rubbing his head.

"The bloody ladder hit me on the head," said Joe. Jack gaped. There was blood across Joe's shirt.

"You're hit!"

Joe's headache retreated in panic as his hands felt across his body, looking for wounds. He felt the damp shirt but quickly realised he was feeling no actual pain, other than from the bump on his head. The blood wasn't his. He kicked with his foot at the lunatic on the floor, twisting his torso. The Nazi was dead. A bullet in the chest had taken him, blood seeping all down his front.

"That's not good," said Joe. "We should get out of here before the police arrive."

"Why? It's 1945; no one is going to care about a dead German. I've always wanted a Lüger. Baggsey his gun." Jack bent over and slid the Nazi gun down his pants.

"The guy was a nut. It's clearly not 1945."

"Oh yeah?"

"Yeah."

"Take a look around, Joe. This is the same room as before,

only before. That crazy old man sent us back in time. We've not moved anywhere. The clock is exactly where it was before we left, only now its 1945." Jack waved his hands around at the décor as if to prove his point through mime.

"You think we've travelled through time? You are as crazy as the old man. Time travel is impossible."

"Come on then. I'll prove it." Jack wandered over to the door, the one they came in through sixty odd years later if Jack's theory was right. He gave it a gentle prod with his finger. "Let's go have a look-see outside." The door swung open and Jack sauntered through it into the hallway beyond. With petulant reluctance Joe skulked after his surprisingly feisty brother and caught him on the stairs going down. They'd come up these very same stairs earlier on in the future. It even seemed to have the same carpet now as it did then.

The brothers opened the outer door and stepped onto a cobbled alley. Joe blinked with surprise. Jack had been right. They weren't in Kansas any more, so to speak. The alley led to a street which Joe knew should be in the centre of the Scumsville estate. But this time he couldn't see a shell suit anywhere. Instead a whole raft of jovial working class people jostled busily up and down, putting up home made celebratory banners ready for the official visit of the country's premier. The men, all of them in their sixties, all wore well worn brown jackets and flat caps while the women of all ages wore painfully coloured dresses decorated in the housewifery heraldry of floral flatulence typical to the era, each with an apron tied around the middle. Many of the women had a headscarf tied over their head, often in a similar garish pattern and colour to their dress. A couple of demobbed infantrymen strolled up the road trying to remember which house it was they lived at. Shellshock will do that to you.

The fortified off licence had vanished to be replaced by an old fashioned butcher's shop. Outside a butcher dressed in a white apron was up a short ladder washing his windows with a damp cloth which his wife kept wringing out for him. As no one seemed to be paying the brothers any attention, Jack and Joe wandered over to the shop.

"Jack," said the butcher's wife, which confused Jack for a minute until he realised she was talking to the butcher who it turned out was also called Jack. "We've got a right couple of gentlemen here. Have a look."

"Cor blimey," said Jack the Butcher. "Tha's got a reet jacket on. It looks like t' wife's summer dress." He was looking at his namesake's outer Hawaiian shirt. The butcher was a sprightly man in his late sixties with a crop of grey hair hidden beneath a butcher's cap. He came down the ladder with a wiry speed, passed his wife the cloth and wiped his slightly-red-stained hands dry on his slightly-red-stained apron.

"Yeah, isn't it," offered Jack with vague disinterest. "Can you please tell my brother what year it is. It's for a bet." Jack placed his hands by his side causing his outer shirt to pinch at his waist.

Jack the Butcher's eyes opened wide in surprise. His wife managed to suppress a giggle by putting her hard scrubbed hand to her mouth. "It's '45 of course."

"See, I told you." Jack scratched at his belly button with his left hand, which had the unfortunate effect of revealing the all-too-obvious shape of a German made pistol tucked casually into Jack's supermarket brand underpants. Jack the Butcher's eyes started to bulge out of the top of his head. His face went as red as his hands. He frantically shoved his unsuspecting wife back into the butchery whilst waving to attract to the attention of the two passing squaddies who had just unsuccessfully tried a house two doors down looking for their Mum.

Jack and Joe were oblivious to the ravings of the butcher who they assumed had eaten too much of his own beef and had already started to make their way back across towards the alleyway. Joe was forced to admit to his brother that he might have a point. They had travelled through time. The crazy old man had built a time machine inside a… well, inside a machine for telling the time. And for some reason he'd shoved Jack and Joe in as guinea pigs to test his invention. The thing that puzzled Joe was that the old man seemed to have been expecting their arrival. Something odd was happening, that was for sure.

"Something odd is happening," remarked Joe.

"That's for sure," agreed Jack.

There was a shout behind them. The brothers threw a glance over their shoulders. The butcher had called over the two soldiers and was pointing to the brothers, repeating the word "Germans!" over and over again. The soldiers, who were thankfully unarmed, began pounding up the street in their direction. Jack threw his fingers at Joe's suit lapel and pulled hard. With an unspoken command both brothers began running.

"Why does everybody always want to chase us?" puffed Jack as they reached the alleyway, clutching at his knees with his sweaty palms.

"Hey, you. Stay where you are!" shouted one of the soldiers.

They had no intention of staying where they were. Jack was first to the door which he bundled open. Joe stepped sharply in after his brother and shut the door firmly behind him, but found he couldn't lock it as there was no key. Both brothers' feet tore into the carpet as they leapt two or three steps a time up the narrow staircase and along the landing. Joe suddenly noticed a figure standing in the corridor. Jack had already swept past him, his mind focussed solely on the task in hand. Joe, however, stuttered to a halt. The man was the spitting image of the old man that had dragged them into this whole sorry mess in the first place. Only he looked a lot younger. Not young, exactly. Just younger.

"Erm," began Joe casually as his tugged his suit jacket back into place. "There are a couple of soldiers chasing us for some reason. You might want to lock the door." Joe swivelled on the spot and darted for the clock room before the younger old man could even speak.

Jack shouted at Joe. "Hey Joe! The key!" Joe fumbled into his jacket pocket and tossed the pendant to his brother who defied his lack of grace by catching it at the second attempt. He slotted it into the clock door and clicked it open. Joe slid into the room beside him but stopped stiffly when he heard four familiar words behind him.

"Hands in the air."

Both brothers spun around with their hands held high. They'd assumed the soldiers had caught up with them, but they hadn't. It was the younger version of the old man pointing a six shooter at them at close range.

"Drop the gun," said the old man to Jack. Jack had removed the recovered Lüger from his pants as the pair were running and now held it high in his left hand. He let it clatter harmlessly to the floor. "Who are you?"

"We're your bloody guinea pigs," screamed Jack almost incoherently. It was past his bedtime and he was getting a little cranky.

"We were testing your time machine," quickly interjected Joe. "We were meant to go straight back to the future but it didn't go exactly to plan."

"We fell out of the clock," added Jack, more constructively.

"My time machine?" said the old man. "It can't be. I haven't yet finished the design. But... but it's true that the clock you are standing in front of looks remarkably like a draft blueprint of mine."

"We just stepped outside to check it had worked. It has, so we need to go back and tell your future self."

"Yes, I see. That is indeed excellent news." The old man sounded quite satisfied, although he didn't lower his gun. "Yes, you must return at once to the future. Under normal circumstances I would go along with you. After all it is surely only a matter of time before I complete the power matrix. It is tempting to travel with you to aid my research, but I suppose that would be cheating." The old man sighed. Despite his more youthful appearance (comparatively) Joe noticed he was wearing almost the exact same clothes he'd been wearing in the future. He was out of fashion even in the past. "But there is a problem," he continued. "I locked the front door, as you suggested, but the soldiers are still outside. Once you have gone they will come in here searching for you and instead find poor, dear Leopold. This would be unfortunate." He indicated the dead German sympathiser on the floor.

"So?" crowed Jack. "He wanted to kill Churchill. They'll think you are a hero! You'll probably get on telly. I bet they'll give you a medal and everything."

"It is not so simple. It would be inopportune for my plans if Leopold was discovered here. I cannot be connected with a dead Nazi sympathizer in my parlour. No. In fact I can think of only one solution." As he said this, a loud relentless braying of the front door could be heard followed by a crack, a creak, then a thud. "And as I have a loaded weapon pointed firmly in your direction you will do as I say." He cocked the gun. "I should warn you I never miss."

The old man gave his instructions. Jack and Joe initially protested, but time was pressing. The soldiers were now inside the building and impatiently banging on the landing door, behind the old man. The soldiers sounded in a hurry. Jack and Joe scooped the dead Nazi off the floor and then reluctantly stuffed him into the corner of the clock. They looked to the old man, who with a delicate wave of his gun indicated the next step should be for the brothers to follow the dead guy into the box. Joe stepped in first.

"We'll never all fit," moaned Jack as he dipped his left foot between Leopold's legs. Joe ducked his head under and was cramped up with the machines controls in his back. Jack started to squeeze himself in the remaining gap, far too close to the dead man for his liking; they were cheek to cheek. He breathed in and somehow managed to suck his body into the small space that was left for him. If you listened closely you could even hear the suction noise as Jack's backside made an airtight seal.

"One thing," said Joe loudly, poking his head outwards. The violent calls of the soldiers outside were unnervingly clear. They were battering the door down between shouts. Splinters of wood shot off the inside of the door. Despite this the old man looked impeccably calm. "We'll take the machine back to your future self now. But in the future you need to remember to hire us. We'll turn up out of the blue looking a little flustered. Sign us up!"

"Do not worry, I shall remember you. Now activate the machine."

"You should pay us double for this…" Jack shouted at the

old man as Joe shut the door. Somehow they had all squeezed in.

"It really is bigger in here than you think." Joe was about to press the return button when Jack stopped him by pulling his elbow back into his torso.

"I have a better idea." Jack reached round his brother's neck and grabbed at the dial. "This thing must control the time and date, yeah?"

"I guess so."

Jack spun the dials clockwise as hard as he could and even before the indicators had locked into position he thrust his palm purposefully forwards and pushed the red button. The clock spun, violently shaking its nervy occupants. Leopold's cold head kept bashing into Jack's face no matter how much he pushed at the corpse with his hands and feet. Everything around them seemed to shudder and jerk and it felt as if the clock would break up under the strain of turbulence and spill the human contents out into the infinite wastes of the cosmos.

But of course that didn't happen.

Instead the time clock landed.

Chapter Twenty One – The Far, Far Future, More or Less

Alyssa reached the top step but had to wait a few minutes for Rascal to catch up. Rascal was absolutely knackered and crawled up the last two dozen steps. He almost fell off three times, and probably would have had Alyssa not dragged him along behind her by the scruff of his neck. She wondered why she didn't just let the son of a bitch drop. The Guild had insisted that she take him with her, and Vasgar seemed to trust him completely. She, on the other hand, thought he was a slimy, back-stabbing creep who doesn't know how to keep his hands to himself and she wouldn't trust him as far as she could throw him (which from this height was quite a distance).

Rascal flopped to his knees and got out a bottle of Lucozade, gulping the sticky, orange-coloured liquid down his dry gullet. He was breathing heavily and the thin air this far above the ground wasn't doing him any favours.

"Look, over there." Alyssa grabbed Rascal's frayed jacket and pulled his head up. "The golden egg."

An altar was at the centre of the fifteen foot wide stone platform that the pair were standing on and looked like it had been carved out of the rock itself. Ornate symbols ran down the sides of the altar, perhaps letters from a long dead programming code (Alyssa believed it to be Visual Basic). Sitting atop the grey stone was a sad and faded red cushion, its golden tassels long since disintegrated and its stuffing beginning to leak out of many straining tears in the dated material. Nestled comfortably on the rotten foam was the golden egg itself, glistening slightly in the murky air. The egg was as big as a widescreen television, although Rascal suspected it had probably been made hollow in the middle to save money. *Knowing my luck the bloody thing will be made of chocolate.*

"Now what?" he asked.

"I don't know. The witch didn't say."

"She didn't say?"

"No."

"That was helpful of her."

"She was quiet drunk at the time."

"She's a bloody lush, that one."

Alyssa took a few steps towards the egg. "There must be some clue here, something to show me the way. I must find the secrets of the Code Spell, it is the only way we can break free from the control of the Instructor. The witch said that this egg was the key and that it was important that I come to this place. Although she did also say that she wanted a kebab so it is possible she was taking the piss." She bent down at the foot of the altar and studied the scribblings underneath, but as she did so she felt a sudden and sharp stabbing pain in her back. Alyssa twisted herself around on her heels, spinning a flailing arm out behind her, her eyes blurring out of focus through the agonising pain. She slumped her back against and the altar and saw Rascal a few steps away from her, wiping a bloody dagger against his dank leather jerkin.

"I'm sorry, I really am," said Rascal. "I like you. I really do."

"What...?" choked a very surprised Alyssa. She could feel warm blood trickling down her bare lower back and leaking onto the base of the altar beneath her. *The fucker has back-stabbed me. The cheating, back-stabbing, waste-of-flesh has actually stabbed me in the back.*

"I thought maybe, y'know, we could have been close, you and me." Rascal held up a pair of crossed fingers with his free hand. "And maybe if you hadn't treated me like the shit on your shoe I wouldn't have done this. But that is one big golden egg, and I want it. I want it real bad."

"But... the Instructor," cried Alyssa, a tear rolling down her cheek. She had failed. Slowly her blood swirled unnaturally onto the altar, the dark liquid gently filling the engraved code in the base of the stone. "What about the Game?"

"Not everyone wants what you want, Alyssa. The Instructor knows what he is doing and we should not cross him. There is a reason why he controls the Game and who are we to question him, eh? I mean he's a robot! Surely robots know what they are doing, right, otherwise what's the point of having a robot? That's why... Hey, what's happening?" Alyssa's body had gone into a sudden spasm. Her arms started shaking violently and her head rocked back and forth, bashing into the solid stone behind her. Her pale skin turned a flickering, translucent blue. "Shit. You're blue screening. Someone is disconnecting you. No, no no!" Rascal leaped forwards and thrust his dagger into Alyssa's ribs, trying to make sure he finished the job. He stabbed hard twice, leaving the point in on the second attack. With a blood soaked hand he lifted Alyssa's chin, the whites of her eyes flickering. It was too late, she was no longer in the Game. Someone had pulled her plug. In a flash her body disappeared and Rascal was standing staring at his empty hand.

"No matter," he said to himself, inwardly worried about the possible ramifications of his failed assassination. "She's no longer in the Game so what harm can she do?" He realised sheepishly that he was talking to himself and instead turned his attentions to the golden egg. He moved forwards to pick up his prize. He'd earned it. Unfortunately for the thief he'd not noticed that Alyssa's blood had spread around the altar's edge, gloops of red sticking to the ornate stonework like jam on toast. Unbeknown to the uneducated rogue, the symbols written around the altar edge actually formed a spell, a code created within the fabric of the Game itself, set to trigger should blood be spilt near the priceless treasure. A fiendish trap set to protect the sacred Golden Egg. As the lettering filled with Alyssa's blood the entire stone column began to rock and vibrate, the impending destruction of the entire temple triggered by Rascal's treachery.

Rascal reached his arms forwards to grab the egg, but just as he felt the cool gold at his fingertips the egg rolled away from him and bobbled off the edge of the altar and onto the stone platform. Rascal took a step to one side of the altar, but found it hard to keep his footing as the cave began to crumble around him. He fell to all fours in an effort to keep some kind of balance and scampered towards to the golden oval just a few feet away. The column was swaying from left to right, and Rascal knew it was now or never. He pushed himself forwards and made a leap for the egg. The egg was having none of it and as Rascal fell on his face the egg rolled and dropped off the edge of the platform and bounced out of sight.

"No...!" cried out Rascal, not so much at the loss of the egg but more because he was now tumbling the other way as the column continued to collapse under him. He had nothing to hold on to and with a desperate grab of his right hand he managed to completely miss the last bit of rock under him and began to fall, shards of cave falling with him to an inevitable doom. Rascal had no intention of falling to his death and, whilst in mid-air, grabbed a scroll from his pants pocket. He quickly cast the spell therein, repeating the words quietly three times before vanishing in a poof.

Rascal had recited his recall spell, and appeared in a flash back with his dragon who had been waiting patiently outside. As Rascal lay face down in the damp blue grass, he banged his head against the floor and wondered what the hell he was going to tell Vasgar.

Chapter Twenty Two – The Far, Far Future, Just Before That

"What did you do?"

"We got ourselves a time machine, Joe! I just figured what's the point returning it to the old man? He must be a hundred years old when he finally finished building it and it makes more sense for a couple of younger, braver recruits to do the, you know, travelling in time for him. Hey, this clock is violent when it moves. It'd probably kill him if he ever used it. We're doing him a favour, I reckon."

"Uh-huh," replied his brother.

"So I twisted the timer on this thing as far forwards as I could. We'll nip out, get the upcoming lottery numbers and a Racing Post, nip back again and we'll be rich."

Joe paused for a couple of moments, assessing Jack's latest get rich scheme. It seemed a lot more plausible than his last suggestion of creating a new breed of ostrich by crossing a hen with a monkey. "Fair enough."

Joe pushed at the door gently and it swung willingly open. Both brothers knew from their limited travels so far that although the grandfather clock moved in time, it didn't actually move in space. So they knew that they should be in the exact same room that they'd just left, only this time much, much further in the future.

Jack pushed himself out, Leopold slumping out behind him.

Jack quickly tried to wipe the stench of death from his face although he stopped midway through stroking at his cheeks when he suddenly became aware of the acute oddness of the location about him.

Joe emerged slowly and looked around. The pentagonal room had gone, perhaps demolished in some day gone by, long after the old man had died from, well, from being old. Instead they were standing in large circular dome made entirely of blinking light emitting diodes and metallic coloured sheets of fibreglass. The curved walls were broken into sections, each containing coffin shaped pods jutting out to differing degrees suggesting the architect had played too much Qbert as a child. Each coffin shaped pod was glazed with a frosted crystal through which the spooky suggestion of a human shaped shadow could be seen within. Both brothers shivered involuntarily. It seemed like they were standing in some kind of futuristic mausoleum. An expanse of two tone flooring lay before them. Joe almost took a step forwards before his brother cried a warning.

"Wait. My spider-sense is tingling." Jack didn't really have a spider-sense, although he was once bitten by a radioactive ant. However he did have an uncanny knack for knowing when to tread lightly and Joe had learnt through painful experience to heed such calls of warning. Jack heaved the prone Leopold upright and gripped tightly at the dead man's jacket. Jack's well bitten fingernails made the task that little bit harder and his grip that little bit looser, but he managed to hold on. His plump knuckles began to turn white as he heaved upwards and then launched the corpse forwards. The effort caused Jack to drop to his knees, his heart pounding heavily. Jack clutched his left arm with his right hand and breathed heavily, blinking the sweat out of his eyes. He'd done too much exercise already today and he didn't like it. He knew one day that all this exercise would kill him.

Leopold's cold, dead body thudded forwards forcefully, his jawbone clanking down hard on the riveted metallic flooring that served as a criss-cross gantry between the various pods. The lifeless corpse flopped to the floor, the fragile bones in the neck cracking violently leaving Leopold's head at a peculiar angle to the rest of his body. If he wasn't dead before he definitely was now. A low hum tripped into life as Leopold's hand set off a sensor and a faint beep-beep-beep was heard. To the keen ears of Joe and Jack it was an instantly recognisable sound. It was a burglar alarm deciding whether or not to start a wailing warning to whomever or whatever owned this corner of the future.

The brothers held their collective breath and kept very, very still. Jack hoped the owner had a cat and was used to the alarm beeping at irregular movements.

A moment passed.

The beeping stopped. The brothers breathed out in unison.

"What is this place?" Joe scratched at his itching chin with his forefinger. He liked to keep clean shaven, but since being evicted from the office he'd not had chance to put a razor anywhere near his face. Jack, of course, never shaved yet somehow his beard never amounted to anything more than untidy stubble.

"It's the future and I don't like it,"

"Why does the future look like the set of a bad seventies sci-fi television drama?"

And it was a good point. Jack had no idea how far he'd spun the clock's dial into the future. He'd pretty much just twisted the thing all the way around. The dial had numbers on it but they were Roman numerals and Jack was no good with his Xs and Vs. Or any other letter for that matter. So perhaps they'd zapped themselves far, far, far into the future, as far as it was possible to go, and the visionaries of early science fiction movies were right. Everything in the future did look shit.

"Retreat gracefully whilst we still can?" suggested Joe as he straightened his tie.

"I'm still up for finding a Racing Post." Jack dropped to his knees and peered around where the body of the Nazi sympathizer had landed. "We just need to find the sensors for the alarm. We're not setting it off but the dead guy here tripped it straight away." Jack removed a pen knife from a hidden pocket he'd got sewn into his pants and flicked it open. He kept it hidden for emergencies. The blade was rusty and broken but there was enough metal left for him to have a good poke around the monochrome tiles that lay underfoot. He gently prised one up slightly and, with his face pushed plush against the cold floor, peered underneath.

"Pressure pads, fairly primitive. The future sucks." Jack lifted a few more of the pads and came to a disappointing conclusion. "The black ones are alarmed and the whites ones are okay."

"That's pathetic."

"Yeah."

Gingerly the brothers stepped forwards ensuring their feet stayed only on the white squares. They managed reasonably well in getting to the other side of the room, only setting the alarm off twice, once after Jack tripped up over Leopold and once more when Jack tripped up over his own loose shoelace. There was an almost-but-not-quite-metallic looking door-shaped door standing in one corner with a small hand-sized panel at one side. Door reached, Jack pressed the panel.

"Shum," said the door as it opened revealing a glass-sided corridor that gradually spiralled upwards towards a mezzanine balcony. The pair strode in confidently and began to climb the slight incline. Jack tugged at his brother's sleeve to try and get his attention. At first Joe ignored him because Jack was always tugging at something and Joe usually found it best to turn a blind eye.

"Take a look will you. Every which way you turn in this place it's the same. Dead bodies everywhere." Jack had a point. The walls were lined with 'em. Row after row of corpses stood upright in frosted, glazed caskets. The two brothers took a moment to stop about halfway along the spiralling corridor. Jack put his face near to the glass and squinted hard. Frowning, he pulled one of his right shirt sleeves over the ball of his palm and wrapped his fingers tightly round the cuff. He then exhaled directly onto the glass in front of him and rubbed his makeshift cloth vigorously in vague circular motions. This, for the most part, had no effect whatsoever. Jack wrinkled his eyes one at a time and as he did so he noticed a blinking box to one side of him. He quickly checked with a suspicious side glance to see if Joe was paying him any attention. Satisfied he was not, Jack flicked open the box and quietly pressed the blue button hidden underneath. He was almost knocked backwards off his feet as the glass in front of him shot upwards at a rate of knots and disappeared out of view.

"For God's sake, stop pressing things," yelped Joe. Well, it started as a yelp. He kind of trailed off as he got to the end of sentence and his jaw drooped to the floor. Jack and Joe stood silently a moment, unsure what to make of the half frozen and distinctly naked female figure they had just uncovered. She was generously proportioned with reddish and worryingly brittle hair and so light skinned that you could almost see the blue of her veins. She was standing upright with her arms by her side and was held in place by a couple of thin metal straps that were helpfully positioned to maintain the lady's dignity. A myriad of cables and tubes encircled the female, some of which were actually directly plugged into the female through her almost translucent skin. The tubing carried a clear gloopy liquid that sloshed around in a way that suggested it shouldn't actually be a liquid at all and as soon as it got half a chance it bloody well wouldn't be.

Jack and Joe stared dumbstruck for perhaps five minutes.

"Maybe we should be getting back now." The pair shuffled their shoes backwards, somehow unable to pull away their transfixed eyes from the naked frozen woman. Which was unfortunate because this was the exact moment that the woman chose to wake up from her enforced slumber. She moaned as she awoke, although the moan didn't sound human. It didn't sound like anything at all. It was as if she had never used her vocal chords before. She was obviously trying to say something but somehow couldn't quite figure out how to make the actual sounds correctly. Her eyes blinked feverishly open and closed, unable to cope with an intensity of light that she just wasn't used to on the grounds that she had never used her eyes before either. She pushed forwards (causing both Jack and Joe to jump backwards) with her arms bending underneath the metallic clamps that held her in place, her hands and fingers stretching out at the two human shapes her blurred vision could make out in front of her. Jack and Joe bumped helplessly into each other each urging the other to go the opposite way as their initial shock turned into their initial panic and, let's be honest, had all the hallmarks of turning into their initial terror. The female meanwhile had just about worked out how to manipulate her vocal chords and managed to dribble out the first words she had ever spoken out loud.

"For pity's sake plug me back in. I need to rescue the golden egg and unlock the Code Spell, before that bastard thief steals it!"

Jack and Joe had no idea what the deranged redhead was jabbering about and had by now made a collective decision about the way they wanted to run, which was downhill and back to the room where the oversized grandfather clock stood quietly ticking away, Leopold still slumped silently dead at its base. However before they'd even taken two steps in the downwards direction, they unanimously decided in an unspoken agreement to change direction and run upwards, veering around the deranged, strapped-in woman as they did so. At the foot of the spiralling corridor they had seen a figure dressed in a dark blue robe pointing at them with a silvery skeletal hand. The figure didn't have a face, just a mesh of metal on top of which were three sinister, swirling and circular eyes. The brothers had no idea who or what the figure was but they had no intention of finding out. Without looking back Jack slammed open a door at the end of the corridor and barrel rolled through it, Joe leaping over him as he did so. Jack swivelled around faster than should be reasonable for a man of his girth and grappled the lower part of the door with his sweaty fingers, swinging it shut. He slumped breathing heavily with his back to the door before turning himself around to find out where they now were.

The door had led them into a large antechamber filled with over sized computer systems. On one wall several reels of brown tape ran backwards and forwards around plastic wheels, with large lights underneath signifying some kind of unknown and presumably sinister activity. A constant stream of ticker tape twisted towards the floor forming a loose pile. Similar machines were doing similar things all around them. However, in all fairness, Jack and Joe didn't particularly notice this as they were transfixed almost immediately by a ten foot tall oval shaped archway that dominated the centre of the room. A rippling sheet of translucent green stretched across the centre of the shape and flickered violently, giving the brothers the somehow distinct impression that the world around it was warping in and out of existence in the wink of an eye. The brothers approached gob-smacked.

"I've seen this on Stargate," said Jack. Joe didn't respond. He edged closer to the portal as if drawn in by some unknown power. For a moment his mind drifted away from him. He could hear laughter. He saw several children running through autumnal woodland; he could hear their soft voices singing songs into the crisp breeze. He could smell the leaves as they fell to the ground, and felt a familiar crunch under his feet as he took a step closer. He started to reach out to touch the image in front of him before he was rudely interrupted by the sound of gun fire and in a green-tinged flash the image was gone.

Joe swirled round snapping himself out of the enchanting vision. He looked around but just couldn't believe his eyes. Two of the three goons who had followed them earlier in the past were standing in the room! He had no idea how they got into the room, there was only one door and that was still shut tight. Joe forced his eyes to blink as if trying to work out exactly what was real and what was in his head. It made no difference. The goons were still in the room and grinning at him with violent intent. No doubt about it. It was two of the three self same goons that had caused them no end of trouble several times today already. Not today. In the past. But today for the brothers. Oh, you know what I mean.

"Who are you?" growled Goldfish, the shortest goon (about six foot five), as he held an oversized pistol pointing in the direction of Jack's chest cavity. The goon rolled his cigar in his mouth, ash dropping to the floor like mouldy snowflakes. A small scurrying brick-shaped robot rolled around after him sweeping the ashes up with a tiny robotic broom.

"Get away from the time portal," cried Jug who was standing directly opposite Goldfish, perpendicular to the brothers. Both goons cocked their quadruplet of pistols with a satisfyingly round of deadly clicks. Jack looked at Joe. Joe looked at Jack. With a bang, flashes of blue flame erupted from the nubs of the pistols pointed at them. Strangely, time seemed to almost grind to halt around the siblings. Time has a habit of doing this just when things get interesting. And for Jack and Joe things were very interesting. The goons had opened fire.

Chapter Twenty Three - The Far, Far Future, Ten Minutes Later

The Instructor looked over the strange clock with an unhealthy interest. His third eye swirled into action, erecting fully and closing to a tight focus on the deep grain of dark wooden casing. The clock was as tall as a tall human, but something seemed odd about it. For one thing it had just one hand. And for another it had slightly too many numbers on the face. The face itself looked like it had been carved from crystal and was secured above an elegant wooden rectangular frame. A rimmed door ran down the front of the frame, perhaps a little over five foot high. There was a slot for some kind of key in one side. The door was locked shut and for some reason no matter how hard anyone pulled, picked or bashed at it, the door would not open...

The Instructor couldn't shake a nagging feeling of déjà vu.

Chapter Twenty Four - The Past, Before All This

Joe picked himself up and brushed his suit down. He'd lost count of the number of times he'd brushed his suit down today. Actually he had no idea if it was still today or, in fact, a different day. Either way he needed a change of clothes. And possibly a wash. And he was dying for a piss.

He looked around at a surprisingly familiar sight. Only seconds ago he and Jack had taken a wild leap into the swirling vortex they'd stumbled upon in what must have been the future. It was either a leap into the unknown or suffer a whole hail of lethal bullets from the goons whose repeated attempts to kill both him and his brother were quite frankly getting on his tits. The brothers had leapt through the wibbly wobbly portal and in a blinding flash they had been transported inexplicably to a point exactly two and a half metres above the sand-cum-dirt of a greyhound track the pair recognised only too well. Naturally gravity didn't quite like having two heavy humans hovering aimlessly above the ground and therefore took immediate steps to ensure that both brothers thudded into the earth with a healthy crunch.

Jack, who had recovered from the fall first, ran back across to Joe. He'd nipped over to a newspaper vendor near the side of the track who was just getting ready to open up for business.

"Joe, look at this. It's Tuesday. We're back where we started." Jack waved the paper close to his sibling's face but was waving it too fast for Joe to focus. Joe quickly grabbed hold of Jack's wrist and held him still. He wanted to double check the date on the paper as Jack could only have dated the rag by looking at the picture of Mick the Miller on the front cover. He'd seen the very same picture when he'd placed a few bets with Denny earlier. Only it wasn't earlier. It had suddenly dawned on him. It was later.

"Shit. We've not even been here yet today."

"What?" Jack pushed his baseball cap to the back of his head and tugged at several dangling bangs of greasy hair.

"We're back in time. We leapt through the…" the words to describe the portal escaped him. "…the thingy in the future. The swirly wotsit. And it sent us back in time. That's how those God damned son of a bitch goons get here. They didn't manage to kill us in the future so they come chasing after us in the present."

"Eh?" counter-argued Jack.

"We should get out of here." He started to stomp firmly in the direction of the exit but stopped suddenly, causing Jack to bump into him. He felt at a blue biro he still had in his jacket pocket and slowly pulled it out into the light. He held it up and looked at it. A curious second thought hit him. "It was me."

"Come again?" Jack had got his role in the current dialogue down pat.

"It was me. I marked the winning dogs in the paper! Or I will do. Hang on." Joe opened the appropriate pages of the paper and quickly circled as many winners as he could remember. He folded the paper and walked with purpose over to the newspaper vendor who he suddenly recognised as the chap he bought the paper from earlier on later. "Do me a favour mate. Keep this paper for me when I come back in a few hours.

I'll even pay you again for it. But you really need to make sure I get this very same paper, understand? The very same paper."

The squat and bearded newspaper vendor looked puzzled but nodded. He didn't speak because he wasn't paid enough to have any lines. Joe handed the confused man the newspaper and then, after a hesitation, the blue biro.

"You might as well have this. I'll buy it back from you later on too." With that he turned and walked towards the exit, his brother jogging behind him to keep up.

"Okay, I get it, I think. You buy that paper and biro when we come here later, which to us was earlier on. And that's how you picked out all those winning dogs. One thing I don't understand though."

"What?"

"What'll happen when the blue biro runs out of ink?"

Chapter Twenty Five – A Short Stroll Later

Donatello Vamenti was not pleased. His Ma was in a rage because she was still in hospital with her legs in the air having been shot in the thigh. His Ma was not a nice person when she was angry. She wasn't much better when she wasn't angry, as Donatello would readily admit, however this was beside the point. Donatello still had a score to settle. No one shoots a member of the family, unless also a member of the family. And Jack wasn't a member of the family. And as soon as Donatello and his hired henchman could find Jack, Jack would be dead. Very dead.

He'd received a call not long ago from an informant at the dog track. Someone had seen Jack and his brother freefall onto the dog track. Donatello grabbed the Yellow Pages and called in a professional to make sure Jack got what was coming to him. But before that could happen he had to make sure Jack knew who it was that had arranged for his imminent and excruciatingly painful death. Otherwise he'd never hear the end of it from his Ma. He'd also brought along his Polaroid camera so he could take some pictures for his album.

The dirt brown Winnebago Donatello was driving turned the corner onto the narrow one way street that ran between the corrugated steel fencing of the dog track and the yellowing plastic barrier that bordered the yellow plastic factory (the fifth biggest employer in Scunchester). He'd timed it perfectly. Jack had just trundled out of the greyhound track's car park, following his brother. The Winnebago rolled silently behind them, the slight downhill gradient allowing Donatello not to have to use the vehicle's accelerator. Donatello held up his camera and with his left elbow squeezed down on his horn.

Jack and Joe instinctively swivelled around. As they did so Jack began to sweep low into a cower, his natural reaction to the sudden sound of honking behind him (he'd once been attacked by a gaggle of geese; a story for another day perhaps). Both brothers' eyes opened wide with surprise when they finally noticed that a rather large and dirty Winnebago had somehow sneaked up silently behind them. Their eyes opened wider still when they realised the driver was Donatello Vamenti, one half of the town's prolifically dangerous Mafiosi twins (his very slightly older brother Leonardo was currently inside doing a ten year stretch for excessively flouting VAT laws).

Donatello squeezed his button and flashed. Joe tried to turn away but it was too late. Jack tried to bury his head between his legs but it was no good. Donatello had already clicked the button. He tossed the camera carelessly into the passenger seat and put his foot to the floor, heaving right on the steering wheel. He applied the brake with a sudden bash of a limb and screeched the vehicle to halt to the side of the dazed brothers. He was smiling his biggest smile. He winked at Jack whilst at the same time raising his left hand. With his index finger extended he quickly whipped up his wrist to simulate the shooting of a gun in Jack's general direction. Donatello blew gently over the tip of his finger before revving his engine and skidding away. Beside him an instant photograph had slowly slid out of the camera and the colour of Jack's surprised face was beginning to appear on the surface. Donatello now had the photograph to give his hired hitman. The hitman would now know his mark. And the mark would know that it was Donatello who had marked him. All he had to do now was give the photograph to the hitman. And the hitman he had hired was the best there was.

Harry Mantei.

Chapter Twenty Six – So Soon After The Last Chapter It Was Barely Worth Starting Another

"Oh my God," panicked Jack in a sudden sweat. "Vamenti marked me. The bastard. The fucking ignorant, immigrant bastard." Jack had grabbed hold of Joe's lapels and was vigorously shaking him.

"Calm down, let's not jump to racism."

"That's easy for you to say! Vamenti took a picture of me, not you. They didn't find the last guy that Vamenti marked." Jack let go of the lapels and Joe stumbled downwards, catching his fall with his hand.

"Yes, they did. In the canal."

"That was just his head! Where was the rest of him? Doesn't matter. I don't want to be found, in bits or otherwise. We need to lay low and fast. I don't know how quickly Vamenti can get a hitman over here, but…. Run!"

A meticulously polished metallic indigo Mercedes had quietly turned onto the street a little ahead of where Jack and Joe were ruminating. Jack couldn't tell who was in it through the darkened windows but he wasn't going to wait and find out. He'd seen plenty of cars with darkened windows already in the last few days and none of them had brought him any good news. As soon as he'd cried out he spun on his heels and charged forwards like a rhinoceros on heat trying to get to the lady rhinoceroses before they'd all been claimed by all the other rhinoceroses and he was left saddled with a hippo. He swiped at his brother as he tore past, forcing him to join in with the fleeing.

The driver of the Mercedes seemed rather cool about it all. He was after all a trained hitman, and it made no difference to him if his target ran away. In fact it usually made it more interesting. *After all,* he thought, *I'm a hunter not an assassin.* The idea of sitting on a rooftop with a rifle sniping off an unaware target had no appeal to a man like Harry. No, he preferred a hands-on approach. He'd got a sharpened machete under the back seat for just such a killing. *Perfect.*

The Mercedes accelerated towards the hapless brothers who were zigzagging between each other unable to make a rational decision about how best to deal with a homicidal maniac in a car. Twice the brothers had actually crashed into each other. In fact it was turning into a bit of a farce. The brothers had lost their usual super-chilled level of cool and had entered into a blind, fevered panic. The car revved hard and shot forwards at ramming speed. Jack jumped left and Joe jumped right, the Mercedes shot straight through missing both by a whisker. Mantei applied the handbrake and skidded to a stop facing sideways into the pavement. The road was a narrow one and the sheepishly embarrassed hitman, who had hoped to swivel the car the full 360 degrees, had little choice but to go into reverse and perform a three point turn.

"I just realised something," said Joe, a sudden rational thought hitting his brain.

"Yeah," panted Jack, circles of sweat drenching the armpits of his inner Hawaiian shirt.

"Foreign plates."

"Now is not the time to go car spotting. Come on." He

made to jog off. Joe followed.

"The car look familiar?" he said between breaths. "It's the one we broke into earlier on."

"Eh?"

"The one from the warehouse."

Jack swivelled his head around like an owl to get a quick glance. Mantei had finished his three point turn and was lining up for a second ram.

"But... how?"

"I don't know but I have an idea. Left now!"

Joe leapt left, followed swiftly by a confused Jack. Mantei missed again by inches but brought the car back under control and turned down a side road to the left. Jack and Joe had jumped over a low wall into a multi storey car park. Mantei slowly rolled the car up the appropriate ramp and towards the barrier. He unwound his window to grab a ticket but instead rolled his eyes. He couldn't quite reach the ticket machine. He was having one of those days. Reluctantly he reversed a few feet and made a second pass, this time gaining entry. It reminded him of a painful experience with his last girlfriend.

Mantei stopped the car as he rounded the first corner. Joe was standing dead ahead with nowhere to run. Joe waved his right hand very gingerly before raising his hands into the air and shrugging slightly. Mantei pulled the car forwards and checked left and right searching for the missing brother. He pulled the handbrake and unfastened his safety belt. As he opened the car door he grabbed an ASP baton he'd confiscated earlier from a police constable who had carelessly dropped it (after Mantei had shot him).

"Where is he?" Mantei asked Joe as he approached gently tapping the ASP into his offhand palm. He noticed that Joe looked uncomfortable, evidenced by a roaming eye which kept twitching to the left.

"Who?" replied Joe, his lip quivering slightly. "I don't know what you are talking about."

Mantei was good. He sensed the movement behind him almost before Jack had made the mad lunge. Joe had been the decoy for Jack to sneak around the back and clobber the would-be assassin over the head with a wheel brace Jack had liberated from somewhere. Unfortunately it didn't go to plan. As soon as Jack made his move, using the stealth technique of running-up-behind-someone-screaming, the game was up. Mantei swung his baton to his left shoulder and caught Jack full on the head. Jack fell to the ground with the sickening thud of bone crunching on stone.

Joe made an attempt to open negotiations. Mantei didn't even hear what Joe had to say. In one swift move he threw the ASP forwards in the air. In his youth Mantei had trained in a circus as a knife thrower, but he got sacked because he never missed. The ASP hit Joe right between the eyes. Joe didn't know what hit him. (He'd never seen an ASP baton before; he thought police officers used truncheons.) The last thing Joe could remember before he lost consciousness was Mantei walking slowly away from him and opening the car boot.

Chapter Twenty Seven – Not Long After That, In A Car Boot

"My head hurts." There was a subtle suggestion of an engine humming deep in the background interrupted by occasional and markedly less subtle bumping. Jack couldn't tell if his head was still spinning from the thud of the baton or if he was trapped in a washing machine. And on top of that everything was dark. He assumed the hitman must have cut out of eyes. He tried to raise his hand to feel for his eye sockets, but he couldn't. "And I think my arm is broken."

"It's about time you woke up."

"Where are we?" He could hear his brother very close by but couldn't see him. He tried to make a furtive search with his remaining good hand but discovered he couldn't move that hand either. All he could do was scratch away with his fingers but he didn't like what his fingertips had found so far. "Is this heaven or hell? I'm confused. I was expecting more clouds and less felt."

"This is a boot," Joe said deadpan. "We're in the boot of Mantei's Mercedes."

"In the whose-what now?"

"The hitman is called Harry Mantei. We met him before. Ironically in this very boot."

"He must have banged my head harder than I thought. I've no idea what you're on about."

"Mantei! He's the guy who attacked us and is presumably now driving to a place where he can dump our soon-to-be-lifeless corpses." There was the sudden juddering of a car going quickly over speed bumps. "It was Harry Mantei. This Mercedes is his car."

"Mantei? Wasn't he the dead guy."

"Yes."

"Oh."

There was silence for a few minutes. Joe wasn't sure if it was because Jack had grasped the implications or because he'd fallen back into unconsciousness.

"Let me get this straight," continued Jack eventually. "The guy we found dead is now alive?"

"The guy isn't dead yet. We travelled further back than we wanted to when we jumped back in time. At some point in the next twenty four hours this guy is going to get shot and be dumped in this boot."

Another pause. Joe could hear the tick-tock of an indicator.

"I hope he gets a move on then."

The car pulled over and the engine stopped. A door slammed and Jack and Joe could hear the crunch of footsteps getting closer. Light returned painfully as the boot was opened. Mantei was standing threateningly overhead and grabbed hold of Jack's outer Hawaiian shirt. He pulled hard, rolling Jack's ample frame out of the boot and on to the floor. Jack rolled on to his bruised arm and cringed in pain. Mantei repeated the action with Joe so that both brothers were sitting side by side on the dusty floor.

Both Jack and Joe looked around in some surprise. They'd been here before. It was the scrap yard next to the warehouse that they had broken into to get hold of Mantei's lifeless corpse in the first place. Joe looked around to see if anybody passing might be able to help but Mantei had selected a secluded spot and the nearby street was obscured by a tottering tower of rusting Datsuns.

"This is where it gets messy. I need to make sure the police can't identify your bodies. So please remove your clothing." Mantei smiled a bit too widely and started to sharpen a machete on a whetstone he'd fished out of his coat pocket.

"If you've got a great plan now would be the time to suggest it," stage-whispered Jack as he unbuttoned his inner shirt with difficulty. His hands were shaking almost uncontrollably. On the plus side he was almost sure his arm wasn't broken but it still bloody hurt. He needed Ibuprofen and fast.

"No plan." Joe put his jacket on a solitary nearby truck tyre. "Best we can hope for is for whoever it is that shoots this son of a bitch to turn up and shoot this son of a bitch."

Unfortunately it became quickly apparent that this wasn't going to happen and pretty soon Jack and Joe were naked save for their underpants. Normally Mantei would insist his marks remove all garments but in this case he'd make an exception. He'd seen quite enough. His plan was to kill the brothers, chop off any part of them that might reveal their identities and then dump the bodies in the boot of a scrap car. Neat and tidy with no loose ends. Mantei popped his Machete on the floor and removed a pistol from an inner pocket before slowly screwing a silencer into place.

"This won't hurt a bit."

"Fuck you."

"Congratulations. You get to go first." Mantei said this in response to the shivering Jack. He moved closer, raising the gun, and pushed the nozzle firmly into Jack's forehead. Sweat initially caused the gun to slip out of place, but second time the hitman got a good grip and slowly he squeezed on the trigger.

But then he stopped and lowered the pistol.

"Remove the necklace. I want nothing to tie back to you."

"Eh?"

"He means the key," explained Joe. The key to the grandfather clock was indeed tied around Jack's neck. He'd put it on for safe keeping after the encounter with Leopold.

"Oh, no way that's coming off. It's my good luck charm!"

Mantei swung the butt of his pistol forcefully into the nose of Jack. A red torrent erupted upon impact and sprayed a circle of blood around Jack. Mantei reached and pulled the key towards him. He studied it a moment before clasping his hands around it and yanking forwards with the intention of ripping it away from the now-silent brother. Unfortunately the chain was stronger than he thought and he succeeded only in pulling Jack towards him. Jack, in some pain, lurched involuntarily forwards and his bleeding head rammed straight into Mantei's chest.

"Hey! This is my good suit," growled Mantei as he shoved the pistol once again onto Jack's forehead. Mantei grasped the chain, wrapping it around his gloved fingers. Jack jerked backwards as Mantei yanked forwards and this time the chain gave out. Jack fell on his backside with an undignified yelp. Mantei casually pocketed the key and again raised the gun aiming it carefully at Jack's head. "Any last words?"

Jack gingerly raised his weary head upwards and shrugged. "Look out behind you?" he offered calmly.

"Eh?" came the response from the hitman. But it was too late. In the kerfuffle over the key Mantei had not heard the stealthy approach behind him. And he'd certainly not heard the spade swing through the air into the back of his head. He spun around under the force of the blow and was surprised to see a short stunty male who smelt vaguely of cooking oil grinning at him. Mantei rolled his eyes as unconsciousness took him and he fell, firstly onto his knees before finally settling face-down in the dirt.

Jack scrambled to his feet wiping his bloody nose on one of his loose shirts. Joe shook his head in shock and waited for his brain to catch up with his eyes.

"It's you!" Joe said.

"'ave we met?"

"Yes! I mean no. Not yet. I mean, thanks for your help."

"No probs. Figured 'e were a copper. See ya." The stunty male picked up the spade which had dropped on impact and wandered off as silently as he came.

"That was the burglar from before!" Jack suddenly remembered the male who'd given the brothers burglary tips whilst they staked out the warehouse before they'd broken into it. Only that hadn't happened yet.

"I think this is going to get very confusing."

"Let's get out of here before Mantei wakes up." Jack quickly shoved a foot into his jeans and picked up his other shirt.

"No wait." Joe quickly pulled up his trousers. "The key."

Jack jumped towards the prone Mantei and turned him over. He was about to rummage for the key when a better idea popped into his head. He pulled his foot back and kicked Mantei's torso as hard as he could. "Stupid arse pointing your stupid gun at me. Stupid."

Joe finished putting his clothes back on before putting his hand on his brothers shoulder. "The key?"

Jack nodded and slid his hands into Mantei's pockets. He rummaged as much as he dared and with some relief clasped hold of the key in his good hand. He pulled it free and made to move away just as fast as his little legs would allow him. He did not want to be around when Mantei woke up. He was going to be really pissed off and Jack had a fair idea who Mantei would like to take it out on. Jack decided he would like to keep his brain inside his head and therefore decided that they should scarper sharpish. Unfortunately for him Joe had other ideas and Joe's fingers gripped firmly onto Jack's shoulder, preventing a quick escape.

"We can't leave. We've got things to do. We've got to make sure the future happens as it happened earlier, right?"

"What you talking about?" Jack shrugged violently in an effort to shake his brother's fingernails out of his shoulder blade. "Fuck the future. Let's get out of here before shit for brains here wakes up and finds out he's not dead. This time travel thing must be rotting your brain." Jack's throw away comment was more pertinent than he realised although neither brother would notice the cranial degradation for quite some time. Or, more accurately, they would never notice at all. The ironic thing is that the worse the brain gets the less capable you are at noticing the difference. That's why alcoholics don't realise they are crap at sudoku.

Joe got his brother to pass him the key which he then waved in Jack's face. "We've got to deal with this. Mantei has to eat this key and then at some point get shot and put in the boot of his car. If we keep hold of the clock key then Mantei can't eat it and my guess is he won't get shot until he has eaten it. And if he doesn't get shot then you better believe he'll keep coming after us. Someone paid Mantei to do a job and he wouldn't want a botch job on his C.V. Now stop shivering and pass me your belt."

"Why does this always happen to me?" whined Jack as he reluctantly removed his trouser belt. Joe had already done the same and used the two belts to bind tightly Mantei's hands and feet. Mantei was still unconscious so Joe had little resistance from him as he carefully opened his mouth and pushed in the key.

"Jack, hold him tight. This is going to be a struggle!" Joe brought one hand tightly around Mantei's chin and once he was happy that the whole key and chain was in the hitman's gob he used his other hand to pinch Mantei's nose tight. Meanwhile Jack got hold of Mantei's body and braced himself. Joe pulled Mantei half upright and raised his chin upwards to encourage him to swallow.

The key had edged to the back of Mantei's throat. The pressure applied by Joe meant that Mantei suddenly wasn't getting the oxygen he was used to and Mantei's subconscious mind wasn't happy about this. His brain began to send urgent nerve signals around his body looking for a solution to this previously unencountered problem. Mantei's eye suddenly opened wide as he awakened from his slumber. To say he was surprised by what he saw was an understatement. And to make matters worse Jack's beltless trousers were wriggling slowly down his legs as he no longer had a free hand to hold them up. There are some things you just don't want to see under any circumstances.

Mantei tried gasping for breath but couldn't. His nose and mouth were held firmly shut by Joe, who Mantei couldn't actually see. Mantei violently tried to kick and punch himself free but he couldn't move his arms or legs. He squirmed left and then right, up and then down, back and then forth, but it was no good. He was held firm and turning bright pink. He tried to suck in air as best he could through his clenched teeth but something was stuck at the back of his throat. Mantei did the only thing he could do to free his airwaves. He swallowed and he swallowed hard.

Joe felt Mantei force the key down his throat and allowed himself to relax his grip as he did so. Once Joe was sure the key had been swallowed he let go so that Mantei would be able to breathe freely. He found the exertion had taken it out of him and he was sweating almost as much as his red-faced brother who still had hold of Mantei's legs. Then he heard it. Something had gone wrong. Mantei hadn't swallowed the key after all. Mantei was in fact still desperately trying to get air into his lungs but just couldn't. The key and chain had lodged itself deep in his throat and Mantei was in fact choking to death.

"Jesus," blasphemed Joe as he rushed back into position behind Mantei. "He's choking!"

Jack loosened his grip and raised an eyebrow at his brother. "So? That's what you wanted isn't? Mantei had to die, you said." Despite his choking, Mantei's eyes opened wide at this throwaway comment. He was beginning to panic a little and tried to plead for mercy with just his eyes.

"I did not say that! I said Mantei had to get shot. He doesn't choke to death, we saw that." Joe pulled hard on Mantei's chest trying desperately to emulate the Heimlich manoeuvre which he had seen Bill Murray do in some film or other. Nothing much seemed to happen. Mantei was turning a kind of purple colour and did not look good at all.

"He chokes, he gets shot, what's the difference? Either way he dies and we put him in the boot. Job done!"

"You don't understand." Another unsuccessful abdominal thrust. Mantei had lost consciousness now, his brain shutting down non-essential functions in an fruitless attempt to save itself from impending oxygen starvation. "We can't change the future because we've seen it happen already."

"Oh and you're the expert on time travel are you, Einstein? I forgot about your Ph-fucking-D."

Joe ignored his brother and squeezed hard one more time but he knew it was no good. His plan had gone horribly wrong. He could squeeze as much as he liked, it wouldn't make the slightest jot of difference. Mantei was very, very dead. And to be honest he was quite pissed off about it.

Chapter Twenty Eight – Straight After That

"I don't know why but I expected something dramatic to happen then."

"Shut up, Jack. Just shut up. Let me think." Joe paced rather edgily between various piles of scrap motor vehicles, with his right hand rubbing vigorously at the throbbing veins in his forehead. Joe had done a lot things in his life but he'd never actually killed someone before. Alright, he figured, Mantei had it coming and the hitman had tried to kill both Jack and Joe only minutes before. And Joe knew Mantei was going to get shot soon anyway because he'd already seen him dead in the future. But that wasn't the point. Joe had killed someone. He was responsible for the death of another human being. And not only that, he had also by a freak mischance managed to change the future. He knew that this was probably going to be a bad thing.

"Does it really matter how he died? Let's just dump him in the car and have done with it."

Joe couldn't actually think of any reasonable alternative plans and with some serious trepidation decided to go along with his brother for now. Mantei had parked his car discreetly close by, which helped. Joe got hold of Mantei's shoulders and Jack gripped hold of the corpse's pants, near the ankle. On the count of three they heaved the corpse clumsily into the boot. Jack had to bend Mantei's knees to get him to fit properly. Job done the pair stepped back and admired their handiwork. Joe looked at Mantei and frowned. It was odd, but Mantei looked almost exactly the same as when they'd found him when they opened the boot in the past (or, for poor Mantei, the future). There was just one thing missing. A large gun shot wound. Joe crinkled his forehead and bit his bottom lip as an intriguing thought occurred to him. He looked left and raised an eyebrow at his brother who had by now picked up Mantei's dropped pistol and was currently scratching his belly with it. Joe looked back at the corpse. And then to Jack. And then back to the corpse.

Some ideas take a while to get through the brain's veto system.

"Jack. I've figured out how Mantei gets shot. You shoot him."

"I do what now?" replied a puzzled voice.

"You've got to do it because we've seen the results already," Joe said rather too eagerly. "Mantei's dead so he won't mind. Just point the pistol and pull the trigger. Simple as that."

"What the hell for? He's dead already. What does it matter if he's not shot?"

"Look Jack, I'm not convinced we can change the future willy-nilly. I've got a feeling the future won't let us. I reckon if we mess with the future then the future will get really mad and take it out on us. There will be repercussions and I'm bloody sure we won't like them."

Jack didn't look convinced but shrugged and pointed his gun at Mantei. He closed his eyes, turned his head away and squeezed slowly on the trigger before finally hesitating.

"You absolutely sure he's already dead? Should we get a doctor to check? I don't want to kill him if we're wrong."

"Of course he's dead!" half-cried an exasperated Joe. "Get

on with it will you." Jack's facial expression demonstrated the doubt he was under and in desperation Joe grabbed hold of the barrel of the pistol. "For Christ's sake, I'll do it."

"No, I got it, I got it," argued Jack. Even though he was a reluctant shooter he was still the older brother after all. He pulled the pistol backwards to get release from Joe's grip. Joe twisted the barrel upwards and tried to get Jack to let go of the handle using his height advantage. Jack jumped up with the pistol still firmly in his grasp and used his old friend gravity to help loosen Joe's fingers from the barrel. The gun squirmed free from Joe's hand but as Jack landed his ankle gave way causing his legs to buckle under him. Not for the first time (and certainly not for the last) Jack crumpled to the floor with a bruising thud. The impact caused him to drop the pistol with a resounding bang. The bang of course meaning that as a result of the fracas the gun had inadvertently gone off.

Joe watched wide eyed as the bullet spun from the muzzle of the silencer in a seemingly random direction. It almost seemed to shoot off in slow motion and Joe found he couldn't even move as the bullet arched forwards and upwards from the weapon. A cloud of red dust exploded slowly from the ground around the area where Jack and the gun had landed. Joe could see the silver streaked trajectory of the bullet as it rammed into the exposed frame of an old Ford Escort just to the side of Jack's fallen body. The bullet ricocheted at a severe angle before hitting an overhead metal crane that was used to lift the scrap cars from one part of the yard to another. The shot took another wicked deflection and seemed almost to curve through the air, defying the laws of physics. Joe felt the bullet whisk past his face missing by a matter of inches before finally and perhaps inevitably finding its target. The bullet struck the already deceased Mantei in exactly the place Jack and Joe had seen the wound when they'd opened the Mercedes boot outside the warehouse. Blood oozed out of the large hole the bullet had created in Mantei's clothing.

Jack clambered around to pick up the gun before rising to his feet.

"Well that makes sense. Now what?"

"Now we move the car onto the road in the position we'll find it in later. Get a move on will you?"

"You know what Joe," said Jack bitterly. "If anyone ever makes a movie about our life story I hope they cut your part."

Chapter Twenty Nine – More Of The Same

Joe was on a roll. He shook his brother vigorously which was quite tricky considering the pair were in a cramped and damp phone booth down the street from the Mercedes they'd just dumped outside the warehouse.

"It all makes sense. You remember the kids in the warehouse? They were working for a Mr. Smith right? That's us! We are Mr. Smith!" Joe started pumping coins into the phone booth.

"We've really got to get a mobile phone," remarked Jack.

Joe dialled directory enquiries and asked to put be through to the address he'd already got for the warehouse that they'd staked out for Drager. Sure enough the voice of a lad answered. Joe tried his best to disguise his voice by dropping it a couple of octaves.

"Is that Martin? My name is Mr. Smith. I work for Donatello Vamenti." Joe made the layabout an offer; he and his gang were to keep an eye on the Mercedes outside the old abandoned warehouse that Martin's gang had turned into a temporary base of operations. In exchange Joe promised one hundred quid for each of them. Joe told Martin that the keys were behind one of the front wheels and that if they had any trouble they should move the car inside the warehouse. He gave the number of the telephone booth as a contact for him. Under no circumstances should Martin or his cohorts open the boot. "Harry Mantei the hitman is in there. He choked on a pendant he swallowed and is now very dead. Tomorrow I will make the necessary arrangements to dispose of his body."

Joe hung up the phone and then began dialling again.

"Who are you calling now?"

"Drager. I need him to hire someone to stake the warehouse out, get it? He's going to hire us. It all makes sense now."

"Maybe to you."

Joe again disguised his voice and introduced himself as Mr. Harry Mantei. Joe arranged for Drager's private detective agency to have the warehouse watched overnight. It took a while to agree terms as Drager was reluctant to accept what he'd consider a small fry job, but Joe convinced him to put someone he could rely on on the job. "I need people there in case something should go wrong. I am purchasing a very expensive, erm, necklace on the black market. If the deal should go sour I will do my best to secure the necklace, even if I have to eat it. In the event of my death you must locate the necklace and ensure it gets to my solicitor, erm... Barker and Hound." Jack had once been defended by Gladys Hound after he'd been caught smuggling an immigrant out of the country. For some reason the name of the firm stuck in Joe's head.

Joe hung up the phone before Drager could question him further. "And that should end that. Come on let's get out of here. We need to lay low until we catch up with the right time."

Jack swaggered out after his brother into the street and followed him half trotting up the road away from the warehouse. "End that? What are you talking about? There are still about a thousand loose ends. What about those guys in yellow who stole the pendant from us whilst we sat in that police cell? What about the old man and that clock of his that we left in the future? I don't think he'll be pleased that we've lost his life's work. What about those goons who keep chasing after us? Eh? Did you think about that? And what about…"

You could almost hear the three dots as Jack stopped whining. He'd also stopped walking, breathing or blinking. To be honest he came within a cat's whisker of fainting. Joe too. Joe shook his head and made a horsey 'prrrr' sound as if to double check that he wasn't seeing things. Jack gave himself a firm, painful slap to the face. Twice.

Ahead of them in the middle of the quiet street in the middle of the run down neighbourhood in which they were standing was a grandfather clock. A grandfather clock that looked remarkably like the one they'd recently been forced to abandon in the far, far future. In fact it was identical. The words 'O.M. (Scun.)' could clearly be seen on the face.

The clock door opened.

Jack fainted.

Chapter Thirty – We Meet Again

"So we meet again. And this time you will give me the pendant."
It was the old man. The same old man who'd got them to test
the time-travelling timepiece earlier in what was proving to be a
very long day for the despairing siblings. Jack by this point had
already sheepishly stood up.

"We haven't got the pendant." Joe considered this point. "In
fact you must have it, you've got the clock."

"No thanks to you two." It was odd but somehow the old
man looked even more ancient than he did before. His wrinkled
skin was now even more wrinkled and sagged just that little bit
more. His head was stooped over his body just that little bit
further. Even his clothes looked just that little bit more worn
than they had done earlier.

"It wasn't out fault. The dial got nudged and we ended up
getting ambushed in the future."

"Yes, yes, I know all that," the old man snapped. "And now I
need the pendant from you so I can rescue my time machine and
return it to myself in the past and hopefully whilst I'm there I
can tell myself what an arse you two make of the job and
remind me not to hire you in the first place." The old man
raised a weapon that looked a little bit like it was from a little bit
in the future. He pointed it pointedly at the brothers.

"I'm really sorry but we don't have it." Jack's already nervy
nerves had been re-ignited by the sight of the gun pointing at

him. His hands were up in the air so high that his fingers were getting altitude sickness.   .

"Where is it?"

"It was either eaten by a hitman or stolen by some yellow guys, depending on which one you want." Jack was now panicking a tad. Beads of sweat trickled down his face and dripped to the floor forming a tepid pool of fear.

"It was the same one," interrupted Joe.

"What?" said Jack, who was getting quite confused by the whole encounter.

"It was the same pendant only later on. There is only one pendant."

Jack shrugged and managed to nod gently towards the old man. "There are three pendants if you include the one he's got".

The old man lowered his gun and sighed heavily. Dust sprinkled from his hair as he shook his head. "Gott in Himmel. I knew I should have made a spare key."

"Hold on," interjected Joe. "This is easy. We just need to figure out who the guys dressed in yellow are right?" Somewhere above and behind Joe's head a security light had come on. Joe had had another bout of inspiration.

"Yeah, but we didn't see their faces."

"That's right we didn't. And tonight we've already been both Mr. Smith and Harry Mantei, right? Let's go the whole hog. We'll be the guys in yellow as well!"

"We'll be the who in the what now?" Jack considered what mental asylums he'd have to visit his brother in once this day was over.

"Err… Old man." Joe didn't know his name but the old man looked up anyway. Joe had an almost possessed look in his eye as he explained his idea. "I reckon we can get the pendant for you but we'll have to come with you and borrow the time clock. I know... I know you aren't happy with us right now but it all makes sense, so hear me out. We found the pendant earlier on before we even knew what the pendant actually was but some guys dressed in yellow tricked us into giving it to them, right? I reckon that me and my brother must travel back to the future with you so that we can rescue the clock that got stuck there. Then me and my brother take that clock to the past and pop to a fabric shop; Jack knows a few. We buy a load of yellow material, wrap ourselves up in it and travel in time to the point when the pendant gets taken from us. You follow? It's us, we take the pendant from our past selves. Then with the pendant secure all we have to do is meet back with you and return both clock and pendant. You return it to your past self who can then at his (or your) leisure come back and do what you are doing now."

"I think I might need you to explain that again," said Jack rubbing his temples with his thumbs. Joe went through the scheme again only slightly more slowly. If Jack were reading a book he'd probably have to go back a paragraph and re-read what had been written just to make sure he'd gotten the details right.

The old man waved his hand. "It won't work. If we travel to the future we'd only have one pendant. The pendant is the key to the clock and we'd need two. We'd have two clocks, yes?"

Joe frowned before suddenly clicking his thumb and his finger held out in front of him. He smiled broadly. "Of course! We'd need two keys. And if I'm right and me and Jack do this then we can come back to a little before this point and..." Joe wandered over to a nearby garden at one side of the quiet road and hopped over the low brick wall. "… and when we steal the key from our earlier selves we can then leave it somewhere for us to collect now. So if I'm right then all I have to do is remember to put the key under, say, this plant pot once we get the job done."

Jack looked to the old man. The old man just shrugged, which came as a relief to Jack. Jack thought it was just him who didn't follow whatever mad reasoning had possessed his normally sensible younger brother. But it seemed even the wizened old man thought Joe was a few marbles short of a Kerplunk set.

Joe meanwhile just stared at the plant pot he'd selected at random in the run-down garden of a boarded up house. If he was right then all that he'd need to do later is make sure that he and Jack take the key from themselves, go back in time a day or two and simply slide the key under the plant plot here in this very same garden. He made a mental note of the house number. Gingerly he pushed the pot backwards, slowly at first with a slight side to side motion as if hoping to wriggle the pendant free. Joe gulped and then, with his eyes closed tight, he whipped the pot up in the air above his head. Joe lowered his head and tentatively eased open a screwed up eye. He could see something on the floor, something out of focus, something slightly shiny. He opened both eyes and nodded to himself in satisfaction. It was the pendant.

The old man spoke first. "I am wondering what would happen if I simply took the pendant from you and left you here." He began to raise the pistol but following a moment of hesitation lowered it again. "Unfortunately your logic is correct. Furthermore I will indeed need your assistance retrieving the stranded clock. Even a man of my intellect cannot control two clocks at once. Very well then. You shall both come with me, but mark my words carefully, should I smell the slightest suspicion of treachery from either of you, I will kill you. And I won't kill you nicely either. Understood?"

Jack and Joe nodded. Jack added another scratch to the mental tally of the number of times he'd been threatened with death today. The old man indicated that the brothers should both join him inside the clock.

"Shouldn't we move the clock first? Y'know, back to your house? We need to get to the right spot before we move to the future."

"The clock you stole was incomplete, an earlier model if you like. I made several modifications when I returned the machine to myself. The clock can travel in both time and space through the simple use of this." The old man held up what looked to be a television remote control in his off hand. "Now you will both enter the clock before I change my mind."

The three figures spent the next few minutes clambering inside the grandfather clock. It wasn't easy, particularly as the old man insisted on keeping his side arm pointed menacingly at whoever tried to throw him a friendly disarming smile (the disarming smile being an oft-forgotten kind of self defence against an armed accomplice) but somehow the three managed to squeeze into the wooden box and just about pull its door to. They were packed in as tight as a tin of sardines. Jack could feel the old man's pistol pushed into his lower spine. At least he hoped it was his pistol.

"There really is more room than you'd think in here," said Joe as he spun the dial back to the far, far future and hit the appropriate button.

Chapter Thirty One – A Moment Later In The Far, Far Future

The familiar churning sensation of time travel was something that Jack and Joe found they were getting uncomfortably used to. Even though the clock spun like a fairground waltzer as it soared through time and space Jack's stomach had somehow adjusted to cope with this and this time he didn't feel as sick as a dog. Mind you he was fairly sure he'd soiled his pants. He'd have to check later to be sure. No one was complaining about the smell and he was pretty sure that if he'd farted in the tight confines of the time clock someone would have mentioned it by now. Either that or they'd have opened the door.

Joe opened the door.

"Thank goodness for that," said the old man. "I thought I was going to be sick. The smell was unbearable." He nudged his pistol into Jack's back causing him to tumble head first back into the room in the future that they'd landed in earlier. Joe flipped out quick as a flash behind, as if he had been sucked out by Jack's personal gravity (not as far fetched as it sounds). Both landed in a heavy heap on top of the plastic pressure pads they'd avoided last time they'd blundered into the room. This had the unfortunately but very predictable effect of setting off the audible alarm system.

"Do not double cross me." The old man nonchalantly slipped his sidearm into his jacket pocket, but he didn't step out of the clock. Instead he crept a pair of arthritic fingers around the rim of the door and pulled it shut. Unseen by the brothers he reset the dials in the time clock and in a puff of smoke the time clock disappeared. To Jack and Joe it was as if the clock had folded in on itself until it was the size of a small ball that then just winked out of existence.

Joe pulled himself upright. Jack stayed prone. He was in no rush to get on with whatever madness had brought him back here and to be honest he felt safer face down on the floor. Reluctantly he cupped his chin in his hands and peered around the room. It looked remarkably similar to the last time they were here other than the fact it had no clocks in it at all. Not one.

"That idiot old man has dumped us at the wrong bloody time."

"No, it's right. Your old buddy Leopold is still here." Joe thumbed backwards indicating that Jack should swivel his head around and look the other way. Jack did this thing only to discover to his horror that Leopold's cold, dead corpse was lying within inches of his left side. Leopold's lifeless eyes were open almost as wide as Jack's.

"Gah," gawped Jack as he paddled away the Nazi body with his hands, his fingers pointing backwards as far as they could stretch. With surprising alacrity he pulled himself upright hopping from foot to foot. He batted his palms vigorously against his outer Hawaiian shirt trying in vain to pound the stench of death from them. He'd gotten too close to Leopold far too many times today already and he decided he didn't like it. It gave him the willies, and he didn't need any more of those. Joe quickly distracted Jack using an old fashioned method an old girlfriend had taught him. He slapped Jack across the face with the back of his hand. It had the desired effect.

"What the hell are you doing? That really hurt." Jack now had both his hands held to his reddened cheeks. He suddenly remembered he'd just used the same hands to fight off a cold corpse and pulled his hands away shaking them vigorously as he did so. "And stop making me touch myself." Joe raised an eyebrow at this ill-thought-out statement but decided to let it pass without comment. It was kinder that way.

Despite the alarm siren there was no sign of any sort of security, so with no choices left a quick decision was made. Without the clock the only way they could get back to where they should be would be to leap through the portal they'd leapt through last time they were here. Hopefully it would bring them right back to the greyhound track, although hopefully not at exactly the same time as before. They didn't want to fall on themselves. It might hurt.

Joe led the way and strolled over to the door. The door slid open with a hearty sigh and once more the brothers were at the foot of a glass-sided walkway that circled far upwards to the room with the portal in it. And possibly the room with the goons with guns in it too. It was this last bit that was causing the most concern for the brothers. With the thought of an imminent, violent and bloody death hanging heavily over their heads the two began to walk warily along the walkway. Both of them were trying to keep up at least an attempt of a show of cool and one or the other would occasionally shuffle ahead for a moment, as if to show to the other that they didn't care one iota what they'd find at the top. However it was blatantly obvious that both were absolutely and positively shit scared and whoever had shuffled ahead would soon shuffle back again. Luckily they soon had a distraction. The naked redhead they'd found last time they'd come this way was still here, and for that matter still naked. Somehow she had been freed from her bindings and was now slumped on the floor in front of the frozen coffin that Jack had inadvertently released her from. The cables and wires once attached to her had obviously been torn out of her battered and bleeding skin and laid around the slumped lady like a load of dead snakes, the semi-solid gloop oozing out of 'em. For a moment Joe thought the girl was dead. When she suddenly looked up at him with cold anger in her eyes he almost wished she was. Her eyes were bloodshot from crying tears that her tear ducts had never been asked to produce before and she looked very pissed off about it.

"You bastards," she spat. "You absolute bastards." She thought about that a moment before continuing her argument. "You complete and utter absolute bastards." She gave a big sniff and curled up into a ball sitting with her back against the remains of the wiring behind her, her hands tucked tightly under her knees.

It was handy at this point that Jack had a wealth of experience when in came to dealing with naked and angry women.

"What the fuck are you whining about? You like being trapped in a frozen coffin, do you? Well, screw you lady. I thought I was doing you a favour. You can rot in there for all I care. C'mon Joe." He tugged his brother and turned his back to carry on his journey upwards to the time portal. Joe was reluctant and didn't budge.

"Can they not, you know, plug you back in...?" Joe bent down, his knees creaking as he did so. He actually managed to look concerned.

Jack rolled his eyes. *This is not the time or the place for this,* he thought.

"No," the lady replied with a sob. "I begged the Instructor, I pleaded with him, to put me back in the machine. I threw myself at his mercy. And what did he do? He just walked away and left me here. He didn't even have the decency to kill me. He'd rather just leave me to starve to death, that's how little we humans mean to him. It's more efficient for him to grow another clone than to patch me back in." She was a little hard to understand as her voice was full of bitter unhappiness, but something tugged at Joe. He couldn't just leave her here, no matter what Jack might think.

"I've no idea what you are going through, but you must know you were just a prisoner in that tomb. Whatever it felt like was happening to you, it wasn't real. This is it, lady. This is the real world. Look, come with us if you want. We can help you, take you somewhere safe, y'know." He glanced up at his brother, giving a half shrug of his shoulders. "This is my brother Jack and my name is Joseph. What's your name?"

The redhead wiped her eyes with the bottom of her right palm.

"My name is Alyssa, High Priestess of the Castle Carranock, Enchantress to the King, level nine Spellchanter."

"You have got to be kidding me," whispered Jack. Joe quickly hushed him and tugged at his brother's clothing.

"Shirt."

"What?"

"Shirt."

"Shit." With an unreasonable amount of reluctance Jack peeled off his outer Hawaiian shirt, leaving him with just the other Hawaiian shirt on underneath. *Never mind the lady, I feel naked myself with just the one layer on.* He screwed the shirt in his hand and thrust it pointedly into his brother's midriff. "Here you go, Joseph." His teeth were gritted and it took two attempts for Joe to shake his brother's fingers off the polyester. Joe shook the shirt loose and carefully placed it over Alyssa's shoulders as he helped her slowly to her feet. She didn't resist, although she didn't exactly help either. She just didn't have any other options. Slowly she fumbled the shirts buttons home. Jack was, to be frank, fatter and taller than she was so the shirt was baggy on her but at least covered all the bits of her that should really be covered. More or less.

"Free humans have no place here, you know," Alyssa sniffed. "Once the Instructor realises we aren't just sitting here starving to death he will kill us. Painfully."

"And yet starving to death sounds so appealing," smirked Jack and he began to walk ahead to the other two.

"Who is this Instructor anyway? Some kind of school teacher?" That was Joe. He slowly led Alyssa along the corridor.

"He's the Instructor. Master of the Earth." Alyssa shivered as she mentioned his name.

"And he keeps you all frozen in coffins?"

"We're not frozen, we're just wired in. He uses the energy that we produce as fuel. That's the only use of a human, we're his batteries." The talk of energy made her suddenly conscious of the dull ache nagging her from where the wires were once embedded into her body.

"That doesn't seem right. Why do people put up with it?"

"They don't have any choice. They are strapped into the Game as soon as they are born. There is no escape from the Game."

"The Game?"

"It's a virtual world, to keep our minds alive whilst our bodies slowly die. I suppose the Instructor designed the Game to keep us all in check."

"Yeah well, what about the free humans? Why don't they do something about it?"

"There are no free humans. Everyone is in the Game."

"Everyone?" Joe was gobsmacked. "How many people is everyone?"

"Twenty billion, give or take."

"Shit." That was Jack. By now they were all standing at the top of the walkway having climbed the swirling walkway to its very summit. And without so much as a by-your-leave, Jack had opened the door.

Chapter Thirty Two – About The Same Time, In The Game

Hector the Invulnerable Warrior, tenth level Castigator of the Queen's Inquisition, looked at his digital watch. "It's almost quarter to three. She should be here."

Vasgar the Tall, minor noble and fourteenth level Paladin, slid down from his dragon and paced over to his comrade on the hill. He pulled thoughtfully on his long beard as he stared into the green tinged skies ahead. "Alyssa is usually most punctual. I am worried. Perhaps she failed to capture her golden egg."

"Alyssa does not do failure. And in any case she could recite recall at will." He fiddled with his sword at his side, tugging the hilt up and down in the sheaf.

"That is so. And yet she is not here. Without her the Guild will fail."

"To be honest it's probably buggered anyway."

The two stood a moment, their dragons' impatiently breathing fire behind them and scratching their talons against the red grass of the heath. One of the dragons began to head butt the floor, an early sign of the inevitable Dracon Spongiform Encephalopathy that all dragons suffer from eventually (that's Mad Dragon's Disease to you and me).

"Incoming," remarked Vasgar pointing skywards, in the direction of the Moon of Gonfall. Hector squinted into the sky, his laser eye surgery having only partially rectified his short sightedness. He watched a dragon shape grow in the sky and within moments a third Guild-Rider parked up beside them. He put twenty pee in the meter and pinned the ticket to the dragon's ear.

"Rascal the Light-fingered, welcome." Vasgar helped Rascal fall from his dragon with a Featherfall spell. Rascal, normally lithe and merry, was as white as a ghost and was sweating profusely. As was his dragon.

"Alyssa," Rascal panted. "She is gone."

"Gone?"

"Game over. She blue-screened and left the Game."

"She blue-screened?" That was Hector, his mouth gawped open wide. He removed his ear piece as he had got his Ipod on and wasn't sure if he'd just misheard his colleague. "She was unplugged?"

"It seems so," replied Rascal.

"Then the prophecy was right after all," intoned Vasgar. "We were fools to fight it."

"And what next then?"

"I'm afraid the next part of the prophecy doesn't make much sense."

"What does it say?" snapped Hector impatiently.

"The prophecy, as told by Waylinda the Witch of Fornication, seventh seer of the Island of Galkulla, third of that name, says that unless the enchantress can release the Code Spell then Jack and Joe are truly fucked."

Chapter Thirty Three – Back to Reality

The same room that they'd seen before was ahead of them. It had the same reel to reel tape players, the same ticker tape tickers and all the other bits and bobs which suggested the decorator hadn't really got any idea of what the future should look like when he or she designed it. The room also had the same big shimmering portal bang in the middle exactly in the place it was last time Jack and Joe fled from the future. In fact only two things were different. Firstly the time clock was standing a little to the left of the portal. It had obviously been hoicked up here by the goons at some point. The presence of the time clock would on the face of it be good news, but the problem was the second different thing. The Instructor was standing just beside the time clock.

Alyssa shivered and fell to her knees quickly. "Lord Instructor," she managed to bleat out before Jack could get his sizeable hand around her mouth to shut her up. This achieved, he gave a panicked look over towards the Instructor who he recognised immediately as the three eyed robotic finger-pointer that they had run away from once before. It was turning into a long and confusing day.

And then suddenly nothing happened. Joe looked at Jack. Jack looked at Joe. Joe looked at his watch. Still nothing happened. The Instructor didn't speak. The Instructor didn't even move. Jack let Alyssa go from his grip and went to stand next to his brother.

"I think he's been switched off," said Joe.

"Yeah?"

"Yeah."

"That should make things easier then."

"Yeah."

"Yeah."

"Good."

Neither of them had moved any, untrusting the mysterious figure standing not twenty metres away from them. Alyssa struggled fitfully to her feet, pulling her shirt at the hem to keep it appropriately positioned around her thighs. She noticed the shirt whiffed ever so subtly of unclean man.

"The Instructor sleeps perhaps?" she offered, as she tried to convince herself it was safe to stand in the jaws of a devil. She clung onto Joe's arm, something she would never have done inside the Game. She just knew that any moment now she was going to get bitten by the Instructor. And possibly chewed up and swallowed as well. She took a deep breath.

"I have a bad feeling about this." Jack got the gun he had taken from Harry Mantei out from his trouser pocket. He had no idea how to use a gun in a combat situation but guessed it was just a kind of point and pull the trigger arrangement. He'd seen it on movies and it didn't look that hard, although at school his P.E. teacher had told him that he had the hand-eye coordination of a drunken chimpanzee. He actually wasn't sure if that was an insult or a compliment but if his P.E. teacher was in the room right now he'd have probably shot him anyway just to prove a point.

"Okay, very slowly we should make our way to the clock." Joe fished the key out of a pocket and got himself ready to insert it should they get near enough to the clock door. He held out the key as if the lock was already in reach, but yet the three of them hadn't moved any closer to the silent and still Instructor who was standing in their way. The Instructor's head faced downwards and it really did look like he was just sleeping whilst upright, much like he was in a queue at the Post Office waiting to collect his pension.

Carefully six lots of feet began to shuffle forwards towards the clock. Jack pointed the gun in the vague direction of the Instructor and Alyssa held fast onto Joe's arm like it was her Jewelled Staff of Enchantment. As the number of metres to cross the room lowered in number the confidence of the gang increased, as did their speed. The Instructor didn't seem to bat an eye. Not that he had eyes. Well, not proper eyes anyway. Jack was first to the Instructor which with hindsight was probably a bad thing. He'd gotten a little cocky by now and decided to have a closer look at the mysterious nemesis.

"I don't know what we were worried about." He prodded the Instructor on the shoulder with a grubby finger causing the robotic creature to wobble slightly. "He's out of juice."

"Leave it alone Jack," said Joe. Joe placed his hand gently in the curve of Alyssa's back and guided her towards the clock. She threw nervous glances back at him (as you would if some nut tried telling you that his grand escape plan was to climb into a locked wooden box in the heart of the enemy's lair). But Joe simply nodded calmly. *It is going to be alright. Trust me.*

Jack turned to follow but before he could move a millimetre a silver hand launched forwards from the previously still body of the Instructor. The movement was so fast that Jack didn't even see it. He was so surprised he dropped his gun, which was perhaps unfortunate. The hand grabbed hold of Jack by his large but ultimately flimsy neck and the steel fingers grasped hard and began to steadily squeeze. The Instructor's face shot upright and swivelled around, his robotic eyes swirling in and out of focus as he assessed the three targets that had disturbed his sweet control-alt-delete. If he could have smiled he would have. He had inadvertently captured the keepers of the key and he had done so whilst in stand-by mode. His minions may have failed him, but the Instructor did not fail even when he was off.

"Give me the pendant. I want the key." The Instructor's robotic voice grinded violently as it strained its way through his artificial voice synthesizer and out of the metal mesh grills that sat a few inches below his multiple eyes. The eyes flickered in colour from purple to green and back to purple again, an indication of just how excited the Instructor was at that particular moment. Honestly, if he could have had a hard-on right at that moment he would have. For some unknown reason when he was built his creator decided not to give him that facility. *A pity,* he thought, *it might have come in handy.*

"No," said Joe as he backed off, pushing Alyssa behind him. He was having difficulty because Alyssa was crying and had dropped to the floor chanting "Oh Instructor please forgive us" or some such gibberish. She was having a right funny turn and Joe didn't know what to make of it. The two somehow backed off despite this, but unfortunately this meant they were moving away from the time clock. "Release my brother, and you can have the key. I don't care."

"Give... him... the... fecking... key," choked Jack. His feet were actually off the floor. His fingernails clawed at the metallic fingers, desperately trying to prise them off even if just for a moment, trying to let the smallest gulp of air through his windpipe and into his pleading lungs. But it was no good. The grip was vice-like. Which is, of course, what the robotic hand was designed to be in the first place so you had to be impressed with that kind of detail. Not that Jack was in a fit state of mind to admire the workmanship. Not with the funny colour his face was currently turning. "Key... fecking... key.... you... feck."

"Give me the key or I will kill this human. Then that human. Then you. To be honest I may kill you all anyway. Either way I get the key." Joe wasn't sure exactly what was scariest about this moment, but the pure lack of emotion in the tinny voice sent shivers down his spine that he wouldn't forget (unless he got killed, that is). He found that he had his left hand close by his side and Joe raised it a moment as if considering whether this was going to be worth the trade off. The Instructor lifted Jack further in the air. Jack gasped like a goldfish that had discovered to its cost what life was like on the other side of the glass bowl. Joe knew he had no choice. No choice at all. He threw the key directly at Jack's head.

The Instructor, not caring one bit about the meaningless humans, dropped Jack to the ground by simply releasing his grip. He swung the hand in the air (his brain had quickly calculated the trajectory of the key, his keen targeting system following the object as if it was travelling in slow motion) and, switching on an insta-magnet, the key got sucked straight onto his palm. He left his hand held up in the air with the palm pointing forwards, like a bizarre Nazi salute. And sure enough a key dangled mockingly from the hand. He gave it a little satisfying jingle. Jingle jingle. The bastard.

The Instructor turned to move towards the clock, eager to crack it open and see what lay inside. He stopped with a bang. Then another bang. And a third one. Most puzzling. His logic circuits kicked in and he began to compute the current scenario.

Within a microsecond the results surged through his neuron circuits, and he swivelled eerily around using his waist gyroscope (which meant that his feet were now facing the wrong way). Only a yard in front of (behind) him Jack was standing with his legs akimbo holding his quickly recovered pistol in both hands. Jack had a worried face. He'd just fired three bullets at point blank range with no effect whatsoever.

Bang. Bang. Bang. Click. Click. Click... Click!

Jack dropped the useless gun to the floor with a clang and in a mad and mindless panic ran in a random direction away from the Instructor, with his arms flapping up and down at his sides. He looked like he was trying to take off and fly away. He also looked like he was going to cry.

The Instructor felt another bang as something else hit him in the side of his head, although not a bullet this time. He swivelled his torso around some more and this time ended up facing Joe, with Alyssa on the floor at Joe's feet rocking back and forth and murmuring madly in what seemed to be binary language. Joe in desperation was grabbing hold of the circular reels of brown tape that were spinning wildly on the machines behind him. He flung a reel like a Frisbee in the Instructor's direction. It span through the air with loops of brown tape trailing behind it and cracked firmly into the Instructor's face. The reel dropped to the floor having had no effect on the Instructor whatsoever. However the absolute failure of a tape reel as a weapon didn't stop Joe having another go. He kept on grabbing and throwing.

"Initiate program Omega. Terminate all humans. I no longer need them." The Instructor ignored the continued brown tape assault and issued his instructions to whatever computer it was that controlled the Omega program. A blue light came on a large data bank situated on the other side of the portal.

"Omega program authorised. All humans will be terminated. Commencing purge. Please wait." The friendly female voice of the Omega computer betrayed just how many people would soon be very dead. Disturbingly the computer piped tinny hold music over a tannoy as it politely prepared for total annihilation.

"C'mon, let's get out of here. The portal!" Jack had recovered some of his very few wits and dived around the Instructor trying desperately to reach the portal. He ducked to his left and barrel rolled forwards, the Instructor lurching at him as he did so. The Instructor was now standing in front of the portal, blocking Jack's way. Jack backed off quickly out of reach and stumbled back to his brother, falling as he did so on top of the big pile of ticker tape on the floor.

"No," cried Alyssa, lifting her head up. She pushed herself half upwards so she was on one knee with her knuckles on the ground. She looked a little like she was about start a hundred metre sprint. In a swift movement she thrust her arms forwards and gave out a yelp of excruciating pain as a sudden burst of blue flames spurted and crackled from her very fingertips and arched across the room, directly into the chest area of the Instructor, forcing him to stagger clumsily backwards. The Instructor was a little shocked by this and his logic circuits went into overdrive.

"That does not compute. Your magic should not work here. It is not possible. You are human." Black smoke drifted up from the singe on his metallic ribcage.

"I... am the Code Spell," Alyssa spat out, although it didn't sound like Alyssa was speaking any more. The voice sounded distant, distorted and... distinctly not human. She thrust forwards once more, a second sheet of blue fire racing from her fingers, through the air and into the Instructor's midriff. The robot bounced backwards, his feet no longer able to maintain purchase, and landed very close to the shimmering surface of the portal. Jack became suddenly alert to a potential problem. The Instructor was precariously close to the portal's edge and he could still see a jangling silver key hanging from the Instructor's metallic hand.

"But you are outside the Game, your spells cannot work here," remarked the Instructor as his leg robotics spurred him back to his feet. But Alyssa did not heed his words. It was true that her spell-casting ability was actually a facet of the Game and therefore had no application in the so-called real world. However the black smoke drifting upwards from her scalded fingers told her all she needed to know. Somehow she had learnt the fabled Code Spell whilst she was in the Game and she'd be damned if she'd let something as insignificant as the laws of physics get in the way now. The Guild had been right. The days of the Instructor were all but over.

"I banish you. I banish you," chanted Alyssa through clenched teeth as she let loose for a third and fourth time. Jack charged over leaping manically through the air in a bid to knock the redhead to the ground before she inadvertently pushed the Instructor through the portal. But it was too late. A fifth streak of blue lightning ignited the air as it powered towards the helpless robotic enemy. The force of the impact toppled the hapless Instructor directly into the power vortex behind him and as Alyssa and Jack crashed to the ground in a heap of brown and white tape, the Instructor was gone. And so was the key.

The power vortex exploded.

Chapter Thirty Four – Seconds Afterwards

"What the hell just happened?" Jack was shouting to Alyssa over the tinny hold music that had somehow got louder as the Omega computer began to launch. Jack, Joe and Alyssa were all frantically turning every switch, dial and knob they could lay their hands on in an attempt to find a way to turn the program off before twenty billion people were deleted on a whim of a deranged and thankfully now departed robot. "How did you do that?"

"Does it matter? Help me yank this cable out." Joe had grabbed a thick rubber cable that he thought might be the electric. He pulled at it but it barely gave at all. Jack jumped to his brother's side and curved the cable around his elbow to get some extra purchase. Both yanked, tugged, pulled, strained, wrenched and heaved with as much energy as they could muster, but it didn't seem to make any difference. The cable was not going anywhere in a hurry.

"Omega program is now ready," said the friendly female computer. "Purge is commencing." Jack picked up a nearby automated sweeping robot that was busy minding it's own business, trying to make the place tidy. The robot was shaped like a brick with wheels, which was handy because a brick was exactly what Jack felt he needed at this point. Jack leapt at the Omega computer with the robot in hand and bashed hard at the machinery with a very loud clang. Alyssa, who had been flicking switches, didn't expect the sudden noise and jumped backwards, grabbing hold of Joe's arm. *That's the third time*, thought Joe. Jack bashed hard once more and an outer casing of tempered glass shattered into a million tiny fragments, give or take. The fragments dropped to the ground in one dramatic shower.

"Warning," chirped up the cheerful female computer voice. "Damage to outer casing detected. Possible security threat detected. Speeding up purge program to compensate."

Wide-eyed, Jack bashed again with the reluctant robot before dropping it to the ground. Jack grabbed hold of a handful of exposed wires inside the casing, whilst the little robot got back to its job and immediately started sweeping up the shards of glass underfoot. Ignoring a sudden shock of electricity Jack pulled the cabling back, ripping a rack of flashing diodes free from the computer terminal. He flung the component to the floor near to his brother who immediately stomped hard with his heel causing the rack to crack.

"Diode damage detected, defence system activated," reported the merry voice of the Omega computer happily. "Self destruction initiated. Nuclear warhead is now primed and will detonate in thirty seconds. Have a nice day."

Jack hopped from foot to foot to foot in a mad panic as the computer began its countdown, digital numbers lighting up on several display panels. He'd done a lot of panicking today and was getting quite good at it. He pounded at a random panel repeatedly with his right fist, causing a small dent in the framework and some light bruising to his fist. The flashing lights of the Omega computer flicked rapidly off and on as a result.

"Detonation in ten seconds," corrected the Omega machine in response to Jack's repeated violence. Jack pulled out a further rack of wiring, ripping it free from the casing, and almost immediately the computer chimed in with a very calm "Five seconds."

"This is it," Joe said in a remarkably dead-pan fashion. "We're going to die".   Several stray thoughts flew through Joe's head and he turned to look at Alyssa who was standing quietly, seemingly resigned to her fate. He put his index finger lightly on her chin and turned her to face him. He decided he didn't have a lot to lose. He didn't have a lot of time either. He leaned forwards, puckered up and gently joined his lips with hers. She blinked a moment but didn't resist.

"Three seconds… two seconds," counted the sweet voice of Omega.

"For God's sake you stupid piece of computer shit," screamed Jack. "Shut the fuck down. Turn off! Do you hear? Turn the fuck off you fucking fucker fuck." He kicked hard at the computer with his right leg. "Turn off!"

"Omega program deactivated at your command," said the Omega computer helpfully. "The nuclear warhead has been disarmed. If you need further help with the human annihilation program please ask. Have a nice day." Jack slumped backwards to the floor and breathed heavily, his heart pounding like it had been wrenched from his chest and used as a football.

Alyssa pulled back from Joe's embrace and slapped Joe hard across the face. "What do you think you are doing?"

"I don't know," said Joe as he rubbed his reddened face. "I thought maybe that you, you know, liked me. And we were about to die, so I thought what the heck." Alyssa turned and stormed off to another corner of the room where she promptly sat on the floor and curled into a sulky ball. Her blackened fingers hugged her knees tightly. Jack, still flat on the floor, turned his head to his confused brother and laughed loudly at him, whacking his hands on the cold surface underneath him. After a moment or two he managed to compose himself. He wiped a tear from his eye as he pulled his body upright, an arm stretched out behind him.

"Hey, Alyssa," Jack shouted. "Good going with the Instructor. Nice trick that, whatever you did. But you zapped our key back in time with him." Alyssa didn't respond, but Joe turned to his brother and smiled thinly. Joe fished into a jacket packet and pulled out a key which he swung in his fingertips for his brother to see.

"No she didn't, Jack. Look what I've got." Joe looked quite pleased with himself.

"The key! Then what did you chuck at the Instructor?" Jack stood upright, shaking bits of glass from his Hawaiian shirt.

"The keys for the Maestro," Joe shrugged. "I switched keys on him. For a robot he wasn't very observant."

Jack jogged over to his brother and the pair sauntered over to where Alyssa was sitting.

"You might want to tug the shirt just a little to your left," said a grinning Jack helpfully to Alyssa. "I'm getting a view of the Grand Canyon here.". Alyssa rolled her eyes and pulled the shirt tightly over her knees, holding it in place with her forearms.

"Thanks," she conceded snarkily.

"Look, I'm sorry about before," said Joe, his fingers tugging nervously at the hem of his jacket. "I was caught up in the moment. It won't happen again." Alyssa nodded unconvinced but didn't comment. "We've still got the key to our time machine. You can come with us, we'll take you wherever you want to go."

"What about the Game?"

"What about it?" replied Jack. "You don't want to go back, it's not real y'know. Think of all the things you've been missing out on in the real world, eh?" Jack wandered over to the dropped gun and picked it up, frowning. He shrugged and tucked the pistol into his pants.

"If the Game isn't real, then this place isn't real either." She gestured around her. "The Code Spell I used on the Instructor was a hack, exploiting a bug in the software. If this is real life then the Code Spell shouldn't have worked."

"I don't know about that, maybe this is real, maybe this isn't. But you know you can't go back, right? We've no way of figuring out how to plug you back in anyway." Joe crouched down and tried his best to look sympathetic. Alyssa nodded dumbly. "Look, stay here if you want. One of these computers must power the software. We could turn it off, turn it all off. We could free twenty billion people."

"No. No, don't do that. There is nothing left on this planet - no food, no resources - and without the Game feeding and maintaining them, most of 'em in there would starve to death. Most of the population are brain dead anyway. The human brain was always an optional extra to the Instructor."

"Then please, come with us. We'll make sure you are alright." Joe held out his hand and, to his surprise, Alyssa took it. He helped her up and she held on to his arm again (*if this isn't sending mixed signals then I don't know what is,* thought a very confused Joe). Joe led her and Jack over to the time clock and opened the door. He lifted her carefully over the rim at the bottom of the door and she slid into the time clock on the far side.

"Don't worry. There's more room than you think."
Jack pressed himself in so he was face to face with Alyssa, trying

desperately not to tread on her bare feet. Alyssa found it easier to put her feet on top of Jack's. Joe clambered in afterwards and inadvertently banged Jack's head into Alyssa's, but somehow the three of them squeezed into the tight space and Joe shut the door. Joe swivelled the dials around and pressed the green button. The time clock jumped up, spun around and in a blinding flash popped temporarily out of existence.

Chapter Thirty Five – Back In The Present

There are times when it is difficult to keep a low profile no matter how hard you might try. This was one of those times.

Jack, Joe and the still half naked Alyssa walked very slowly down a fairly busy suburban main road, half carrying and half dragging a very large and very heavy grandfather clock. Many a passing car driver did a double take as the three of them walked by. There were a few shunts that day I can tell you.

They'd materialised not thirty minutes before just around the corner from the old man's house at the edge of Scunchester's roughest estate. They could have, of course, chosen to pop back to see the old man and return the clock as promised, but on the flimsy premise that doing so would mean they'd be endangering an exposed female in a rough part of town Jack and Joe decided to steal the clock for a second time.

"We're not stealing it anyway," argued Jack. "We'll bring it back eventually. Hell, we can even return to this exact moment and return it, so the old fellah won't even notice we've taken it. It's more important we get somewhere safe with Alyssa." Alyssa wasn't really listening. She was too busy trying to keep the clock from falling over. She was also in a little bit of shock. She'd never seen the real world before and she didn't expect it to be so noisy, so busy and so lacking in dragons. There were people everywhere. And cars. So many cars. More cars than people, which seemed rather odd but she was sure that there'd be a good reason for it which she'd probably discover later on. Her eyes were wide open as she stumbled along taking it all in. If it wasn't for the painful gravel underfoot she'd have even forgot her half-nakedness; that's how excited she was about the hectic world that she'd been thrust into. *And to think only this morning I was riding dragons and chasing a golden egg.*

Before too long a flat back truck had pulled up and offered assistance. The driver that is, not the truck. The truck didn't have a say in the matter. To be fair the driver probably only offered to help so he could get Alyssa up in the front with him and the truck was pretty happy with that arrangement too. Jack and Joe were made to sit in the back holding the clock in place. The driver, who introduced himself as Steve, had asked the brothers where they wanted to go, which confused them because they hadn't actually decided yet. Pushed for a destination they decided to head for Charlie's for no other reason than the Maestro was holed up there and if Charlie had got it up and running again then they'd have more options. Joe did wonder if they'd be able to get the car going without the key, but Jack told him not to worry about it.

Ten minutes later Steve dropped off the three of them outside Charlie's garage and even helped them shift the reluctant clock inside. Of course he was a little put out when Aylssa refused to give him her telephone number. She explained as gently as she could that she couldn't do that because she didn't have a telephone number, but Steve just thought she was blowing him off. Which ironically was kind of what he wanted in any case. With some reluctance and a heavy heart Steve finally buggered off.

Bronzer, the oil-monkey, was first to meet the arrivals and quickly eyed the clock (he also eyed Alyssa, but he definitely didn't do that quickly). Joe began to offer some odd lie about how they'd stumbled across the clock. He'd come up with a whole back story as a cunning cover to explain their current predicament. The story was quite convoluted and he was actually disappointed when he didn't get chance to tell it. Instead Bronzer simply hushed him up with a shrug, and called for Charlie. "Charlie. You weren't joking. It's time."

Bronzer rubbed at his hands with a cloth, but the cloth had as much grease on it as his skin so had no discernible effect other than perhaps smudging the grease about a bit. He walked backwards to the door of the small office at the side of the workshop through which the tall and stubble-bearded Charlie entered, a cuppa in hand. In his huge fingers the mug seemed very small, like it had been plucked from a child's kitchen play-set. He had a sup of the hot brown liquid within and swirled it thoughtfully in his mouth a bit.

"Mon, I wondered how long it would be before this day would come." He took another sip, but didn't offer to make one for anyone. Jack was gagging for a drink of something. It had been some time since he'd replenished his strength with a cup of boiling something or other. He was almost at the stage where he'd kill someone if he didn't get some caffeine soon.

"Eh? What day?" That was Joe.

"Leave your clock there. Follow me." Charlie walked towards the rear of the workshop, passing the corpse of the fridge. Jack bowed his head respectfully as he walked by. At the back of the shop was a row of unused lockers from days-gone-by, browning posters of busty girls from a previous decade sellotaped loosely here and there. Charlie smiled and gave Jack his half full mug to hold. Jack duly nicked all the contents held there within. Charlie applied his considerable weight to the side of the lockers, his brow creased with the strain of effort, his knuckles turning white as his fingers gripped tightly onto the cold metal frame. With a rusty screech the lockers slid reluctantly to one side. Behind the lockers was an open doorway criss-crossed liberally with yellow 'do no enter' police tape. Jack and Joe exchanged quizzical glances. Alyssa was standing a little way behind, with Bronzer just behind her. Bronzer kept glancing casually down to see if he could get a view of her arse.

Charlie pulled the tape from the doorway with his hands and then indicated that it was safe for the brothers to enter. He smiled and nodded as a very confused Jack and Joe entered. The doorway led to a short corridor, with a stairway leading upwards half way along. A closed door was at the other end of the corridor.

"What's going on here Charlie?"

"Trust me, will you. Up you go," Charlie frowned as Jack handed him back his now empty mug. "I'll be up in a minute."

Jack and Joe went along the corridor and up a flight of stairs that twisted around, leading them presumably to whatever rooms were on the floor above the garage workshop. Alyssa carefully followed behind, but was conscious that Bronzer was at the foot of the stairs as the shirt was offering her only limited protection from his beady eyes. Sensing her discomfort Charlie shooed a disappointed Bronzer back into the workshop.

At the top of the stairs was a dusty glass panelled door. The door had writing underneath the years of grime. The brothers couldn't quite make out what the words said, but even under the dirt the shapes looked oddly familiar. Joe curled the cuff of his jacket around the palm of his hand and brushed in circles at the window until the words became readily readable. Joe blinked. Jack blinked.

The writing said simply "Jack and Joe - Private Detectives."

"What the...?" Joe turned the handle and the door swung open revealing a sizeable room, a desk immediately to their left as they entered. Behind the desk a door led off to a side room. On their right hand side were standing a number of grey filing cabinets, menacingly eye-balling them as if to challenge the brothers to just try and do any filing. Just beyond the cabinets several wicker chairs sat around a sad looking plastic plant that was no longer green, and therefore no longer qualified as a plant look-a-likee. It was difficult to tell what colour the carpet once was. It not only needed a clean but also a thorough disinfectant, and possibly cataloguing by the National History Museum as a number of new uncategorised life-forms now lived deep within its frayed threads.

Ahead of the three there was an open set of wide double doors, a couple of grey and holey decorator's sheets draped over the top of each. Joe was first to stumble his way through, Jack and Alyssa close behind him. The doors led them to an office in the centre of which was the very table from Jack and Joe's old office (they'd had to abandon it there when the bailiff's chucked them out). Jack and Joe exchanged confused glances, not for the first time. The table had chairs around it. Jack walked behind a springy red chair and rocked it with his left hand.

"This is my chair." And it was. It was the chair from the office they'd been evicted from days before.

"Same here," said Joe, gazing at the familiar broken leather of his chair. He lowered himself into the seat with a satisfying flump. He wriggled his bottom around. It felt good. His bottom let out a satisfying 'Ahhhhh' and Joe hoped no one had noticed.

"What is this place?" asked Alyssa, as she looked around at

the faded walls and half boarded up windows that surrounded them.

"It seems to be our office," said Joe as he kicked his shoes off and leaned backwards, his fingers interlocking behind his head. "Only we've never been here before. We've used Charlie as our mechanic for years and he's never mentioned this place."

"Yeah, what's his game?" asked Jack. Joe couldn't give him an answer.

"What's this?" Alyssa had wandered over to the table as the brothers talked. On the table, next to a small cactus and a rusted hole punch, was a three pronged star made of black plastic. On the side of the star several lines of ridges ran up about an inch before the plastic curved inwards towards the centre. In the middle was a flat circular disc with several red buttons dotted around its circumference. Jack looked at the device, shrugged and then pressed some of the buttons at random. A light flickered quietly from the flat disc and Jack pulled his hand back quickly, unsure as to what he had just done. A bead of light from the centre of the star jumped up as if it was trying to escape from the plastic underneath. Several other beads of light leapt up to join the first. The beads began to swirl around each other, getting faster and faster as they did so. As the speed increased it quickly became impossible for the gathered watchers to follow the individual lights and instead they suddenly realised they were actually seeing an image. And worryingly the image was of Joe. Or at least it was an image of what Joe would look like if he was a lot older and only a foot high.

The image of Joe coughed. "Is this thing on?"

"What the…?" Jack looked to his brother who was watching his older self mesmerised.

"Hi. It's Joseph here. By now you should have discovered

175

the office. I hope you like it. This is important, you must remember to at some point go back in time and set this up. This office will give you a base of operations. Get the clock set up and you can travel back and forth in time from this location and, for the most part, you shouldn't have too many problems." The image of Joe didn't look entirely convinced by this last statement.

"What's going on? Can you hear us?" asked the real Joe, sitting behind the desk. He leaned forwards intently with his fingers wrapped around the edge of the desk.

"No, Joseph, I can't hear you. I am just a recording."

"Eh?" asked a confused Jack.

"I am you, Joseph, so I knew you would ask me that question. So you can ask your questions, and so long as I remember them I can answer you. If I ignore you it's because I've forgotten what you asked."

Joe reached over to the image of himself and gently poked at it with a finger. The beads of light broke up around his finger and the image distorted. As Joe pulled his finger back the lights danced around each other once again and the image quickly re-assembled.

"Alyssa," carried on the older Joe in the image. "I know things are confusing right now, but you will be looked after. Behind the desk in the reception room is a door. Pop in there and you'll find a bedroom with a wardrobe. That's for you. You'll also find a working shower, spare clothes and whatever else you'll need. Help yourself." Alyssa looked up from the image to the real Jack and Joe, who responded with a shrug and a nod. With that she turned away and went back out to reception and disappeared into the side room.

"There are further rooms for yourselves through the door to

your right." Jack and Joe looked right and indeed saw a door leading off. Strangely they hadn't noticed this door when they came in. Nor had they noticed the hole and pole situated in the corner of the room, like the kind you'd find in a fire station for fire-fighters to slide down. It looked oddly out of place in a private detective's office, but whatever.

"Beneath the office you have a garage lock-up that comes out on the lane around the back of Charlie's garage. I'd put the clock down there if I was you, which of course I am. The pole will give you easy access. And finally, this recording device. I have made a number of recordings on here. When you feel you need to ask me something just hit the buttons and hopefully I'll give you some insight into what might be happening to you. Y'know, if you ever get stuck, or are in some trouble for example, or if you lose an elephant. I just hope I recorded this thing in the right order. It got a bit confusing after a while."

"I gotta question for you now. Where am I? I mean, I can see you, and you've got old. Where am I?"

"Jack, if I remember rightly, you are now asking where your future self is. Unfortunately I cannot answer that right now."

"What do you mean? What's wrong with me?"

"And that's that for this recording. I don't say anything more now as I recall. Now, how do I turn this thing off? I think it might be this button." The small figure in front of Jack and Joe leaned forwards as if to press a switch at waist height in front of him. Unfortunately for him the image didn't disappear and instead he looked around confused. "No, that's not it. Have you got the instructions there? Look, forget it, just pull the power cable out will you? Yes, that's it, give that a yank. Yes, that's…"

The image suddenly jumped up and distorted, the beads of light breaking free from their loop and this time dancing slowly downwards back to the flat circular disc at the centre of the star, falling like snowflakes. One by one the beads of light disappeared as they fell until the last one bounced around uncertainly, as if trying to find where all of its friends had gone, before finally winking out of existence.

There was a pause, a lull, if you like, as both brothers eyed each other suspiciously, throwing sly occasional glances at the metallic pole twinkling at them from the corner of the room. On an unspoken command both brothers bolted for the pole, arms flailing at each other in an effort to keep ahead in the short sprint. Despite his woeful lack of fitness, Jack was first to the finish line, perhaps in part because he'd elbowed Joe to the floor in the final few steps. In triumph Jack grasped the shiny pole. He was not ashamed to admit that having his hands wrapped around such a considerable girth was a joy and he savoured the moment, caressing his hands gently up and down the shaft. Unfortunately this gave Joe time to recover from his prone position and Joe flung himself at Jack's legs which were poised carelessly at the edge of the metre-wide circular hole in the floor. Jack's legs buckled and his bottom half flew forwards, flapping in mid-air as he tried to get a grip on either the pole or the solid floor but achieving neither. Jack's significant body weight suddenly realised that gravity wouldn't let him hang on forever, particularly as the silver pole was almost frictionless to touch. Jack's hands began to claw upwards at the pole to try and stop the descent he wasn't ready for, but it was a losing battle. Gathering momentum he slid down the pole and, unable to control his fall, he fell into a blubbery heap at the pole's base, face up and spread-eagled. Joe slid down in a rather more graceful fashion a moment or two after. He smiled happily as he placed his feet on a spot of ground between his brother's legs.

Joe had a look around as Jack slowly groaned himself upright.

The pole, it seemed, was the quick way to get to the lock-up garage situated bang beneath the office. There was a set of double up-and-over doors to one wall, some outside light spilling in through the narrow uneven cracks between the door and frame. At the right hand side was a vehicle-shaped shape sitting underneath an old grey cloth. At the left was an empty space with a well worn darkened rectangle burnt into the middle of the floor. The rectangle was a strangely familiar size. On a wall behind the pole was an internal door which opened almost as soon as the brother's looked at it. In the doorway appeared the heavy face of Charlie, sweating slightly. He nodded, grinning broadly, and then turned away. He grunted and groaned just out of sight and slowly trundled backwards into the garage, his legs akimbo and his large hands holding the head of the grandfather clock. This in turn had been placed on a short, wheeled truck which was reluctantly bearing the clock's weight. Behind the clock, pushing and panting, was Bronzer, shunting for all he was worth. After a few moments of painful exertion the clock was in and dumped unceremoniously into place. It fitted the rectangle shape in the floor perfectly. To the millimetre.

"That's that, mon." Charlie patted his oversized hands together as if wiping oil from them.

"What's this all about Charlie?"

"You've not figured it out yet? You own this place. I rent it from you. You told me years ago that one day you'll turn up with a big clock and on that day, and not before, I should make sure you get your office back." With that he threw a small set of door keys to Joe. Joe caught them and put them in his jacket pocket without looking.

"So that's why you always let us slide on our payments,"

chipped in Jack helpfully, before waving to the old cloth. "Hey, what have we got under here? Is this ours too?"

"Sure."

With the wrist action of a practised magician Jack whipped the cloth from its resting place and held it to his side like a triumphant matador. Revealed was a slightly battered but seemingly intact vehicle.

"What the hell? We go to all the effort of travelling back in time to set up our own office and this is the vehicle we leave ourselves?"

"Yup. Isn't she a beauty? She has been serviced every year and works just fine."

"A hearse?" queried Jack, his voice hoarse with disbelief. "What the hell do we want a hearse for?"

"It's got a big boot," offered Charlie cryptically.

"So, what now?" asked Jack as he shifted his weight from one foot to the other. Joe shrugged.

"Hey, guys," came a voice from above. All looked upwards and saw Alyssa's head sticking down through the pole hole in the ceiling, her freshly showered hair falling shabbily about her head and dripping drops of water onto everyone's shoes. Her fingers clasped onto the rim of the hole like she had rigor mortis, her nails digging in to keep her from tipping too far forwards. "The telephone was ringing and you'd all disappeared. So I picked it up."

"Erm. Good?" offered Jack.

"It was someone called Mrs. Gilhooney asking if you've found her missing cat yet."

"Tell the old biddy to get lost will ya?" cried Jack as he turned himself away and took a step towards the car. He was instantly seized upon by his brother who stopped him dead in his tracks.

"No, wait," Joe shouted to Alyssa as he held his brother firm. "Tell her we've got a good lead and we're on it. Tell her she'll need to get our cheque ready. We're going to get her cat."

"What?" asked Jack incredulously. Joe placed his hands on his brothers arms and shook him as he responded.

"This is it Jack. We're back in business. And I know exactly where to find Mrs Gilhooney's cat. Right where she left it. Come on!" Joe twisted himself and pushed past a rather amused Charlie. He took hold of the handle of the clock and the unlocked door swung easily open. Joe shoved a foot in, and nodded firmly to his stammering brother indicating he should just shut up and do the same. Jack looked up at Alyssa, shrugged, and with as much petulant reluctance as he could muster he stepped forwards and followed his brother into the time clock. Charlie, who was somehow giving the impression he had seen this all before, calmly shut the door behind Jack.

"Good travels, guys," he said tapping his hand on the door before grabbing Bronzer by the scruff of his neck and pulling him back into the garage. Behind them the time clock leapt inches into the air and swirled, shaking violently, shades of blue and yellow fighting in an orbit around the clock as it slowly worked up speed. In an impossible flash the clock blinked out of existence.

"No, honestly," continued Alyssa to no one in particular, still clinging to the rim of the hole. "Don't mind me. I've no idea where I am or what I'm doing, but hey, its okay, just leave me here." She got up off her knees and looked around the dirty, dank and dusty office she'd been left in. "Arseholes."

Chapter Thirty Six – A Little While In The Past, But Not Too Long Ago

The clock door cautiously opened. An eye peered out. Followed by another eye. Followed by a head. A neck wasn't far behind that, and once that was out a torso followed bringing with it a pair of arms. One thing led to another and well, to cut a short story short, Joe got out of the clock. As did Jack. And, as expected, they were in the exact same place they were a moment ago. Only they weren't, of course. They'd travelled back in time only a couple of months and to be frank it wasn't immediately apparent that they'd travelled at all. But Alyssa's head had vanished from upstairs and no one else seemed to be around, so they must have. Jack was far from convinced but Joe assured him that this was all very normal and he shouldn't worry about it.

"I won't."

Joe looked at the keys he'd been given by Charlie but couldn't see any car keys on there. Jack shrugged and tried the hearse door. It wasn't locked and disappointingly (for Jack anyway) the car had the keys in the ignition so he didn't even need to try and hot-wire it. Instead he turned the key and the engine started second time with no problem. Joe meanwhile had opened the garage doors revealing a short, unmade lane that ran the length of the rear of Charlie's garage.

"We'd better take the clock." With a unhealthy degree of

unwillingness Jack got out of the car to help his brother heave the heavy clock into the rear of the hearse. It took a bit of shunting to get the clock on the ramp that they'd rolled out of the back of the car, but they'd had plenty of practice at shunting today already so it didn't take too long to get the thing loaded up. A host of elastic straps wrapped tightly around the woodwork to hold the clock in position. Wasting no more time they set off, not exchanging any words for the first ten minutes of their journey.

"I don't know where I'm going by the way," Jack said eventually. Like most of his gender he didn't like to admit such things and was annoyed his brother hadn't said anything to give him a clue.

"Mrs. Gilhooney's house." Another silent ten minutes or so passed. Jack drove on, keeping to the more minor roads.

"I don't actually know where Mrs. Gilhooney lives."

"Jesus," wept Joe. "We only went a month ago. Don't you remember climbing that tree?"

"I remember falling out of a tree. And I remember waking up in a hospital bed with a bandage over my head. Pretty much everything else is a blank."

"Take a left at the lights." Jack turned the corner and as an afterthought flicked his indicator in the appropriate direction. Joe gave his bro a direction or two every so often and eventually told him to pull the car up discreetly at the end of a pebble-dashed cul-de-sac (the houses were pebble-dashed, not the cul-de-sac. That would be stupid). They got out and Jack slammed his door shut with a unnecessarily loud thud. Joe threw a growl in his brother's direction.

"This has to be discreet Jack. We cannot let Mrs. Gilhooney see us."

"Why not?"

"Because we are about to steal her cat."

"Eh?"

"C'mon, it's blindingly obvious. We steal her cat and take it to the future. We return it to her and get paid, a job well done."

Jack frowned as his brain computed the notion. After a moment a light came on at the back of Jack's skull and his frown quickly became a manic grin. Pleased with this idea, he eagerly grabbed his brother and dragged him down the dead end street. "Which house are we looking for?"

Joe pointed out a tree just ahead of them. Jack winced. He remembered climbing the branches looking for the damned moggy the last time they'd been here. On that visit he'd put his right foot on a branch which immediately snapped under his weight and he'd tumbled gracelessly to the ground, cracking his head painfully on the pavement underneath. It hurt. It hurt a lot. And sure enough sitting high in the tree was a carefree black and white cat licking it's sock-like paw. It was as if the cat was trying to taunt him. Jack wished he'd not left Harry Mantei's gun in the car.

"Second time lucky?" Joe raised his eyebrows and looked thoughtfully at his brother.

"No fucking way am I climbing that tree. You can climb it if you think it's so easy. Go on, I'll watch. I know the way to the casualty department, don't you worry."

"Maybe not then," Joe conceded. He needed another plan. He stroked his chin with his forefinger and thumb, the grimy stubble of his face's unshavenness becoming more beard-like with every passing hour. *What do cats like? Milk? Mice?* He needed something to lure the pussy down from its perch, something like... It was at that point that something whizzed past Joe's head at a hurtling speed. Something small, grey and stone like. He turned his head quickly, eyes wide with surprise. Although he really shouldn't have been surprised.

"What?" Jack had picked up a handful of stones from the roadside and was hurling them at the cat. He didn't wait for Joe to respond. Instead he lobbed another missile in the cat's direction and, amazingly, was bang on target. A bull's eye (so to speak). The cat shrieked and hissed, his back arching upwards and his fur suddenly standing on end. For a moment Jack thought the critter was going to attack him, but the cat swivelled, leapt down the side of the tree and started running along a green-daubed fence into one of the many grassy gardens that lined the street.

Jack and Joe bolted into the garden after the feline, leaping over a low stone wall - thankfully the owner had never replaced the missing iron railings, long since chopped down as part of an over zealous war effort during the Falklands crisis. Jack got his shoe caught on a rose bush and had to tear himself free. Joe squelched on gooseberries before getting to the relative safety of a garden lawn. Out of the corner of his eye Joe could see an elderly gentleman wearing thick rimmed spectacles standing at the lounge window of the house goggling at him, mouth gaping wide open. Both brothers raced down the side of the house along crumbling stone paving. They could see the cat whip up and over a greenhouse, jumping beyond the back garden and out of sight. Unfortunately this meant that the brothers had to navigate over a six foot high wooden fence to keep up.

"I'll give you a leg up," Joe shouted to his brother behind him. He knelt down near the fence and cupped his hands together to form a makeshift platform for his brother's foot.

"Sod that," gave Jack in war cry as he raced forwards. Instead of trying to clamber over he simply leapt at the fencing, thrusting his right shoulder forwards. He hit the fence with a sickening crunch and the weak panelling gave way, splintering left and right under Jack's barge. Jack kicked with his feet to finish the job and, unhurt, raced on into a muddy field of makeshift allotments. Joe followed quickly behind, waving an apologetic shrug to the old fellah who was now in his back garden waving a fist in the air and shouting expletives that need not be repeated here (but believe you me you'd be blushing right now if you'd heard them).

Jack spotted the cat hiding amongst the cabbages and made for it, darting left and right between the irregular rectangular vegetable patches that dotted the landscape every few feet. Joe leapt over a strawberry plot in an effort to keep up. The cat made for a snicket that ran between two bungalows and it was all the brothers could do to keep sight of the damned thing. The snicket came out onto a road, several be-hooded youths loitering around smoking cigarettes and sniggering to themselves. The cat ran past the youths and downhill, darting between parked cars, and was by now a good way ahead of Jack and Joe. Jack, always good at thinking on his feet, attacked one of the youths who just happened to be sitting on a bicycle. He pushed the young lad firmly in the chest and the lad tumbled to the floor almost swallowing his cigarette in surprise. Jack yanked the bike, a small wheeled, florescent green BMX, from between the kid's legs and hoisted himself quickly onto the hard plastic seat. One of the other youths made a grab for Joe but narrowly missed, however the effort left the second youth's skateboard exposed. Joe grabbed it, throwing himself forwards on to the four wheeled frame. As the two brothers raced down the hill the youths stood a moment, unsure what was going on, before

186

deciding to give chase. As they raced away the old gentleman arrived in the snicket sweating profusely and wondering if he'd taken his heart medication that morning. He held a foot of his broken fencing in his hand and waved it angrily.

Joe had no idea how to control a skateboard and he'd landed on it on his belly anyway, thus making steering largely academic. All in all it was a bad combination and he basically careered downhill at a speed he couldn't control. Jack was having a little more luck on his chosen transport, but the bike was way too small for him and he wiggled it violently from side to side in order to keep it going at any significant speed. This had the unfortunate effect of loosening his already very loose pants to the point that a healthy portion of his backside crack was exposed to those giving chase, hairs and all. To the youths it looked like he was deliberately mooning them.

Jack could see the cat sitting quiet and still on the edge of the pavement on a corner just ahead, licking his paw and seemingly oblivious to Jack's sweaty efforts. Jack smiled as he saw a window of opportunity and he swung his bike quickly leftwards to get behind his four legged nemesis. His eyes narrowed as he focussed in on his foe like a hunter stalking his unsuspecting prey. Unfortunately this meant that Jack did not see the flame pink Vauxhall Corsa pulling out of a side road and he hit it hard to the front wing. He blinked tearfully at the arrival of the sudden and surprisingly painful pain. The BMX spun backwards into the air, its wheels twisting and spinning freely. Jack's torso equally twisted as his back legs lurched upwards over his head. His body and chin dragged along the sloping bonnet of the car and he felt like he was moving in slow motion (which is odd because in these situations it is often best to get it over with). His legs made contact with the windscreen which shattered into a trillion pieces much to the surprise of the teenager sitting within the vehicle. Jack's body carried on moving and slid silently off the other side of the Corsa, dropping to the floor in a heap of bruises. The BMX hovered in mid-air as it tried to decide where to land. Obviously the bike hunted for the safest, softest place to land - right on top of Jack. Its front rubber wheel bumped Jack's skull before the back wheel came to rest at Jack's side, with a bent pedal digging in to his rib cage.

The driver of the vehicle didn't like this situation one bit, not least of all because he'd only stolen the car a few minutes ago. He really didn't want to be also involved in a fatal road accident at this early stage of his criminal career. The Courts frown upon that kind of thing and he might end up getting some kind of (shudder) community order. There was only one thing for it for the spotty youth. He revved his foot to the floor and spun off down the road. He didn't need this, he decided. He'd reckoned he'd go and pick up some impressionable teenage girls instead and see if couldn't get one of them pregnant.

Joe missed the back end of the Corsa by a matter of mere inches but, as previously mentioned, he had no control over the steering. He couldn't avoid ramming head first into his prone brother even if he tried. Which he did. He tried with every muscle he could muster to change direction, but the skateboard obviously had a death wish. Joe slammed into Jack, the skateboard skidding sideways causing sparks to fly in the air as the wheels ground into the ground. As if to show off the skateboard, now under its own control, flipped backwards landing on its front end and span three times before tilting back and landing wheel-side down. Tony Hawk would have been proud.

Joe groaned, but his brother didn't respond. Joe tried to pick himself up, pushing his gravel burnt hands into the rough road surface underneath but he didn't have the strength. Which is just as well. He became suddenly aware of a number of shadows falling over him. His eyes, still at floor-level, could make out probably half a dozen feet all wearing various makes of trainer. Mostly Adidas. It was odd that he should notice silly things like the make of the footwear. That was probably his detective training kicking in. He needn't worry, he'd soon get a chance to inspect each pair of trainers close up. He'd even get some footwear marks to keep, imprinted heavily into his skin. He was about to get the shit kicked out of him.

"What have you done to my bike! My Nan got me that!" This youth was the first to get a boot in but the other lads didn't need much encouragement. A whole mass of different sized feet swung into the prostrate bodies of the two brothers, accompanied by a lot of swearing, shouting and jeering. Luckily for Jack and Joe the kicks weren't particularly well aimed and most of the lads were scrawny runts so it could have been much worse. And to be fair to the lads there was very little stamping. So you see, there is always a silver lining. Although you probably wouldn't tell that to Joe's bent, bloody nose and Jack's cracked ribs (luckily they were spare ribs).

The lad who owned the BMX recovered it, and a second kid grabbed back his skateboard. With disgust and a moderate amount of spitting the lads began a trek back uphill to continue the important business of hanging out at the end of the snicket, intimidating the local residents and generally breaching their collective ASBOs.

"Are you all right Jack?" Joe shook his bleeding head and trails of gloopy red spray liberally painted the road underneath. Jack didn't reply. Joe again made to push himself up despite the pain he was feeling in nearly every part of what was left of his body. As he did this thing he became aware of yet another shadow falling quietly over him. He almost didn't dare look, but curiosity got the better of him and he shifted his eyes left a little revealing a couple of well worn brown brogues.

"Break my fence will you..." were the last words Joe heard before a long length of fencing cracked him on the back of his head, banging his already badly bruised nose into the terra firma underneath. He lost consciousness at that point so didn't feel the next few whacks as the old man took his revenge on the two still bodies on the floor. Satisfied with his work the old man threw the wood to the ground and stomped off back up the hill. He shouldn't really have been outside anyway because of his ASBO.

The cat observed all of this with interest. *What fun!* He wandered over from his vantage point and had a sniff around purring contently. He ran his rear end against Jack's still shoulder and then, daringly, had a lick at Jack's head.

"Gotcha!" yelled Jack as he flung his forearms forwards and grabbed the cat by his midriff. Jack pushed down hard to prevent the cat from wriggling free. "Who's laughing now, eh? Dumb animal. Do you think you are dealing with a couple of idiots?"

Chapter Thirty Seven – Not Too Long After Before

It took the brothers a while to get back to the car. Partly because Jack was holding a cat that really wasn't happy about being held. And partly because they both had quite nasty injuries that would probably require medical attention sooner rather than later. But it was mainly because they were a bit lost and didn't want to go back the way they came in case they bumped into the local youths and the old chap. Neither of them could face another kicking. But after a few wrong turns and having to ask twice for directions they got back to their car. Joe opened the boot and pulled the ramp out, ready to remove the clock. Jack couldn't help as he had hold of the cat and Joe only really had one working arm so it was a struggle, and to be honest they had to have assistance from their old friend gravity to get the clock out of the rear of the hearse. Somehow Joe managed it, although the clock ended up prone on the floor rather than its more usual upright position. Well, you can't have everything.

Joe locked the car and tottered back to the clock, heaving open the door. He helped Jack put a foot in and lowered him down to his arse. The cat made several attempts to break free, making multiple swipes with its socky paw. The cat was causing damage to Jack's Hawaiian shirt and he was just beginning to slightly lose his cool about it.

"Stop scratching me, you flea ridden, mangy, four legged sack of shit." Jack shuffled his backside down the back side of the clock one cheek at a time. When his feet finally reached the footwell he laid himself flat down like he was in a coffin. A couple of passers-by passed by and gave the two brothers the strangest of looks. "Have you never seen two guys getting into a clock before? No? Well, bugger off then." The passers-by buggered off hurriedly, the first tugging at the coat of the second. The expression on their faces showed that they'd applied the typical British solution to having a bizarre encounter, that is to pretend they haven't seen it.

Joe leaned over the clock and made an adjustment to the control panel before putting his first foot next to his brother's shin. Joe had less room than usual to squeeze into the clock but somehow he managed to slide in sideways, his face jammed right up against the side panelling. The brothers had some difficulty closing the clock door on themselves (they'd tried to make the clock go with the door open, but it refused to budge no matter how hard Joe prodded the 'go' button). Joe tried to lift the door using various appendages but he couldn't lift the door high enough for gravity to help it on its way. Eventually and after a lengthy argument they managed to persuade a further passer-by to close the door for them.

"What, close the door on ya, in that box?" asked the perplexed passer-by.

"Yes. It's not complicated."

"S'a joke, right?"

"Does it look like we're joking?" Jack was losing his temper, and almost frothing at the mouth. The cat wasn't much happier.

"Well, yeah, it does. This is a wind up, right? Is it gonna be on T.V.? This is a prank show, yeah?" The passer-by, a greasy haired male with bad breath and a duffel coat, looked anxiously around for a television camera and was fairly sure he could see one in a nearby bush. "Where's the camera? Is that it, in that bush? I can see you! Hello Mum!" He waved cheerfully at the bush. The bush vibrated nervously.

"Yeah, if you like, it's a T.V. show, right," lied Jack. "We can't fool you! Just close the door will you? And keep smiling."

"Sure mate. Is you Jeremy Beadle? That's a crap disguise." The man was smiling and gently lifted the clock door, expecting any moment for the trick to be revealed.

"Yeah, mate, I'm Jeremy Effing Beadle. Shut the door and shut your gob, right?"

"Keep calm, Jeremy." That was Joe. Joe turned his head to the stooge. "You're doing a good job, this will be on television in a few weeks. It's a magic trick okay? We're going to make the clock disappear. Please shut the door and then you can watch the magic, okay?"

"Alright mate, whatever ya say. Cor, wait 'til I tell the missus." The male swung the door over and shut it, only just avoiding getting his dirt infected fingernails caught in the slam. He took a few steps back and watched the magic trick. The clock jumped a few inches in the air, rocking its head and base into the ground as it did so. It tried to spin, but the closeness of the floor made this impossible and instead it shook violently from side to side, crashing into the floor with each vibration. The passer-by thought he could hear someone being sick. In fact he was fairly sure he could also smell it. Although it could have just been his halitosis. Either way he was certain he could hear someone screaming like a girl.

The clock jumped a little higher with each vibration until finally it had enough room to spin, defying gravity and pretty much every other law of physics it could think of. The air seemed to turn blue around the clock, crackling like electricity, before suddenly the clock winked out of existence, folding in on itself like a piece of bad origami. Blink. The clock was gone.

"Nah, that was crap," said the passer-by to no one in particular. "Bloody obvious how they did that. Load o' crap." He blew a raspberry in the direction of the television camera hidden in the bush, picked up his bottle of white cider, and carried on his way.

After a couple of minutes a bald, gaunt looking man stepped out from the bush holding a video camera. He was looking intently at the footage on the little camera screen as he rewound his tape. He paused when he got to a clear shot of the brothers. No doubt about it. It was them.

"Jack and Joe. I can see you. You've been very naughty boys." The bald man smirked at the still image before getting an out-of-date mobile phone the size of a house brick out from his jacket pocket. With a spare finger he pressed a speed dial button, pulled out a thick plastic coated aerial and put the phone to his ear, camera tucked under his arm. The man sniffed through his painfully red nose as he spoke. "Drager? Yeah, it's Brownlow. I've got a tape you might want to see."

Chapter Thirty Eight – The Present

Jack and Joe really felt that one. Joe pushed the door open and scrambled out, almost rolling straight in front of a passing car. The driver was very surprised by the sudden and quite unexpected appearance of the grandfather clock in the middle of the street and put his foot down, driving quickly past. The car's bespectacled driver repeated a panicky mantra to himself. "I didn't see that. I didn't see that. I didn't see that." His psychiatrist was going to have a field day.

Jack leaned forwards and gripped the screeching cat hard. The cat was quite perturbed because Jack had thrown up in mid-spin. As there isn't much room in the inner workings of a grandfather clock the cat had taken most of the damage and was trying to shake its coat dry of the foul toxin it was unhappily dripping in.

"Jeez, Jack, did you have to do that?" Joe didn't escape the fallout and was doing his best to wipe himself down. The main problem was the horrendous smell. Someone was going to have to wash the clock out before they used it again. *It damned well isn't going to be me,* he thought.

"I didn't mean to, Joe, give me a break. Come on, let's just get this thing done." Joe nodded in response and heaved his brother out of the clock, Jack somehow keeping hold of the desperate moggy.

"We need to put the clock back in the car." The brothers had travelled forwards in time to what was, at Joe's best guess, the present. Surprisingly, perhaps, their hearse was sat in the same spot they'd parked it in the past with only minor vandalism.

"I can't help with this cat in me hands. We'll have to do it later."

"Some bugger'll steal the clock if we just leave it."

"Who'd steal that thing? It weighs a ton."

"We did."

"Fair point. But we know what the clock does, and we've got the key."

"Someone'll pawn it or something," countered Joe. "Mind you, it smells so bad right now we might get away with it." Jack screwed his face up, but the two decided that they had best lock the clock in the car. Joe could think of only one way of keeping the cat from escaping. The brothers shut the cat inside the grandfather clock and boy, the cat was not happy at all about it. A cat's nose is far more sensitive than a human's. The cat screamed and screeched, jumped and bumped, and scratched and bashed until it was blue in the face. Not that you could tell under its fur, in the dark and trapped inside a grandfather clock. A significant number of people wandered along the pavement as the brother's struggled with the clock and were growled off by Jack.

"Now what?" Jack asked after the clock was loaded up. Joe hadn't thought that far ahead and wasn't sure how to stop the cat bolting off as soon as they open the clock door. Joe bit his lip in thought.

"I know," he said finally. "You get in the car and shut yourself in. Then when you open the clock the cat can't escape."

"What? Why can't you get it this time?"

"You're scratched up already, Jack. No point in both of us getting our clothes ruined."

"No, I suppose not," admitted Jack, his voice heavy with sarcasm. However, as always in these situations, Jack admitted defeat and got himself into the car. He shut the car door and very carefully lifted the lid of the grandfather clock an inch or two. The cat bashed hard trying to force the lid wide and get away from the intolerable smell. Even Jack had to agree, it stank. He was almost sick again. In fact he was sick, but only a very little bit. He managed to swallow it back down, the foul taste causing him to pull a variety of funny faces. Joe raised an eyebrow, but watched intently as his brother finally opened the clock door allowing a ball of fur to zip out of the box at the speed of light, claws flashing everywhere. Jack made a grab with one hand and missed, but not before he managed to drop the lid on to his other hand. He yelped and pulled the hand free.

Someone tapped on Joe's shoulder.

"Yes?"

"Excuse me, sir," said a nasally voice. "I'm from the Scunchester Animal Welfare Society, and we've had an anonymous report of cruelty to animals."

Joe swivelled himself around at a speed that didn't seem humanly possible. He made himself as wide as he could, trying (and largely failing) to block sight through the hearses' many windows. A blonde haired chap from the animal society tipped at his official issue cap and leaned to his left and then right in an effort to get a view of what was going on inside the car.

And what was going on inside the car was this; Jack was losing. The cat darted back and forth under the seats, and leapt up and over Jack whenever he attempted a clumsy grab, the cat usually managing to draw blood with a claw as it tore by. The cat flung itself at the car windows, desperately seeking an escape route but finding them all blocked. However that didn't stop the cat from trying. It hissed as it swirled around the inside of the car like a Tasmanian devil running late for an important meeting. All Jack could do was try to minimise the damage he was taking. His hands were protecting his face as best as they could, although he already looked like he'd been an extra on the set of Enter The Dragon. *This is a really embarrassing way to die,* he thought, *I won't be able to live down the obituary in the local paper.*

"Animals?" offered Joe, trying his best to maintain an expression of innocence.

"Animals, sir," repeated the official suspiciously. He frowned as a blur of black and white slammed into the driver's door window and then immediately disappeared from view. The official could see Jack throwing his head around and moving from seat to seat. "Or rather animal, singular, in particular one black and white cat, trapped in a large wooden box and being loaded into a car matching your description."

"Matching my description?"

"Matching the description of your car, I should say, sir." The man took a few steps to his right to get a better view and peered down his thin nose. Joe quickly shuffled down the side of the car to continue to block the official's line of sight. "I think you should step aside, sir."

"I think you've got the wrong car. We've only just got here."

"If you like I can call the police and ask them to sort this matter out?"

Joe stuck his tongue to his top lip for a moment as he considered whether police involvement would make things worse or, well, much worse. With a quick smile, he pushed himself away from the car and waved his hands out wide at his side.

"She's all yours. I was just passing by, as it happens, nothing to do with me." Joe took a few steps backwards, making to cross the road. The official didn't stop him so Joe hopped away before mounting the pavement on the opposite side of the street to the car. The official made a quick detour to his van, parked unnoticed a few feet behind the hearse. He removed a plastic cage and a large net on a stick. He opened the cage and placed it on the floor just outside the driver's door, standing over it with his net held in place to limit the cat's escape options. Satisfied that his tools were ready he reached with his right hand and pulled the car door handle upwards. The door clunked free and the blonde haired official inched the door open.

Boom! The door was bashed open with a surprisingly large amount of force for a small cat. A black and white blur shot out of the car at an uncontrollable speed and, as luck would have it (for the official, not the cat), the cat ran straight into the waiting cage. The official slammed down the lid of the trap and locked it tight shut in one swift and obviously well practised movement. The official smiled at a job well done, tucked his net under his arm and picked the cage up, whistling to himself all the time. He walked, almost skipping, back to his van.

A battered, bruised and heavily scratched Jack slumped head first out of the open car door, banging his skull to the ground with a loud groan. His arm sloped down onto the road, his feet half caught in the seat belt behind him. He tried to pull his tangled foot free with the little strength he had left before gracelessly admitting defeat. He lay collapsed and waited for his surely imminent death, or a beer, whichever came sooner.

"Wait," shouted Joe from across the road to the official. The animal man threw an arched eyebrow in Joe's direction as he opened the door to his van, the cat by now firmly secure in the rear. "Where are you taking the cat?"

"The rescue centre." The man tilted his head as he planted a foot in the footwell of the van. "People like you shouldn't own cats. You make me sick."

"No, that was Jack!" But the man didn't listen. He'd gotten back in his vehicle and was already spinning his van around. Joe took a few steps in a futile chase, but the van was having none of it and was soon away and out of sight. The cat was gone.

Chapter Thirty Nine – Ten Minutes Later

Ten minutes and an unnecessary amount of struggling later and the brothers were sitting in the two front seats of the hearse wondering exactly what they should do next. Jack and Joe were (in no particular order) tired, bruised, battered, fed up, sober and, to sum up, pretty miserable. And to be honest, so was the hearse. The cat had made a right mess of its plastic leather seating, and the stink of sick seeping from the horizontal clock tucked up in the back didn't help matters. So, yes, the car was miserable too. In fact, in the interests of telling a complete story, it should be noted that the clock was also pretty pissed off. Ho hum.

"Let's just go," said Jack, his neck cranked backwards to try and stem the blood pouring from his nose. "Who cares about a sodding cat. Let's go back, get Charlie to wash out the car and clock, and we'll wait for the next missing cat case to come through the door."

"You don't get it, Jack. This is our chance to make it, our chance to finally build our reputation. This is it, our one opportunity to make something of ourselves. No more living hand to mouth. No more defrauding the tax man. No more claiming benefits for dead former employees. This is it. This is finally it. With this clock we can achieve anything." Joe didn't even blink as he spoke to his brother, pointing his finger into the dashboard to emphasise his point.

"I don't think Mrs. Gilhooney is going to help improve our reputation."

"If we can't even catch a missing cat before the cat is reported missing, what the hell chance have we got with anything else?"

Jack shrugged. "We can still get the cat."

"Eh?"

"Eh? It's obvious isn't it."

"Go on," said Joe with just a hint of nervousness. It was never a good thing when Jack came up with a plan.

"We wait until dark, find the cat rescue place and bust the cat out. What kind of security they gonna have anyway?"

"What kind of dumb idea is that?"

"Better than whatever you've got." Jack rummaged in the glove compartment of the hearse and was pleasantly surprised to find a Hawaiian shirt stuffed in it, obviously left by himself at some point in the future/past. He pulled it free and popped it on.

"Hmm," conceded Joe eventually. "Start the engine." Jack did so and spun the car around, heading gently in a picked-at-random direction until Joe decided to furnish him with further instruction.

"Further instruction would be nice."

"The nearest animal rescue centre is the one in the town centre. Head for that."

"Eh? I thought you didn't like my plan?" Joe didn't pass comment. Jack silently carried on with the driving, only speaking twice. Once to ask his brother for directions when he got lost and once to apologise to a cyclist he knocked over en route. But aside from such minor encounters the brothers arrived at their destination unscathed, which makes for pretty boring narrative but what can you do.

The animal rescue centre was a custom built modern building and yard just outside the Scunchester ring road, next to the derelict discount store that shut down after being extensively looted during the Scunchester riots the year before last. The centre had a breeze block perimeter wall with curly wurly barbed wire running along the rim to prevent the local villains from climbing in. It also had several security cameras pointing in several directions and two security guards doing a regular patrol of the perimeter. One of them, a squat, bob-haired lady, had a big and nasty looking dog.

"What kind of rescue centre is this?" asked Jack after the brothers had watched the building from a distance for an hour or two waiting for darkness to descend. The place had finally shut for the evening. Jack and Joe even saw the blond haired official from earlier heading home for the night which was a bonus. ("I'd rather take my chances with the security guards and the big dog," remarked Joe at the time).

"This place has a lot of security for just cats and dogs."

"We're not getting inside in a hurry."

"No."

"No."

"Hmm."

"So, let's give this up, yeah?" pleaded Jack, easily dissuaded. "We can just steal a different cat. Mrs. Gilhooney is nearly blind anyway. Face it, she's not going to notice if we give her the wrong moggy. And even if she does notice she'll just forget about it what with the Alzheimer's and everything."

"Hmm." Nothing more was said for about half an hour, until Joe continued. "It's getting dark. Put this on." Joe pulled out a pair of balaclavas from an inside coat pocket and pulled one over his head.

"Jesus," blasphemed Jack despondently as he popped the woollen hood over his head and topped it off with his baseball cap. The brothers got out of the car, Jack discreetly sliding Harry Mantei's pistol into his pants for safekeeping. They had parked several buildings away outside a local plastic bottle top manufacturers. The pair shuffled their way down the mossy grass verge that decorated the side of the road and pressed themselves against the outer wall of the animal sanctuary. "This is stupid."

"Yeah," agreed Joe as he peered around the corner of the breeze blocks. The yellowy glow of nearby street lighting gave Joe a good view of the front of the rescue centre, but equally it meant that the number of shadowy places to hide was limited. Not that that mattered particularly as Joe's peering balaclaved head had already been spotted by a grey haired patrolling security man.

"Hey you!" yelled the ageing sentinel. The old fellah waved a torch in Joe's general direction and began to break into a very slow run. To be honest he'd have been quicker if he'd just walked. Jack and Joe grabbed hold of each other and swivelled around running as fast as their little legs would carry them. The guard gave brave chase but didn't get too far before he was too knackered to carry on. Instead he waved his torch in the air after the disappearing shapes of Jack and Joe. "Bloody kids."

Jack and Joe had hidden themselves discreetly around the corner and behind a grey and overfull wheelie bin, breathing heavily. Both brothers pulled their balaclavas upwards. "We are not getting past that guy."

"No way," agreed Jack. "That guy is a professional. I don't like this."

"No, we need a better plan. Come on." Joe grabbed his brother and pulled him in the direction of the hearse in a half jog. Upon arrival Joe pulled open the boot and began to slide out the clock. "Grab the other end."

The clock was placed upright at the back of the car and the door swung open. Inside was not a pretty sight and Joe made his feelings very clear. "You have got to be joking? I am not getting back in that thing."

"It's the only way, Jack," reasoned the stony-faced Joe as he pulled out a compass from an inside pocket of his jacket. "We zap back in time to before this building was built, move the clock so that we are in position inside the grounds of the sanctuary, and zap back to now again."

"That's stupid."

"Yeah?"

"Yeah."

"Well then. I'll get in first shall I?" Joe plopped his foot inside the clock, his shoe sliding slightly on the slop that had dripped to the clock bottom. He grimaced but with a sturdy determination pulled his second shoe inside and stooped into position. Jack, complaining all the while, followed close behind and pulled the door shut.

"Jesus, it stinks in here. Get a bloody move on will ya?"

"How far back do you reckon we should go?" asked Joe.

"Fuck it. Give it a good twist backwards. We don't want to run into anybody."

"Okie dokie." Joe twisted the dial for all he was worth and slapped the 'go' button. The clock hopped up into the air and whirled itself out of existence in a flash.

Chapter Forty – Meanwhile In The Present

Alyssa had dried her hair and put some clothes on. She felt a lot better because of it. Almost human. The side room of the office-cum-flat was quite well stocked with a double wardrobe stuffed with a wide variety clothing. Why Jack and Joe should require quite so many items of female clothing in their office she dared not make a guess. The only thing that troubled Alyssa was that she wasn't sure what clothing was actually appropriate for this world. In the Game she would wear the robe of an Enchantress over strappy leather armour with an orbed shield for protection. But here? She'd dug out a tasteful pale blue blouse and a pair of cream linen trousers, which she felt was suitably restrained for the odd world she was now in. Of course she'd put a cape and sword belt on over the top of her outfit, and it was just a pity she couldn't find an actual sword to go with it. *No matter,* she thought, *I'm sure I'll be given one in due course.*

She had a look around the office whilst she had the spare time (and to be honest she had a lot of spare time right now) and had even tidied it up a bit. And by the Gods she was bored. Charlie had sent her up some food, which she thoroughly enjoyed eating. After all she'd never eaten anything before. Not real food anyway. When she was in the Game she was fed gloop in a tube and knew little about it. And now she'd eaten a Big Mac and fries. She'd chewed each gorgeous mouthful, savouring every single morsel as the taste tickled her tongue and the food rolled down her gullet. It was magical.

She sat in a chair pondering what to do next. She'd been told not to leave the office until Jack and Joe got back. But bugger them. She didn't owe them anything, she reasoned. Not really. In fact she reckoned it was their fault she was bored. She was never bored in the Game. And here she was with a whole new world to explore, a world of things to touch and taste. She'd wasted enough time in the office, she'd finished the vacuuming and had scrubbed the bathroom so hard that you could now see the tiles, so she decided that she'd go for a little walk.

She got up, tugging her cape in her arm as she did so, and strolled mock-confidently over to the door. She hesitated as she got to the doorknob, her freckled hand hovering over the plastic handle. Alyssa ground her teeth together and steeled herself, her heart pounding nervously for reasons she couldn't quite put her finger on. With sudden determination she pushed the handle down and opened the door, but instead of stepping out from her self-made prison she simply gawped in surprise and stumbled backwards. Standing at the other side of the door was a man holding a pistol.

"Where are they," demanded the man in a squeaky voice about an octave higher than would be deemed reasonable when pointing a gun at someone. "Where are Jack and Joe?"

"What's going on? Where's Charlie? Charlie!" yelled Alyssa. The bald man in front of her just grinned, the gap in his yellow teeth making his reaction all the more mocking.

"Yell as loud as you like. Charlie won't hear you." The bald man give a snort-cum-chortle that sounded more like he was choking than laughing. A little white foam edged the rim of his purple lips. The chortle stopped and the man's eyes rolled upwards as a thought struck him. "No, actually, that's not true.

What I mean is he will hear you, but he isn't in a position to do anything about it." More rasping chortles followed, so much so that he struggled to get his words out. "Charlie is... tied up... at the moment." He obviously thought he was funny. Alyssa did not see the joke.

"What do you want?" She edged backwards. The male followed cautiously.

"Where are Jack and Joe? I've seen the clock. I want the clock."

"You've seen the clock?" managed Alyssa. She'd backed up to the desk at the far end of the office, her backside poking into the wood. She lifted herself onto her toes and pushed her back backwards, edging her hidden left hand to her rear searching for something, anything, she could grab hold of and use as a weapon. The short, bald guy didn't really look the physical type and Alyssa was confident she could overcome him if she could just get past the pistol in his hand, so long as the stench of the man's bad personal hygiene didn't make her puke. Perhaps they didn't have mouthwash outside of the Game. "Who are you?"

"The name is Brownlow, Miss. Arnold Brownlow. And all I want is the clock. Where is it? I won't hurt you, Miss." His words were not all that convincing, particularly as Brownlow chose that moment to cock his gun with a shaky thumb movement. The click made Alyssa gulp hard, small beads of sweat trickling mischievously down her brow. Her hand discreetly moved a few millimetres to the right until her fingernails made contact with an object. She scratched the object closer to her so that she could get a hold.

"Jack and Joe will be back soon. You should ask them. I can... er... take a message?"

"No, Miss, I don't think so." Brownlow took a couple of

steps towards Alyssa. Brownlow wiped his red, running nose with the sleeve of his free hand and then sneered. "I think you'll have to come with me."

"No, I don't think so." Alyssa give a defiant laugh, although inwardly she was shaking. She was unsure how much strength she had in the real world. Brownlow took another step forwards, his chin raised in disappointment. *Just a little closer,* thought Alyssa, *just one more step.* She held her breath.

"It seems I have the advantage here. I have the gun. Now please, out." Brownlow flicked the gun barrel a couple of times to indicate that Alyssa should walk slowly around him and move towards the door. Brownlow took a step closer to the girl.

"If you say so," began Alyssa, but before she'd even finished speaking her left hand lashed forwards, swinging around with it a potted cactus she'd picked up from the desk behind her back. How she'd managed not to cry out when her fingertips jabbed the prickly spines she had no idea, but now she flung the cactus as hard and as fast as she could at Brownlow's bald head (a big target; he might as well just paint a bull's eye on his forehead). The plant span like a green shuriken through the air. Brownlow tried to use his gun arm to block the missile but he wasn't quick enough and Alyssa scored a direct hit. Brownlow plucked the cactus from his scalp and threw it to the ground. Small drips of blood ran down his forehead from several holes. Brownlow wiped his head with one hand and waved his gun with the other looking for Alyssa. Her saw her head disappear down the circular hole in the corner of the room.

"Shit," cursed Brownlow as he ran forwards towards the silver pole, initially tripping up over the floored cactus but soon regaining his balance. Brownlow leapt at the pole. Unfortunately leaping down a pole when you have a gun in one hand and blood all over the other is not a very sensible thing to do. Brownlow dropped the cocked gun almost immediately and it hurtled down beneath him, going off with a violent bang as it hit the floor, the bullet just nicking Brownlow's big backside before embedding itself in the ceiling above. Brownlow half slid and half fell down the pole, leaving a trail of blood behind him. He saw the door against the back wall swinging shut and made for it, picking up his loose gun as he did so. He pushed the door open, leading him back to the office stairwell and then on into the garage where he'd successfully managed to tie up the two mechanics only minutes before. The pair were still there, tied to two rickety wooden chairs with grey tape binding their hands and mouths.

Alyssa had run over to Charlie to try and rip the tape from his hands, but almost as soon as she'd started tugging at the tape Brownlow appeared at the doorway, droplets of blood dribbling to the floor from his circular face. Charlie's eyes were wide open, his eyeballs dancing in their sockets. Alyssa assumed incorrectly that this was in fear. Alyssa mouthed the word 'sorry' to Charlie and turned to run from the approaching Brownlow. Unfortunately she ran straight into the arms of a second man who had somehow sneaked up behind her. Alyssa screamed in sudden shock as the man took hold of her with a firm grip. Alyssa kicked hard with her flailing feet but could not get free, and with her strength ebbing out of her, she finally gave up. She was feeling dizzy, she realised. She was feeling sleepy. Sleepy and dizzy, almost as if she'd been drugged.

"She's a feisty one," chortled Brownlow as he limped over, clutching at his various nicks and scrapes.

"I've given her a shot," said the second male in an accent that was almost, but not quite, American. "She'll be out in a minute.

Shhh, little one." The last bit was to Alyssa.

"Who... are... you?" asked Alyssa, her eyes half shut. Her body felt wobbly and she could no longer support her own weight. Her head reluctantly balanced on the chest of the man she'd run into.

"My name is Drager."

That was the last thing that Alyssa heard before she went under.

Chapter Forty One – Long, Long Ago

"This is the past, is it?" asked Jack as he urinated on a small shrub a few paces behind the clock. He'd been holding it in for some time. "Doesn't look much."

"Yes. No," agreed Joe as he glanced around him. It was pretty damned bland, he had to admit. He wasn't sure exactly what he expected to find in the past but it wasn't this; nothing at all. All he saw was just a vast vista of wilting shrubs and broken bracken on rolling hills in a murky morning haze that lingered overhead like pipe smoke. No trees. No people. No animals. No nothing. "Can you hear that?"

Jack shook himself dry, put the Little General away and zipped up his flies. He listened intently, screwing his face in semi-concentration, wiggling first one eyebrow up and then the other. He shrugged and wandered over to his brother at the other side of the clock. He listened again, just in case he needed to be this side of the clock to hear whatever his brother was on about.

"I can't hear anything," Jack concluded finally.

"No. Me neither."

"Oh. Well. Good job you brought it up then."

"No, I mean I can hear nothing at all. No planes overhead, no power cables crackling, no birds tweeting, no wind blowing. Absolutely nothing. Just listen. This is what pure unadulterated silence sounds like."

"Hmm." Jack pondered a moment and gave this some thought. "Loser."

"We must have gone pretty far back in time."

"Yeah, I'd have expected to see some Roman gladiators fighting some cavemen or something. Y'know, some proper history, like what we were taught at school."

"Uh-huh," managed Joe in a vague response. He'd pulled out a compass from a jacket pocket and was trying to work out which way they'd need to move the clock to get to where the animal sanctuary would eventually be built. After a bit of umming and arr-ing he decided on the general direction. "I reckon we need to move the clock that way about a hundred and fifty metres."

Jack rubbed his hands as he got into position ready to hoick the clock across the rough terrain. He wasn't looking forward to the graft but he knew that the only way Joe would let them go back to the future was to get the job done, no matter how stupid the job actually was. Jack pushed from one side to topple the clock to the horizontal, Joe acting as a support to prevent it crashing to the ground. The pair then heaved from behind to slide the clock forwards along the decaying grass. Recent rain had wet the ground just enough to provide a little lubrication and the brothers made light work of the task right up until they ran into their first and only obstacle; a giant crater.

"What the...?" asked Jack. The crater was at least fifty metres in diameter and just a little scary. Jack peered over the rim. "Don't tell me. The rescue centre is down there."

"Yeah. At least, it will be one day. I'd guess we'd have to be bang in the middle of the crater. Dead centre. Doesn't that strike you as a bit odd? A strange coincidence?"

"I dunno, but I've got a great idea." Jack grinned his

broadest grin as he pushed the clock so the clock face was almost-but-not-quite hanging over the crater's edge. He opened the door to the clock, letting it flap to one side, and stepped inside. "Come on. Don't be a wuss." Jack sat himself in the clock and pressed his back against the base. He left just enough room for Joe to sit between his legs at the top end.

"You have got to be kidding," called Joe, although apparently his objections didn't stretch so far as to actually stop himself from climbing into the improvised toboggan. He sat himself just in front of his brother and took several deep, deep breaths. "This is insane."

"Yup. When I say rock, we rock ourselves back and forth until we topple over the edge, right? Just like when we were kids and we had that sledge, remember? We went down the ridge over Bollingswood Hill, no problem."

"I broke my arm when we crashed into that big tree at the bottom of that hill! I was in hospital for three weeks! I've still got the pins in my arm!"

"Rock!" Jack shunted himself forwards hard, then gently backwards, and then forcefully forwards once again. Joe was too busy gripping for dear life to help, but Jack's weight was enough to inch the clock forwards until the magic of gravity kicked in and took the clock down the crater's slightly damp slope. The clock slid down the crater's edge at a surprising speed, bumping over every shrub and rock and threatening to turn over and spit the brothers out at any moment. The back end swung out as they neared the crater bottom before the inevitable happened. The clock jumped up over a small stone and twisted in the air, spilling the brothers who simultaneously rolled forwards as they hit the turf. The clock bounced onwards, its door somehow swinging itself shut. The bottom corner of the timepiece banged hard into a stump of dead wood sticking out from the wet earth and the clock leapt further through the air, spinning counter clockwise for a moment, before landing base-down in the soil with a splintering thud. The clock came to a standstill. Somehow it had managed to land bolt upright. It took a moment for the dust and debris around it to settle, but after a few seconds the door simply swung open as if inviting the brothers inside for their next journey.

"That was a dumb idea. Idiot." Joe wiped the mud from his jacket as he stood up, not that it made a jot of difference. He pulled a mound of moss from one of his pockets and tossed it to one side.

"What do you mean? That was bloody ace! Let's go again!" Jack had leapt to his feet, ignoring the gash to his hand and holes over his knees. "I don't suppose you saw where my tooth went?"

The brothers approached the clock and checked for damage. They found none. The clock was completely intact with not even a dent. However Jack did see something unusual as he circled the clock. Something that seemed quite out of place and yet oddly familiar.

"What's that?" asked Jack, nudging his brother in the ribs with a frayed elbow. "To your left. Is that a body?" Joe looked to his right (Jack rarely gets it right) and saw sprawled on the floor a pair of booted feet no more than ten metres away. The rest of the body was covered by a cloak and an inch of dirt. Joe took a step towards the body, Jack tried to hold him back.

"I don't know about this."

"Your spider-sense tingling?"

"No. But it's usually bad news whenever we find a body."

Joe shrugged and trudged over to the boots. He tapped a

boot with his toecap, but the boot didn't respond. Joe knelt down and brushed away some of the dirt and debris. He could feel something solid underneath. Something far too solid to be a body. He pulled at one side of the cloak and twisted whatever it was over. The sight of what lay underneath the cloak made Joe's legs turn to jelly. He tried to speak but couldn't, a garbled scream coming out of his mouth as he tried and failed to kick himself away and instead he landed on his backside only inches away from the uncovered body. The body sprang to life and sat upright in one sudden, jolting movement.

"Hello?" said the body.

"Jesus!" yelled Jack loudly as he pulled Harry Mantei's empty pistol out of his pants pocket. The pistol came out the wrong way, so that he held the barrel pointing at himself. He quickly twisted it round to point the right way, but the sudden shock had shot his dexterity causing his clumsy fingers to drop the gun to the floor. He quickly swooped to the floor and picked up the weapon. "It's the bloody Instructor! What the hell is he doing here?"

"Where is here?" asked the Instructor as his three swirling eyes tried to focus on the two humans at once, almost as if he was trying to remember the two vaguely familiar shapes. Joe threw a desperate handful of wet grass in the Instructor's face and scrambled backwards, panting hard as he did so. He expected to receive pain as he stumbled his retreat and was surprised when he received none. The Instructor merely sat and watched.

"Look, just let us go, right. Take the clock. Just don't kill us." Jack squeezed at the trigger getting ready to fire, a pretty futile gesture considering the gun was empty.

"Clock?" asked the Instructor. "I have an in-built clock. I do not need another."

"Then what do you want?"

"Want?"

"Yeah, what do you want?" This didn't get a response.

"How did you find us?" asked Joe, as he found his way to his brother's side.

"Find you? It appears that you found me. I do not know you. I do not know how I got here," came the metallic voice. Somehow the voice was not quite so harsh as the brothers remembered it. The Instructor didn't sound quite so... fatal. "I remember a flash, and then darkness. And then you turned me over. Are you my creator?" He was nodding towards Joe.

"Your what?"

"What is my purpose?"

"You're the Instructor!"

"The Instructor?" The Instructor seemed very baffled by this information, almost as if he had never heard his own name before. His circuits began to mull the new information over, the clockwork interior of his delicate brain clicking quietly in circles.

"This doesn't make any sense," complained Jack to his brother, his gun still waving hopelessly in the air.

"Does that gun have any bullets?" asked Joe calmly.

"No," hissed Jack quietly. "But he doesn't know that."

"Then put it away. Don't you see what's happened here?"

"Does it look like I know what's going on?" Jack's wild eyes told Joe that he didn't.

"Alyssa blasted the robot through the portal in the future," Joe replied, "and it sent him here to the past. Obviously the power has frazzled his circuits because he has no idea who he is or what he's doing. His memory has been wiped."

"So... so he is not going to kill us then?" stage whispered

Jack.

"No."

"No," mimicked the Instructor, his keen robotic hearing able to pick up every word of the muted conversation. "Unless you want me to, of course."

"No, no, I'm fine, thanks," quickly replied Jack, tucking the pistol back in his pants.

"As you wish. Please let me know if you change your mind."

Chapter Forty Two – Later On In The Present

Alyssa woke with a start, staring wide eyed about her. She was in an office and sitting uncomfortably on a chair. *Another bloody office. Typical.* She'd never seen an office in her entire life whilst she was in the Game and within a very short space of time in the real world she'd been in two of them. Her hands were behind her back, for some reason. She tugged at her wrists but with no joy. She swivelled her head around to try and see what the problem was and she could just make out the frayed ends of a rope holding her hands together. *Some bastard has tied me up.* Her ankles were similarly bound she noted with a serious amount of disdain. Two bloody offices and she'd been a prisoner in each one. *At least Jack and Joe hadn't tied me up,* she thought, *although they might as well have.*

The room around her was decorated with books. Actually, that's not quite true. The room was decorated with an off white wood-chip wallpaper that looked like it had been put up quite some time ago by someone who didn't really give a fuck. But immediately in front of the wallpaper pushed tightly against each wall were several racks of shelving on which were a lot of books. A glass-topped desk was only a few feet in front of Alyssa and she could see a number of items on it, including, tantalisingly close to the edge of the desk, a telephone. She looked around and saw that the only door into the room was shut, no movement evident through the door's frosted glass.

Alyssa leaned forwards so that the chair was on it's tip-toes and hopped for the desk. The chair made a loud bang on the floor as she bounced forwards and instinctively she twisted her head to the door to look for any signs of life coming from outside. Not even a flutter of movement. Satisfied it was safe to carry on she bounced further forwards so that she was just at the table's edge. Now for the difficult part. She had to pick up the phone and dial for help (not that she knew anyone's number) with her hands tied behind her back whilst restrained to a chair.

Alyssa twisted herself around so that she was now side on with the desk. She slowly lowered herself over, worried somewhat about toppling over like a tortoise and not being able to right herself after, but she knew she needed to be on her feet if she was going to be able to do this. Taking a deep breath and a leap of faith she tippled herself further forwards and hopped painfully onto her feet. She darted quickly forwards and backwards with her toes trying to find her centre of gravity and, after a few worrying moments, she finally managed to find her balance. She pressed herself up to the desk edge so her hands were level with the phone. Alyssa had to bend over quite a way to achieve this but she used the weight of the table to help keep her upright. At this unusual angle she couldn't actually see her hands anymore and so inched them blindly onto the desk, trying to find the phone. Her bindings made it painful to stretch her delicate fingers too far from the back of the chair and Alyssa could feel the rope chaffing into her skin as she scratched her way along the desk. With the very tips of her fingers she could feel something solid but try as she might she just couldn't get any purchase on the item, whatever it was. Knowing her luck she reckoned it wouldn't have been the phone anyway. She'd have gone to all this effort and end up holding a vase behind her back.

Reluctantly she knew she needed another plan. She let her fingers drop from the table edge, happy for the instant relief from the pain of the ropes. She hopped to one side so that she could twist her neck, looking for movement at the door once more. As she did this thing the legs of the chair caught the edge of the table with a rickety creak, a sound that suggested that the wooden chair she was strapped to wasn't quite as sturdy as perhaps it might have been. Alyssa saw no movement through the glass door and shrugged. *In for a penny,* she thought before she twisted herself round and swung with all her might, letting the chair's legs move behind her and bang hard into the edge of the desk. She heard one leg splinter loose and clatter to the floor. Inspired with this success she swung a further two or three times into the table until the whole bottom end of the chair had broken off in a rotten heap. Her ankles, freed suddenly from their bindings, allowed her better balance. She wriggled at the ropes behind her and with a little effort the chair bottom dropped free. She turned herself around, now upright, and used the top of desk to batter away at the chair back, soon having the desired effect of loosening the bindings to her hands. She worked her right hand free, despite considerable pain to her thumb as she pulled her hand through, and with one hand out she could pull the other to her front, with the remains of the wooden chair attached to it. She picked at the rope with her free fingers and soon shook off the shackles that had temporarily bound her.

"Ha!" she said to no one in particular, very satisfied with her exploits in escapology. She twirled herself around to the desk and snatched the phone. In the Game telephones like this had an operator who would connect you to whoever it was you wanted to speak to. Even better you could also travel down the phone line, should you wish, and materialise at the other end and be none the worse for the journey. She hoped this was the case in the real world too. She pushed the phone to her ear. It rang briefly. "Hello?"

"Uh.... hello?" came a confused sounding nasally female voice through the earpiece. *Must be the operator,* reasoned Alyssa.

"Hello operator. Put me through to Joe please. Or Jack."

"Uh... yes." It almost sounded like the lady was holding her nose. "I'll, umm, just try the line for you. Please, umm, hold?" The female voice disappeared before Alyssa could reply and was replaced by hold music, a tinny one tone affair that sound like a child had recorded it on a Casio keyboard. Alyssa let her eyes drift to the door as she waited and she thought she saw a flicker of movement, just out of the corner of her eye, as if someone had put a hand to the door handle and then quickly thought better of it. What was going on here? Why was she still on hold? *I should have been transintergrated by now.*

"Operator, quickly," demanded Alyssa in a low whisper. The hold music faded as she spoke, and a polite sounding male voice, a recording obviously, piped up.

"At John Drager's Private Detective Agency we are available around the clock whatever your needs. If you want help, we can provide the solution. Please ask about our very competitive prices." Alyssa dropped the phone before the voice had even finished speaking. She suddenly realised she had not been speaking to the operator at all. The phone line was connected to someone to do with the man who called himself Drager, the man who had kidnapped her, tied her up and done Gods know what else. She darted forwards, lunging an arm low to pick up the sturdiest looking of the fallen chair legs and gripped it purposefully with her right hand. She swivelled around to the room's only window and pulled a hole in the blinds with a couple of free fingers, a shard of light beaming into the room through the gap. Alyssa narrowed her eyes but saw instantly that she was not on the ground floor and it was too high to try and jump. Which meant there was only one way out. Through the frosted door. She heard a noise, someone at the door handle perhaps, and she circled herself around ready to repel any attack. She realised her mistake, of course, as her eyes struggled to cope with the semi-darkness in the room after peeking out to the bright blue outside. She blinked hard and tried to squint, waving her leg vaguely in the air in front of her at an unseen assailant. Unfortunately the blind wafting of a splintered stick did her no good, and the wooden shaft was snatched from her. Within a second she had someone's hairy hands holding her in place and from the distinctive smell of stale Hai Karate she knew who it was. The man from before. Arnold Brownlow.

Chapter Forty Three – About The Same Time

Joe opened the door of the clock, relieved to get out of the intensely cramped conditions. He stepped out onto solid ground and strained to see anything in the darkness around him. Quickly Jack was at his heels and flicked a lighter to life. They seemed to be in a storage room, a stack of paint tins to their left and a pile of neatly folded cardboard to their right confirming the theory. Several wooden beams and riveted air ducts ran above their heads, narrow metal pipes and wires criss-crossing this way and that between them. Several feet ahead of them, just visible in the gloom, was a small stairway, only six or seven steps high, that ran up to a wooden door.

"I told you we wouldn't materialise under ground," whispered Joe.

"Mm," admitted Jack. Since the crater was so deep he'd worried the clock would be underground when they came back to the present. Joe told him not to be such a cry baby, but Jack guessed it was better that he was wrong than the alternative. He knew from bitter experience that being buried underground in a wooden box was not a lot of fun... a story for another day perhaps; Jack's advice would be never to get drunk and fall asleep in a funeral home. Subsequently Jack had left his brother with explicit instructions that he was to be cremated should he die, although to be honest he worried if it was possible for even that to go wrong. He'd hate to be burnt to death by mistake.

He wondered if perhaps he should change his instructions and instead ask Joe to leave his body exactly where he found it and to drop off the odd parcel of food and water just in case. Jack stretched his back out and wiggled an arm to his side, cracking his knuckles as he did so. It had been cramped in the clock.

"Interesting," said the Instructor as he took a robotic step out of the clock. "Your machine seems to have transported us to a new world."

"No. Same world, different time," sniffed Jack.

"Interesting," repeated the Instructor in a polite voice. "Also the interior of your clock is precisely five point seven five centimetres bigger on the inside than the outside. A curious thing for a box to be bigger on the inside than the out, don't you think?"

"Could do with a couple more inches I reckon, if we're going to start bringing robotic luggage with us." Jack hoped the robot understood sarcasm. He had no idea why Joe insisted they bring their nemesis with them. He, for one, didn't believe the Instructor's claim that he had no memory of his former life and thoroughly expected the robot to take his revenge on the brothers at any moment. "Make yourself useful and, umm, wait here."

"As you wish," agreed the Instructor, his third eye socket swirling backwards and forwards in the gloom, attempting to find focus.

Jack stumbled around with his lighter held out in front of him looking for a light switch. He found a length of string dangling from the ceiling near to the short stairway and he give this a tug. A solitary, sad-looking light-bulb flickered slowly to life although the pathetic glow it produced barely gave the room more light than Jack's old lighter had done. The musty smell of burnt dust swirled into the occasional nostril. Jack pocketed his rusty lighter and took the first tentative step up the creaking stairway. He gripped the partially painted bannister to try and keep his ample weight from creating too much noise as he steadily climbed the six wooden steps. Joe shuffled to the foot of the steps and watched his brother reach for a plastic handle that would hopefully open the door. Millimetre by millimetre Jack pushed the handle downwards not knowing what was waiting on the other side. He prayed quietly to Gods he didn't believe in, hoping above hope that the big bastard of a dog he'd seen outside wasn't sitting on the other side, waiting bare-teethed and drooling for Jack's juicy leg bone to step carelessly through.

The handle descended as far downwards as it cared to go and Jack pushed forwards as gently as his clammy hand would let him. Initially the door refused to budge, the wood swollen tight into the outer frame. Jack chewed his tongue and wiggled his nose, but he had no choice other than shoving hard at the door. He heaved at the handle and the door gave an inch rubbing against the rubbery floor tiles underneath. Worried that the scraping sound would alert the rescue centre's two security guards of the break-in, Jack paused, hand still firmly on the handle. He could see no light through the crack that had emerged between door and frame. He could hear no movement, no sounds of life and no vicious dog barking, keen to get at Jack's flesh with its glistening teeth. *It could be a cunning trap*, thought Jack suspiciously, *dogs are clever like that*.

Joe thumped Jack's upper thigh with a vicious jab. Jack twisted his torso angrily backwards and mouthed a big, silent "Ow" to his brother. Joe merely smirked and nodded to the door. Jack shrugged, pretending that the sudden bruise on his thigh didn't throb, and pushed forwards, staggering with the door as the friction from the frame finally gave up and the door could swing freely. Jack almost fell as his legs stumbled up the last of the steps but he managed to right himself whilst maintaining his grip on the door handle. The dog he expected to see sat waiting for him wasn't there, and Jack breathed a hearty sigh of relief. His brother was quickly behind him, crouching slightly in the murky darkness.

"Looks like that way," Joe pointed. They had emerged on a short corridor that was being used more as a storage dump than a thoroughfare. Some mops and buckets casually blocked a fire exit at one end. A door led the other way, the glass panelled upper half of which gave Jack and Joe a view of the interior of the rescue centre. Joe crept to the panel and peered through, his shallow breath causing a light mist to form on the cracked glass. The room beyond was a reception area with several other exits leading off from it. At the far end was a large porch that served as the building's main entrance, the dim silhouette of a security guard could be seen in the darkness outside. Two other corridors led off from the reception area, a faint light down one corridor indicated some kind of life down it. The other corridor was dark. In the near distance a dog barked with a high pitched growl, but after a moment was silent again. In the centre of the reception, not far from the porch, was a curved desk, no one sitting behind it. A slight flicker of light from behind the desk suggested that the various screens for the various security cameras lived here. Which was good. It meant no one was watching the place. *Both guards must be outside*, thought Joe with a half-smile.

The door swung open easily on a well oiled double hinge and Joe darted from his hiding place to the edge of the dark corridor. He crouched here for a moment, waiting just in case he'd triggered some kind of unseen alarm, but nothing happened. He beckoned for Jack to join him which he did with as much stealth as a fat man in a bright Hawaiian shirt could muster. Jack panted as he threw himself down to the ground next to his sibling and rubbed at one of his various aching muscles with his stubby, nailless fingers. Jack peered down the dark corridor. His ears pricked up as he heard a faint mewing not too far away.

"I thought I heard a pussy cat," he mumbled, nudging Joe in the ribs with an elbow. "This way me thinks."

Joe followed his brother down the corridor, his back bent as best as he could manage, trying as he was to keep a low profile. Jack flicked his lighter on ahead of him as the corridor veered to one side. A set of plastic flaps dangled from the ceiling, temporarily blocking further progress. Joe reached an arm through, lifting a flap carefully to one side, and peered into the darkness. A rim of slanted windows in the roofing above provided some moonlight. Joe could see breeze blocks down one wall lined with a variety of cages, different sizes to suit different animals. The nearest section seemed suitable accommodation for a cat. Just to the right after the plastic curtains was a set of double doors, a yellowy light shining through another set of upper glass panels that the designer of the building had obviously taken a liking to. Jack frowned and twisted around, the flame from his lighter lightly scorching a plastic flap as he did so.

"I can hear voices," whispered Jack ever so lightly. "Through the double doors."

Joe nodded his response, but still seemed to insist that Jack carry on through. Lifting the flap higher Jack pushed through and pressed his back lightly against the metal lined lower panels of the double doors. The door moved slightly as he did so but he managed to resist putting his full weight on to it. He twisted around and slowly stood up until his eyes just peered over the glass. His brother slid alongside him and joined in with the peering.

"Shit," whispered Jack urgently. "Shit."

"Shit," agreed Joe.

To the brother's eternal surprise the whole of the Vamenti family were standing or sitting in various positions in a loading bay located through the double doors, Donatello Vamenti sitting in the middle on a blue and uncomfortable looking plastic chair, his Ma standing right next to him. The entire clan seemed to be in the room, except for Leonardo of course. Jack recognised Donatello's cousin-in-law Paul O'Gander who was sitting smoking a cigarette near half raised metal shutters at the far end of the bay. O'Gander was a vicious Irish bastard who once lost a tenner to Jack at darts; O'Gander still held a grudge about this and Jack was not keen on a rematch. Over in the corner by an electric heater was the wheel-chair bound Victor, a thug you didn't mess with unless safely on the other end of a long staircase (and even then with care. Victor had once crawled up three flights of steps, dragging himself with his muscular arms, and broke the neck of a chap who'd been cheating on his sister). A few other thugs and devotees of the Vamenti racket dotted the room, each as menacing and dangerous as the next. Jack and Joe slowly lowered their heads and whimpered.

"I think we've stumbled on the secret bloody Vamenti headquarters," moaned Jack so quietly Joe could barely hear him. "I told you this place had too much security for an animal rescue centre."

"Let's just get the cat and get out of here. Very, very quietly."

Joe tip-toed away from the door, keeping his head low and inching himself to the other side of the corridor. Jack kept a hand at the hem of his brother's jacket and winced with every footstep, sure that the squeak of footwear on the concrete floor would give them away and result in a barrage of bullets from the nearby mafia. To be blunt, Jack was shitting bricks.

"C'mon," he whined. "Let's just get out of here, I've got a bad feeling." Joe ignored him and scanned the various caged holes that lined the wall, nearly each one containing a cat of one variety or another. Some of the cats stirred to life and mewed, much to Jack's chagrin. He glanced around, but no movement came from the docking bay doors. Jack tugged at his brother anyway, to ensure he was aware of his heightened sense of impending doom. Joe just shrugged him off and kept his mind focussed on the task in hand.

"This is the one." Joe lifted a latch that held the cage door shut. The cat inside, happily asleep not five minutes ago, jumped to life, the hair on the cat's back standing on end. The cat's tail tripled in girth, and the wild hissing noise indicated the cat's opinion of the sudden rescue. Fierce talons appeared on the pussy's paws. Joe wedged himself tight to the rim of the row of cages and he eased the wire door open, just an inch at first as the cat hissed at him and edged, back arched, so far to the back of the cramped space that the cat's tail curled up and over the rest of it's body like a scorpion ready to sting. Joe opened the cage door wider, just enough to squeeze his left arm through whilst keeping the cage blocked using the side of his body as a makeshift seal. Steadily Joe reached his fingers towards the reluctant pussy (a surprisingly familiar situation for him). Joe received a painful slash across his knuckles as the cat made its feelings about the intrusion perfectly clear (a surprisingly familiar response).

"Err, Joe..." said Jack as he tapped on his brother's shoulder.

"Not now," grimaced Joe. Joe decided that the slowly slowly approach wasn't the best way to go about grabbing a cornered cat and therefore his second approach was more forceful. He thrust his arm deep into the cage and grabbed hard at the scruff of the cat's neck. The cat gave a pained yelp at the unwanted attention, but it's flailing claws could only make contact with the cuff of Joe's jacket.

"Err, Joe... we've got a little situation here..." Jack had stopped tapping on his brother's shoulder, but the high pitch of his voice hinted that there might just be a teeny-weeny problem that might just require Joe's attention. Joe heard his brother gulp but it was too late to stop now. Joe pulled the cat forwards, despite its protestation, and in one swift movement that any street magician would have been proud of, Joe whipped the cat out of the cage and tucked it under his jacket, holding it pressed tightly against his breast. The cat, not keen on the level of intimacy, squirmed and squealed trying to get free. The cat's little wide-eyed head popped out of Joe's collar and hissed. Joe wrapped his other arm around and, once confident that the cat was going nowhere, turned himself around to see what had spooked his brother.

Joe gulped.

Jack was shaking like a leaf, heavy rings of sweat evident around his armpits. He was holding in his hand the empty pistol he'd nicked from Harry Mantei. Jack was pointing the pistol unconvincingly at the menacing mob of Mafia members huddled in the now open doorway to the loading bay. At the front of the mob was the wheelchair bound Victor, with

Donatello Vamenti standing just behind him and looking very pissed off. The other goons had gathered round and growled like dogs, hungry for meat and ready to pounce.

"Here I am," began Donatello, "having a nice chat with my family, sharing with them my concern for animal welfare, when who should I catch breaking and entering? None other than the infamous Jack and Joe, Scunchester's worst pair of private detectives." Donatello leaned in as he spoke, his bristled chin jutting out just above Victor's scarred forehead.

"Times must be hard, eh, boss?" That was Paul O'Gander, his soft Irish lilt adding an air of sinister mockery. "Looks like these two are just a pair of cat burglars."

"Leave the jokes to me, O'Gander." Donatello slapped his cousin-in-law across the back of his head with the back of his hand, eliciting a loud "Ow" from the Dubliner. O'Gander rubbed his bruised skull with the plank of wood he was holding.

"Let me 'ave 'em, boss," grunted Victor, rolling his wheels back and forth as he waited impatiently to be let loose. His hands, both covered in grey-white bandages, gripped hard onto those circular bits of metal at the side of the wheels – these probably have a technical name but Victor was buggered if he knew what they were called.

"Put the gun down, Jack. Make it easier on yourself." Donatello smiled as he spoke, his perfect teeth unnaturally white in the dimly lit corridor. "I've only just bought this suit and I'd hate to get a hole in it." Donatello was wearing a navy blue suit that looked like it had been sculpted to fit his body. The suit contrasted sharply with Joe's suit which looked like it had been chewed up, swallowed and shat out by an angry bear. It didn't help that Joe was wriggling left and right trying to keep the cat hidden underneath.

"No way," cried Jack with bravado that surprised even him. "If I put this gun down you'll set your goons on us!"

"I probably will," replied Donatello smartly. "But, heck, I'll probably set my goons on you anyway. And you'll only be able to shoot one of them. You can't stop them all."

"Yeah, well," gulped Joe hoarsely. He felt backed into a corner and suddenly knew how the cat felt in the cage. "I'm not gonna shoot them, am I? This bullet'll be gunning for you if you don't let us out of here."

"That does it!" screamed a new voice. Ma Vamenti stepped forward, pushing her youngest aside. Ma was five foot one in her heels and was almost as wide as she was tall. Even so, the matriarch had a frightening presence. She stared directly at Jack, her narrowed gold-green eyes piercing him like lasers. She might have a mass of grey hair and be ready to start drawing her state pension, but boy, you do not fuck with Ma Vamenti.

"Ma, I can handle this."

"Can you?" Ma cuffed Donatello quickly. Ma was wearing a sturdy floral dress that circled her body like badly pasted wallpaper. "It doesn't look like you can to me."

"Ma," whined Donatello, "please... Not in front of my friends. You're embarrassing me!" Behind him Paul O'Gander was quietly sniggering gleefully.

"Jack, you will give me that gun now," demanded Ma. She held out a greasy palm in front of her. Jack felt his arm quiver under the sudden weight of feminine pressure. Joe had to nudge him to get him to respond.

"Look, I'm sorry Ma, I am. We just want this cat, and we're gone." Jack took a shuffling footstep sideways trying to get a little nearer to the flapping plastic barrier, Joe keeping tightly to his side. Jack waved the pistol around carelessly. "I honestly wouldn't have hurt little Donatello. I was just joking with him, y'know. This gun doesn't even have any bullets in it. See?" Jack demonstrated that he meant no harm by pulling quickly on the pistol's trigger. Unfortunately, and to Jack's great surprise, a bullet silently shot out of the gun's silenced barrel at high velocity, the soft pfffft somehow managing to echo down the corridor. The freed bullet span forwards in the direction the pistol was absent-mindedly pointing in when the trigger was pulled and lurched forwards. Donatello watched helplessly, eyebrows so high as to be practically above his head, as the bullet travelled directly in the direction of his poor, sweet Mama.

"No...." yelled Donatello in that low and stretched pitch that signifies everything has gone into slow motion. He moved his hands to try and push his Ma out of the way, but his hands didn't seem to want to move with any degree of urgency no matter how hard he tried. It was no good. The bullet thudded straight into Ma Vamenti's thigh, a spurt of gloopy red liquid shooting out from the wound like a badly popped zit. Ma immediately toppled over clutching at her leg and in a great degree of shock. She tried to speak, but no words would come.

Jack looked at the pistol with an even greater degree of shock. He knew the gun was empty. He knew the gun had no bullets 'cos he'd fired them all uselessly into the Instructor in the far, far future. He remembered vividly that he'd clicked and clicked the trigger until it was empty. *What the hell just happened?* All these thoughts would have liked to try and force their way into Jack's mind for consideration, but to be honest he didn't have the time right now. So instead he dropped the gun as if he'd suddenly realised it wasn't a gun at all but a flaming dead rat, span on his heels and ran, Joe close behind him. The pair careered through the plastic flaps hanging down from the ceiling and belted it so fast down the corridor that they almost fell over each other.

It took a second or two for Donatello to understand what had just happened. He knelt, holding his Ma's hand in his. *Jack has just shot my Ma in the leg,* he finally managed to think. *Jack, the little shit, has just shot my dear Ma, my fucking Ma, in the fucking leg. Jack is a dead man.* "Get that son of a bitch!" he yelled at those gathered around him. Victor was first to break away from the pack and rolled his wheelchair urgently down the corridor, his arms spinning so fast that you could barely see them. O'Gander tried to keep up with him, but ended up getting flicked in the face by a plastic flap that Victor had sent flying into the air upon impact. O'Gander clutched at his bleeding forehead and swore loudly in Gaelic as he fell to the floor.

Jack and Joe made the most of their head start and tumbled into the reception area. A short haired female security guard was just making her way into the building through the porch, a large, drooling dog tethered to her by a thick strap of worn leather.

"Hey, stop right there!" the guard cried out in astonishment as she fumbled to pick the right key from a keyring that contained far too many keys to be actually useful. Jack and Joe managed to twist away despite their velocity and the pair headed quickly down the short corridor and even quicker down the short number of stairs to the storeroom.

"Get in the clock! Get in the clock!" yelled Joe as he half jumped and half fell down the stairs.

"Of course," replied the remarkably dead-pan Instructor, who had been happily charging himself up using a plug socket in the wall. The Instructor yanked himself free from the socket, a bright fizzle of confused electricity following him, and he trundled as hurriedly as his little robotic joints would allow him.

He slid himself into the clock at the same time as Jack who had skidded to a halt next to him whimpering something about it all being an accident, a misunderstanding that could have happened to anyone. The Instructor tucked his head under the wooden frame and Jack did the same. *It is most curious,* the Instructor thought, *but the wooden walls of the clock seem to give ever-so-slightly, as if the clock itself is trying its damnedest to give us just that little bit more room. Not much more room, admittedly, but just enough to squeeze everyone inside. Not that the humans seem to have noticed this implausible breach of physics of course.*

Joe arrived at the clock with a thud and a shrieked meow exactly at the same time as Victor wheeled up at the top of the stairs, big bulging veins of hate throbbing down his temples. Victor could see the brothers trying to hide from him in what he thought was a cupboard of some sort. He reckoned he had them now and no stairs were going to hold him back. Victor pulled backwards half a foot, just to get a little ~~run up~~ wheel up to the top step. With all his might he pushed his wheels with his Popeye forearms, yelling a meaningless war cry as he did so. He flung himself, chair and all, off the top step and into the air, for a moment gracefully floating forwards until exactly half a second after take off when his head slap-banged into a low beam that ran along the storeroom ceiling. The force of the blow swung his body around, sending the innocent wheelchair crashing violently upwards into the ceiling and then downwards onto the floor, both wheels buckling at one end or the other. Victor's useless legs twisted up as his head twisted down before smacking into the bottom step, blood dribbling from his mouth as several teeth loosened on impact. His bruised head came to a stop on the cold concrete floor, his numb legs dropping down behind him a second or so later. Unconsciousness did not take him immediately, but Victor knew he must be hallucinating. He watched, unable to move, as the thick fingers of Jack's paw pulled the cupboard door shut. *It's funny,* Victor thought, *but that cupboard looks like a big old grandfather clock.*

The clock jumped up and started to dance in front of Victor's obviously very confused eyes. It hopped from one side to the other before swinging itself in a circular arc, getting faster and faster with each circuit. Flashing lights began to swirl to life as the clock suddenly blinked and disappeared, leaving behind only darkness. Victor tried to focus, tried to work out what had just happened, but his brain gave up and he promptly fainted, finally succumbing to the inevitable unconsciousness.

Chapter Forty Four – Elsewhere, In The Present, Give Or Take A Minute

"Where do you think you're going, Miss?" Brownlow rasped through his purple lips, grinning broadly as he spoke, his voice edged with a subtle hint of sinister sexual arousal. He had Alyssa's hands held behind her back and was standing with his mouth hovering unnervingly close to her right ear. Alyssa felt nauseous as Brownlow's stale breath drifted across her cheek and towards her nostrils. "You're going nowhere until we get the clock from those two clueless brothers. You see, Miss, we'll arrange a little trade. We'll give you up if they give up the clock. Think of yourself as a nice, quiet and well-behaved piece of property and you won't be hurt, eh, Miss?" Brownlow snorted, a faint spray of spit moistening Alyssa's lobe and, to be blunt, creeping her out.

"What do you want with the clock?" she asked.

"I've seen what Jack and Joe have been up to, popping back and forth in time like they own the place. They can't be trusted with such power. Jack and Joe are too..." he struggled for the correct noun "...simple. They cannot be trusted to use the time machine... responsibly, yes?" Brownlow let his right hand slide raggedly along Alyssa's forearm and pushed himself close to her hip, his mouth held so close to her pale neck that Alyssa could feel the damp air shiver down the back of her top. Alyssa decided to respond in a language she was sure Brownlow would understand.

"Fuck off." The words came out quickly, with a steely grit she hadn't felt since she was in the Game. Alyssa growled, giving off a sound that a wolf might make if it got its tail trapped in a car door, and thrust her head backwards with a burst of speed that a slow motion replay would struggle to pick up. The back of her skull crunched into Brownlow's jaw, shattering the surprisingly brittle bone within. Brownlow yelped at the sudden unexpected agony that had exploded in his lower face, and then yelped again at the pain that giving out a yelp caused. Somehow he managed to hold back a third yelp, but the streams of yellowy water running down his broken face told of the excruciating pain Brownlow was in. He let go of Alyssa almost immediately, but was in too much shock to know what to do next and so he just stood there. Unfortunately for him Alyssa hadn't finished yet. She twisted herself around to face her enemy, a grimace of rage torn across her delicate face. Any residue of empathy for her captor had been deleted from her subconscious; she'd had enough. It was time for her to push back. *No one will stop me*, she thought, *no one will touch me again*.

Alyssa launched forwards with the palms of her hands whirling around in a maelstrom of violence, pounding into Brownlow's fragile ribcage. Ripples of loose skin wobbled down Brownlow's sore chest as his ribs loosened under the impossibly powerful barrage. He tried hopelessly to stop the onslaught with his own useless flapping arms. He backed off as fast as his little legs would allow him, but Alyssa showed no hint of mercy. If he hadn't tripped over a wastepaper basket and sprawled backwards on the floor he was sure Alyssa wouldn't have stopped until she held his still-warm and beating heart in her freckled fingers. (Looking back on the incident afterwards

Brownlow was actually quite relieved that Alyssa had *only* managed to break his jaw and five of his ribs).

"Hold it, lady," cried a voice from the door, which had been suddenly swung open and was bleeding an intense light from the foyer beyond. Drager was standing stony-faced holding a pistol confidently in his hand. His nervous secretary could be seen hovering behind him, holding onto a ring binder like it was a shield. Drager cocked his weapon coolly. "You will desist. I will not warn you again. If you do not follow my instructions precisely then I will shoot you."

Alyssa turned to face the private detective, her face snarling like a wild animal. She grabbed hold of the desk that stood between them and flipped it to one side like it was only rotten driftwood. The desk bounced, splintering on the floor, somehow managing to hit the prone and groaning Brownlow only once before crashing into the side wall and knocking several bookshelves and a chunk of plasterboard to the floor. Alyssa took a step towards the detective, driven on by animal instinct, her consciousness long since having retreated to somewhere nice and safe at the back of her fragile mind. Drager didn't hesitate. He'd had a stint in the Bulgarian army in his youth and was a crack shot. He pulled the trigger and a bullet spiralled into the air racing towards the target at the speed of, well, a speeding bullet. Alyssa, if she could still be called that, raised her hand in the air, palm flat and facing outwards, and the bullet stopped, inches from her skin. Literally stopped. The bullet hovered, quivering in mid air as if the laws of physics were desperately trying to apply themselves but, after a short battle, physics capitulated and the bullet simply dropped to the floor like a stone, bouncing twice and spinning to an embarrassed halt.

Drager hesitated.

Alyssa's eyeballs were now as black as the rage that controlled her. She stooped her body low, gazing left, then right. Slowly at first she swung her body around, gathering momentum as she spun in dizzying circles at speeds that shouldn't be possible (or at least not possible without being physically sick). Crackles of blue electricity began to appear at her fingertips, like she was some kind of turbine. Within seconds flames of pure energy burst from her outstretched arms and a spray of pure havoc swirled around the room, burning the walls like they were made of rice paper. Drager, suddenly realising the unworldly danger he was in, made a decision. He dropped his pistol and he ran, not looking back. The secretary threw the ring binder in the air as Drager barged past her. Drager jumped down the stairwell and away from the blue fire spreading from his once immaculate office. Alyssa, if she could be called that, just laughed as chaos spread around her. She laughed. No one would touch her again.

Brownlow slowly pulled his broken body underneath the broken desk and kept himself very quiet and very still. *Why do I never have any luck with women?*

Chapter Forty Five – Before Too Long

Jack and Joe had had a topsy-turvy time of it. Their life had become an ebb and flow of moments of terror, abject terror, pleasure, some more terror, something worse than terror, satisfaction and confusion. To be honest it was all getting a little out of hand. Jack considered whether they should give up being private detectives and go and work in a supermarket or something. At least the hours would be better.

The brothers had returned the ungrateful cat to a very grateful, if confused, owner. To signify her gratitude Mrs. Gilhooney had kindly written out a sizeable cheque to the pair, thus becoming their first paying client for over a year. Things were looking up, or so they thought. The happy mood was spoilt upon their return to Charlie's lock up with the discovery that Alyssa was missing. After a cup of tea and a short nap the brothers followed up this first discovery with a second discovery of a very unhappy and extremely tied up Charlie and Bronzer in the workshop downstairs. Charlie eventually calmed from his anger and told the brothers that their detective rival had caught the mechanics unawares and then stolen away Alyssa at gun point.

And so before too long Jack and Joe ended up standing outside the seedy snooker hall above which Drager's prosperous detective agency was currently burning, flames leaping from the window in an unnaturally bright blue colour. Nearby a solitary fire engine was splashing water at the fire in a half-arsed attempt to douse the flames. Drager was standing near to the fire engine berating a fire fighter and pointing wildly to his offices, but the fireman was having none of it. In fact the fireman seemed rather bored and didn't appear to want to be there, instead he was yawning and glancing occasionally at his watch.

"That's no ordinary fire, Joe," said Jack.

"No."

"It's Alyssa, isn't it? She's using her bloody Game magic."

"Yup."

"Yeah." Jack scratched at his head and tugged his ear, frowning. "Well, then. Bugger Drager. Let's go home."

"No, come on. We need to get her out of there."

"Erm, Joe? The building is on fire? If she is in there, she'll be all melty by now."

"Come on." Joe yanked his brother's elbow and jogged confidently across the road heading for an alley at the side of the snooker hall. A lone fire fighter was standing picking his nose on the corner, blocking the way. He seemed a bit young for a fire fighter, but Joe shrugged and spoke up. "Mind if we, erm, walk down this way?"

"Eh?" replied the fire fighter, genuinely puzzled.

"You know. The fire?"

"Fire?"

"Yes, the fire." Joe threw a puzzled glance to his sibling. "Up there?" The young chap stopped picking his nose for the time being and tilted his chin upwards.

"Shit! That building is on fire! I best tell the chief!" The fireman pushed past the brothers and ran in the direction of the fire truck. Joe watched him a moment, unsure what to make of the conversation they'd just had.

"Something odd is going on here." The pair ran down the alley and found an open fire exit a few metres down, partially hidden behind a sad, yellowing bush.

"We should have brought the robot and sent him in. This is a stupid idea. I don't like getting burnt."

"Yeah, well, put some sun cream on." Joe stepped a foot inside before giving out a short yell. "Alyssa?" He got no response. Jack followed his brother into the building, although he also continued to make loud protestations against a plainly stupid plan. Faint wisps of smoke drifted here and there over the several snooker tables that lined the open plan ground floor of the building. A couple of yellow haired youths were happily playing snooker on a table near a seedy bar, both seemingly unaware of the dangers above them.

"Erm, lads?" asked Jack. "You not worried about the fire upstairs?" The tallest youth looked over at Jack whilst chalking his cue. Blue dust sprinkled to the floor.

"Fire?"

"Yeah, fire. Upstairs?"

"But there'd be an alarm or something wouldn't there?"

"You'd think."

The lad shrugged and took his shot, pocketing a loose red.

"Something odd is going on here. Come on." Jack and Joe walked up the stairway leading to Drager's office. The faint suggestion of smoke didn't seem to get any thicker as they entered the reception. Drager's secretary was sitting behind her desk, happily filing her nails. She looked up at the brothers with severe disdain, her bobbed blonde hair hanging slightly askew above a heavily made up face.

"Oh, it's you two again. Mr. Drager isn't in."

"Hey Noreen," acknowledged Jack with a smile, plopping his

backside on the edge of her desk. The desk creaked under the strain, threatening to topple. "You know there is a fire engine outside? Must be for the fire in my heart for you." He leered in towards the secretary and fluttered his eyelids.

"Fuck off, Jack." She went back to filing her ruby red nails. She too seemed blissfully unaware of the fire that the brothers could see plain as day from outside.

Joe had cautiously approached the door to Drager's office. It was shut. Joe could see a flicker of flame from underneath the door, but only the lightest wisps of smoke came out from the crack between door and floor.

"Noreen, mind if we go in? I think we left something earlier."

"Anything to get your creep of a brother out of here, Joseph," she replied tartly. "Just be quick."

Jack hopped off the desk and over to his brother. "What about the fire?"

"I don't think there is a fire." Joe held his palm to the door feeling for heat. It felt just like a normal door. He pushed it open. "I think it's a magic trick, an illusion."

The office was a mess. The desk was crashed over against a wall and split in two and the plasterboard on the wall was cracked revealing rotten wooden slats underneath. Every cabinet, bookshelf and drawer had been opened, tipped over and emptied, paperwork strewn across the office like confetti at a giant's wedding.

"This reminds me of our old office," remarked Jack casually, a loose hand scratching at his flabby belly.

Joe darted quickly to the centre of the room and knelt down. Alyssa lay on the floor, curled in a ball and crying softly, rocking gently back and forth. Joe placed a hand carefully on her shoulder, and tried to give her a reassuring smile although he wasn't very good at them; he hadn't had the practice.

"I just wanted them off me," cried Alyssa, slowly allowing herself to be pulled upright. "I don't know what happened, I lost control. I don't like it. I want to go back to the Game. Can't you send me back to the Game?" She sniffed continuously as she spoke, tears leaking from her reddened face. "I just want to go home."

"I know," said Joe. "We'll take you home, I promise. Come on." Jack joined his brother and the pair helped Alyssa limp weakly out of the office. Noreen looked over in some confusion as the three re-entered the reception. Her jaw dropped at the sight of the distressed Alyssa held up between the brothers.

"I think you might need to get a cleaner in, Noreen," said Jack helpfully as they made their way out of the office and down the stairs. "Drager looks like he's had one wild party in there."

Chapter Forty Six – A Lot Later On,
Back To The Future

"You know what you are doing, right?" asked Jack in a tone that suggested no answer would satisfy his immediate fears. Jack was strapped into a coffin-shaped pod, several wires pricked precariously into his thick, blotchy skin.

"I have studied the system. This would seem the logical way to plug you into the Game." The Instructor was fiddling with various bits of odd looking equipment, checking the cabling between the three pods that Jack, Joe and Alyssa were all securely strapped into.

"You sure we can trust him, Joe?" He twisted his face right and looked pleadingly at his brother.

"I hope so," came the reply. In truth it had taken them a good few hours just to persuade Alyssa that the Instructor now meant no harm and had, in fact, completely lost any memories of his previous life. But eventually she relented and the four of them somehow squeezed into the clock and returned to the future.

"You hope so? What if this is a trap?"

"Then we have a problem. Not much we can do about it now though. We are strapped in." Joe tried to wave an arm but couldn't move it for the strap across his midriff. "Look, just relax, will you? He's not tried to kill us yet and he's had plenty of time to do so."

Jack turned his attention to his left, where Alyssa was quietly contemplating what she might find upon her return to the make-believe world she had left behind. "Alyssa, you sure you wanna go through with this? I mean, there is a lot going on in the real world you haven't experienced yet."

"I need to go back. I must finish my quest."

Jack rolled his eyes. "Hey, Insty, you're not going to kill us, right?"

"No," replied the metallic voice without looking up. "Not intentionally anyway."

"What do you mean not intentionally?!"

"I have no memories of this place, so as far as I am aware I have never used this equipment before. It appears a logical setup, but it perhaps would be wiser to try it out on some test subjects first in case of a miscalculation."

"Miscalculation? But you are a robot. You shouldn't make any miscalculations!"

"Quite so."

"I tell you what. Try it out on these two first, and if it works then send me."

"Hey!" argued both Joe and Alyssa.

"I rather think it works better if I do it all at once," said the Instructor. "Less chance of a cranial feedback loop that way."

"A cranial what now?"

"Transmitting now." The Instructor pressed a square button on a panel halfway up the wall. The lights of the pods flickered for a moment as the various wires started their dataflow. Gloop started glooping around and a low hum emitted from the panels next to each pod. Within seconds each of the three subjects was unconscious, their heads lolling forwards simultaneously. The

Instructor looked on satisfied at a job well done, and went into sleep mode.

Chapter Forty-Seven – The Game Is Afoot

The three of them were slightly embarrassed and confused about their predicament. They had materialised in the middle of a field, leaving a twenty foot circular pattern in the purple grass around them in a way that should give you an idea of how crop circles are really formed. All three were completely stark bollock naked (or just stark naked, in Alyssa's case).

"Where are we?" asked Jack as he attempted to his hide his embarrassment with a handful of the purple flora.

"The Game. In the fields of Daldaron, I should think."

"Daldaron?" asked Joe, bent double in an effort to hide himself – this worked okay so long as you weren't standing behind him.

"Yes. It's a small settlement designed to greet new arrivals. Look, here comes a greeter now." Alyssa lifted a lithe hand to point out a figure approaching through the grass. "Be wary, these guys are quite patronising. You might feel compelled to hit him."

"Hallo! Hallo there!" cried the figure, a long haired chap in a green robe. He carried a knobbly wooden staff which he used to push himself forwards. He was a young-ish man, with pointy ears and a pointy beard. He spoke again as he got nearer, an overly wide grin on his nodding face. "My name is Garnesshi and I am your guide. Welcome to the Game! Is this your first time?"

"We don't need a guide, so save your patter," commanded Alyssa forcefully. Her voice somehow sounded different in the Game, more forceful and authoritative. She stood up, unconcerned that all and sundry could see her bits. "I am Alyssa, enchantress of the Guild, and I return from the world of the Instructor."

"But... but that's impossible," stammered Garnesshi.

"You shall provide us with robes so that I can continue my quest."

"Yes... yes, of course, this way please... oh my." Garnesshi was clearly disturbed by the news of a visitor returning from beyond, but he did his best to hide it. He walked the three to the edge of the field, to a narrow lane that led to a small settlement in the near distance. Jack and Joe casually hid themselves behind a prickly bush. Parked on the lane, flouting the double yellow line, was a small cart pulled by a large striped cat. The cat was busy licking itself and paid no attention to the naked arrivals. Garnesshi took a rucksack from the back of the cart and tipped the contents on to the floor. Several items of basic clothing tumbled around, and were quickly gathered up by those who needed them. The robes were brown and loose fitting, and smelt vaguely of potatoes. The shoes were not much better, the coarse leather curved upwards at the toe and each had a small bell at the end.

"Do you have a dragon?" demanded Alyssa, who somehow managed to wear her robe with more panache than the others. She looked positively regal.

"Why... no. I am only a poor greeter."

"Then I must commandeer your cat cart."

"But... my livelihood depends on my cart... "

"That is immaterial. I am assuming, of course, that you do

not wish to be turned into a frog or a toad."

"No… no, my lady Enchantress, of course not… my cat cart, by all means, yes." He indicated feebly towards the two wheeled vehicle. Jack and Joe scrambled on to the back of the vehicle and found it hard to keep any sort of balance. Jack fell off twice before Alyssa had even got into the driving seat.

"Yaw," cried Alyssa in cat-tongue. The large pussy mewed to life and pounced onto all fours, springing forwards with surprising energy (for a cat). The cat, muscles well toned from years of fruitless towing, managed to tug the weight of the cart's occupants easily and the cart pulled away at a good lick. Jack and Joe gripped the front edge of the cart and kept themselves low.

"Where are we going?" whispered Jack in a hoarse voice.

"To find Vasgar, and the Guild. And most importantly of all to find Rascal."

"Rascal?" asked Joe.

"He's a back stabbing thief. He stabbed me in the back."

"Well, it is in the job description I suppose."

"He shall pay for his treachery."

"Hey, no fair!" cried Jack. "I thought crime didn't pay."

Alyssa rolled her eyes.

Chapter Forty-Eight – At The Guild

It didn't take too long to get to a telephone booth. Which was just as well as the cat was pooped. Alyssa dialled the local exchange for the Guild headquarters and one by one the party transintergrated (Jack and Joe both needed reassuring that transintergration was a safe way to travel. Statistically speaking, of course, it is much safer than travelling by cart). And so the three sack-wearing adventurers found themselves in the guild hall, a room of opulent dullness. Several dozen paintings of long dead Guild-Riders stared down disapprovingly from the high walls, their faces cracked with age. An ornate stairway led upwards from the guild hall, several doors leading from the landing.

"Vasgar." Alyssa acknowledged the tall man who was standing with his arms folded behind his back. He was dressed casually in a fluffy dressing gown and looked like he'd just been woken up. His hair was all skewiff at the back.

"Alyssa," cried the bearded noble. "You are safe! Rascal told me you had blue-screened. We feared the worse."

"I'm safe. No thanks to that bastard."

"Whatever do you mean?"

"Like you don't know. Rascal betrayed me."

"Now, Alyssa. Rascal is a trusted member of my inner circle. He saved me from the Blunderbeast of Teraal, remember, and sacrificed his own mother to join the Guild. Why ever would he betray you?"

"Once a thief, always a thief. He wanted the golden egg."

"You found the egg!"

"Almost. Rascal tried to kill me for it."

"But the egg was the key to the Code Spell," despaired Vasgar. "Without it we cannot free ourselves from the Instructor's power."

"No matter. I have control over the Code Spell. I can manipulate the Game at will." To demonstrate her powers she raised her right hand in front of her and made a pinching motion with her thumb and forefinger. As she did so she twisted her wrist sharply to the left. A line of reality ahead of her twisted with her wrist, a cylinder of no more than an inch in girth but of infinite length. The whole fabric of the Game along the cylinder distorted and stretched with Alyssa's pinch. Alyssa realised immediately that the little pinch was doing more damage to the Game's programming than she intended, and so she let go. The distortion relaxed somewhat but, as always when something is stretched, the affected area didn't quite spin back to line up as it should, leaving a visible crack in the fabric of the Game.

"My Gods," cried Vasgar. "Such a dangerous power! But if you didn't get the golden egg how did you survive?"

"I was pulled out of the Game just in time by Jack and Joe, here." She threw a thumb in the direction of the two brothers, both dumbstruck by the world they found themselves in.

"This is Jack and Joe?" asked Vasgar. "My Gods! The Prophecy!"

"Prophecy?" asked Jack.

"The witch said that the coming of Jack and Joe would signify the end of the Game."

"Which witch?" asked Joe.

"The seer. She said your arrival would bring the end."

"Isn't that what you wanted, Vasgar?" asked Alyssa. "Wasn't the Guild supposed to bring about the end of the Instructor's reign?"

"Yes, but at what cost? What are we without the Game?"

"Yeah, well, the Instructor is no longer in command, buddy," said Jack as he sauntered around the room looking for things to steal. He secreted a golden goblet about his person whilst nobody was looking. "You guys can do what you like. We just want Rascal."

"Very well, then," said the noble. He nodded to a flunky who was faffing around nearby. The flunky immediately darted to a bone white telephone and placed a call. Within seconds the other Guild members appeared in a digital blur; Hector and Rascal.

"This had better be important, Vasgar..." began Hector before he saw Alyssa. "By the Gods, Alyssa! You're alive!"

"No thanks to him." Rascal's eyes had opened wider than his head as soon as he saw the figure of Alyssa in the room. He was too far from the telephone to transintergrate back, so instead he twisted around and made a run for it, heading up the grand stairway that led up to the balconies above. His plan, as vague as it was at this stage, was to get to the dragon-pad atop the guild hall and fly away quickly before Alyssa could invoke her retribution for his betrayal.

Alyssa reached forwards with her hand and pulled sharply backwards, using her powers to pull the stone floor from underneath the running Rascal. The nimble tea leaf dived to one side as the flags underneath him buckled and bent, folding in on themselves.

"Alyssa, no! The damage!" Vasgar pleaded with her to stop, but rage had taken over the femme fatale. Her eyes darkened, and a shimmering glow of silver circled her body, pulsing violently with every movement. Underfoot the stone floor crunched like fresh snow with every step of her size fives, leaving stoney footprints as she paced in the direction of her prey. Rascal was darting up the stairway by now, springing left and right like a Persian Prince in an effort to keep out of Alyssa's considerable line of fire. Blocks of stairs crumbled as he jumped, Alyssa's arms flinging flashes of unbelievable power.

"Shit," mouthed both Jack and Joe. As one they rushed forwards, trying to catch Alyssa without tripping up over the many stone obstacles that were appearing in her wake. Above them Rascal had made it to the top of the stairs and he disappeared through a hole in the wall where a door used to be. The remains of the door clung to the air as wispy ash, simply zapped out of existence at Alyssa's will (she was aiming for the thief. Unlimited power didn't improve aim, apparently).

Alyssa leapt up the stairs in one impossible bounce. Jack and Joe had to make do with climbing those few blocks of stairway that still remained. Behind them Vasgar and Hector stirred the Guild to life, calling other nameless Guild-Riders to arms. Joe could hear the orders of Vasgar very clearly. Kill Alyssa before she destroyed the Game. Looking at the chaos around them she'd already done a good job in the destruction of the guild hall. If she kept this up the whole Game might fall part.

As Jack and Joe scrambled through the hole in the wall they could see Alyssa ahead of them mounting a large green dragon. A smaller, yellow dragon had already taken off and was flapping madly in order to get some distance. Several people were running around the dragon-pad, flapping florescent table tennis bats and muttering about the dragons not having had clearance. A grey-blue dragon was sitting peacefully to the brothers' right, wondering what all the commotion was about. The dragon was quite shocked when not one but two riders suddenly staggered up its lustrous tail. Jack and Joe had decided to steal a dragon.

"How do you start this thing?" screamed Joe to his brother, hoping that it was as easy to hot-wire a dragon as it was a car. Jack was sitting at the front end of the saddle and picked up a loose set of reins that dangled from the pommel. Joe pulled himself behind his brother and clung on tightly, his fingers clasping around Jack's significant waist.

"Hee-yaw!" whipped Jack, digging his feet into the dragon's back. The dragon, annoyed that his beauty sleep had been disturbed, rose to his feet with some reluctance before beginning a slow bound forwards and finally leaping airwards. The dragon's wide wings made a slow beat as the scaly beast slowly ascended and made chase after the green and yellow dragons ahead.

"Can you make this thing go faster?" yelled Joe over the turbulence.

"Yeah. I could throw you off!" countered Jack.

Ahead of the trailing brothers Alyssa veered left after Rascal. A plume of flame snorted forwards from the green beast's nostrils and singed the tail of its smaller cousin. The yellow dragon wasn't happy about this and began to nosedive, throwing Rascal forwards. The wiry thief grabbed hold of the dragon's ear in an attempt to stay aboard. Dragons, of course, use their ears to balance, and therefore this particular dragon went from a nose-dive into a perilous and out of control spin, fast heading for the ground underneath. Rascal tried to move a hand to remove a magic scroll from a jacket pocket, hoping perhaps to zap himself away from the danger, but he discovered he needed both hands just to hold on to the dragon's slippery skin.

Alyssa brought her dragon into a controlled dive, aiming directly for the belly of the yellow dragon in front of her. She prepared her dragon for another belch of fire, a killing blow at this distance. Suddenly she felt a thud from her starboard, causing her dragon to lose balance. She glanced right and saw that Jack and Joe had used their dragon to ram her.

"What are you doing? I had him!" she yelled, although her words were lost over the wild wind about them. Her controlled dive was suddenly out of control and Alyssa's grip relented, sending her plummeting to the ground underneath. There was an almighty puff of smoke as Alyssa, Rascal and two dragons all hit the ground. Alyssa, her body still shielded by the shimmering glow of the Code Spell, disappeared underground as several foot of earth and rock just gave way as she crashed. Rascal and the dragons had to make do with simply slapping painfully into the purple grass of the hillside they had hit.

Gently the grey-blue dragon flapped downwards and landed gracefully near the crash site. Jack and Joe hopped off, unscathed by their virgin dragon experience. They could see Rascal writhing around clutching his obviously broken legs. The two other dragons looked unhappy but unharmed by the experience, the fat padding in their underbelly taking the brunt of the collision. Nervously the brothers peered into the hole made by the fallen redhead.

Alyssa shot upwards in a flash of light, hovering for a moment, before gradually falling to the soft purple foliage. She stomped towards Rascal, her teeth gritted in rage.

"I'm sorry, okay!" begged Rascal, his tears red with the pain. He tried to drag himself away but every movement was agony.

He raised a hand to protect himself. "I couldn't help it! It's the way I was brought up! I'm a thief, and I'm sorry!"

"Too late," said a voice that sounded like Alyssa had her own personal echo. "You will die." She raised both hands in order to launch a double barrel of devastation in the direction of the downed rogue. Just before she could release her power she crumpled to the ground, a rugby tackle from both Jack and Joe sending her tumbling down the slope of the hillside. The three of them rolled for a few seconds before coming to a halt in a heap.

"What do you think you are doing?" demanded Alyssa as she sat bolt upright, her body still encircled in the power that had taken her. "You shall perish. You shall all perish!"

"Alyssa, wait, wait!" pleaded Jack as he bent to his knees, pulling himself off the ground. "It's us!"

"It's Jack and Joe, Alyssa. Can you hear me? I know you are in there. Alyssa?" Joe pulled himself forwards and looked directly into Alyssa's darkened eyes. "Just let it go, Alyssa. Let it go. We'll help you. Everything is going to be alright."

"Joe...?" questioned Alyssa, her voice tinged with sadness. "Joe...?"

"Rascal isn't worth it, Alyssa. You're hurting the Game. The Code Spell is too dangerous Alyssa. Just let it go. Let it go." Joe smiled peacefully and gently moved an arm towards her, cautiously placing his fingers onto Alyssa's forearm. As he did so the silvery glow that surrounded her slowly dissipated and the darkness of her eyes lifted. Instead her green eyes looked tearfully to Joe.

"Joe... Joe... what have I done?" she cried. She reached forwards and hugged Joe, pulling him close to her and pushing her face into his chest, her fingers tugging tightly on his potato robe. Joe put his arms around her and she wept. "I'm sorry. I didn't mean it. I'm sorry."

Jack stood up and looked at his brother and Alyssa as they embraced. He frowned and folded his arms across his purple-grass-stained Hawaiian shirt. "Typical," he said, mostly to himself. "I fly the dragon and he gets all the credit."

Chapter Forty Nine – A Little While After That

It took a little while to clear things up when they got back to the ranch. The Instructor had unplugged them all from the Game, including Alyssa. It was just too dangerous for her stay. The Code Spell was uncontrollable inside the Game and it was going to take the inhabitants a heck of a long time to clean up the mess she had made.

"Look, its not all bad, Alyssa," offered Jack.

"That's right. The Instructor has arranged for control of the Game to go to the Guild. Vasgar and his pals can do whatever they like in the Game now. They could even start unplugging it if they decide to, free themselves completely from the program."

"I know," said Alyssa. She smiled. It hadn't turned out like she'd planned, but she did complete her quest. The Guild-Rider's were free and Vasgar had promised that Rascal would be suitably punished for his treason.

"And don't worry about what you did to Brownlow in Drager's office. He's a creepy little shit and got all he deserved."

"Drager is after your time machine, you know," said Alyssa. "He's prepared to go to extreme lengths to get his hands on your clock it would seem."

"He'll get the clock over my dead body," said Joe.

"I think that's the kind of deal he had in mind," replied Alyssa. "He fired a gun at me, point blank range. He'd have killed me."

"I still don't get how you can use magic in the real world," said Jack. "The fire illusion and that."

"Maybe this isn't the real world, Jack. If it was then the spells wouldn't work."

"To be honest that would explain a lot."

"What does it matter?" said Joe firmly. "Look, we are back in business here. We've got an office, a car or two, a robot and a fucking time machine. Bugger Drager, and sod everyone else. Jack and Joe's Detective Agency, in association with Alyssa of course, is open!"

"Everything has worked out," agreed Jack with an over-wide grin on his chubby face. "And best of all no loose ends!"

"Just how I like it, Jack. Just how I like it."

Chapter Fifty – No Loose Ends

Mrs. Gilhooney finally found her glasses on the sideboard where she had left them. She struggled with her bent fingers but eventually managed to get the bloomin' arms unbent and, poking her eyes only once, she slipped the semi-transparent grey frames over her wizened and slightly hairy ears. Her hand shook gently as she reached for the tin of cat food and she slowly filled up the off-yellow plastic food bowl. She got about two spoons of the brown meat-like substance into the bowl and bent to lower it to the floor. The cat darted forth and lapped up the delicious entrails hidden within. Mrs. Gilhooney, with her glasses on, frowned and sucked her teeth back onto her gums.

"Hang on a minute here, pussykins. You're not my cat. Oh deary me, they've given me the wrong cat." She hobbled in slippered feet into the front room. "Where did I put that phone? I must call those nice detectives about this."

*

Jug bashed hard on the hand held device he held in his hand. "This is the right timeline."

Bolt scratched at his forehead with one of his oversized pistols. "Errr, are ya' sure boss?" Goldfish said nothing, and carried on oiling his equipment.

"Of course I'm sure. If I can find the Instructor's transponder code then we can follow his signal and find him. Then we re-boot him, upload his memory and the Instructor will be back in business. Just like last time."

"Eh?" Jug smacked Bolt across the back of the head with the hand held device, which gave a loud beep on impact.

"Just shut up Bolt." Jug looked at the device. A bright and flashing red dot appeared on the screen. "I've got him. Load your guns. And remember, shoot to kill. I want everybody involved in this almighty fuck up dead. Seriously dead."

*

The Old Man was standing on the empty street, his clock behind him. He looked again at his fob watch. He had given Jack and Joe several hours now to turn up, as they had agreed, and deliver him the key. He needed the key, of course, to give to his past self in order that he could come after Jack and Joe in the first place. It was all very confusing, and he was getting quite annoyed by the whole thing.

Jack and Joe were obviously not coming. They had stolen the time machine from him. Again.

He had given them their last chance.

The Old Man swore then and there that he would hunt down the brothers and kill them. He would take the key from their cold, dead corpses. *There will be no escape when I finally catch up with the thieves,* he decided, *only pain and death.* And he already knew this would all come to pass because otherwise he wouldn't have been able to return the key to himself in the first place. Or was it the second place.

This was giving him a headache.

"I wonder if there is a Boots open at this time of night," he mused.

*

Donatello Vamenti knelt over the hacked and abused corpse of Harry Mantei, his knee damp in the pool of blood that oozed like rusty oil on the warehouse floor. A single tear ran down his left cheek, following the route of a scar inflicted by his brother during childhood. Paul O'Gander was standing behind him, holding a squirming fat kid in his greasy fingers.

"'ere, get off me!" the kid screamed in protest. "I've told you everythin'"

"You are sure it was Jack who did this. The man in the Hawaiian shirts?"

"I told you already, get off me!" Vamenti nodded to O'Gander who immediately loosened his grip. The fat kid, Billy, picked himself up from the floor and ran away from the warehouse just as quick as his plump and underused legs would let him, although he had to stop several times for air.

"Jack's mocking you, boss," O'Gander offered helpfully, a rueful smile stretching across his unshaven and frankly unattractive face.

Donatello Vamenti rose to his full height, his chin high in the air. In his hand he held the bloody bread knife that Jack had used to cut open the corpse. "First he shoots my Ma in front of me, in the middle of my secret hideout. Then he butchers my hitman, who, by the way, I had already paid up front. Who does Jack think he is?"

"He's a dead man walking boss," O'Gander whistled softly. "Dead man walking."

"No," replied the slick haired Mafioso. "I want Jack brought to me alive, O'Gander. I'm going to do to him what he did to Harry Mantei. I'm going to do it very, very slowly and I'm going to start with the little fucker's testicles!"

*

Brownlow sucked some of his food-shake through a straw as he lay in the hospital bed, various parts of him suspended in the air to aid the healing process. He desperately wanted to scratch his nose, but couldn't get at it because of the mass of wires over his face trying to hold his jaw in a position that could only be described as jaunty; it was the closest the surgeon could get to straight.

"Those bastards will pay for this," said Drager, who had sat himself down at Brownlow's bedside. He tossed one of the grapes he had brought for the injured detective into the air and caught it in his mouth.

"Mmmm-mmm," replied Brownlow, unable to open his mouth to any useful degree.

"We'll get that clock and we'll make sure that Jack and Joe never work again. I'll have my revenge."

"Mmm," agreed Brownlow.

"Not for you, dickhead," came a quick reply. "For my office. They completely trashed my office. All my files, my tax return, my wallpaper, my desk, my books. My books for pities sake! All ruined."

"Mmmm, mmm, mmm!" argued his horizontal companion.

"And I will have that time clock. I will have that time clock even if it kills you."

Brownlow's eyes widened but he didn't say anything. He just pressed the *call nurse* button repeatedly.

*

There was a knock at the office door. Joe looked towards the door suspiciously.

"Relax," said Jack, a foot resting casually on the battered table. "It's probably a new client or something. Don't be so on edge."

The door splintered open violently. A dozen or so armed police officers crashed through, taking up various tactical positions and pointing large automatic rifles at dangerous angles just in case one of the filing cabinets or light fittings might try anything funny. In and amongst them was PC Cadley.

"What's going on?" asked Jack, as he pulled himself upright, hands in the air.

"Jack and Joseph," said Cadley sadly. "I'm arresting you for the crime of escaping from lawful police custody, for the severe damage of a police building and for the murder of seven police employees. You don't have to say anything, and to be honest I'd be glad if you didn't so keep your smart arse gobs shut. Somebody 'cuff 'em and make sure they're on too tight."

"What! That wasn't us!" argued Jack. "It was some guys from the future!"

"Looks like we're going to need a sequel," said Joe quietly to no one in particular.

THE END

1895692R0015

Printed in Great Britain
by Amazon.co.uk, Ltd.,
Marston Gate.